FINDING DAVID

It's About Time Series

Courtnee Turner Hoyle

Pale Woods Publishing

Finding David

It's About Time Series

Copyright © March 25, 2023

Erwin, TN

by Courtnee Turner Hoyle

Library of Congress Control Number: 2023902775

Print IBSN: 979-8-9876468-3-0

E-book ISBN: 979-8-9876468-2-3

This book is a work of fiction. Names, characters, businesses, places, events, and incidents are the product of the author's imagination or used in a fictitious manner. Any similarities or resemblance to actual persons, living or dead, events, or places is entirely coincidental.

Cover Design: Taylor Dawn, Sweet15 Designs, LLC

To everyone who doesn't give up on love, whether it's your family,
friends, or romantic partner
People like you are the reason I have loved ones.

To Tosha and Matthew and Stereling and Kinidy
Your relationships inspire me.

FINDING DAVID PLAYLIST

1. "Where Are You Going?" Dave Matthews Band

2. "All My Love" Led Zeppelin

3. "Runaround" Blues Traveler

4. "Ants Marching" Dave Matthews Band

5. "Barely Breathing" Dunkin Sheik

6. "Linger" Cranberries

7. "The Space Between" Dave Matthews Band

8. "Highway to Hell" AC/DC

9. "Satellite" Dave Matthews Band

10. "Sunday Bloody Sunday" U2

11. "Tangerine" Led Zeppelin

12. "Crash Into Me" Dave Matthews Band

13. "Fade Into You" Mazzy Star

CHAPTER 1

When you know, you know.

Celeste wasn't certain what else she knew, but she was ready to go after the man she loved. Carrying Emma, she tried to shield her from the slanting rain as they crossed the field to the Winsome's house. The blanket provided little protection for the baby, but Celeste was glad she didn't fight against it, especially when the fabric clung to her face.

The wind felt too cold for summer, but Mrs. Winsome had talked about short spurts of cold weather in relation to particular kinds of fruit. She supposed the town could be experiencing a blueberry or blackberry winter.

Celeste put her lips together and swallowed some of the rain that had flown into her mouth, almost gagging in the process. When she'd decided to jump back into David's time frame, she'd selected Caroline's body. Her information had already been in the system, and she'd made an acceptable host in the past. Some of Caroline's habits made her unsuitable, though.

For instance, Caroline smoked, and the nicotine from her last cigarette was laced through her saliva. Celeste hadn't liked coffee when David had offered it to her, but she preferred it over the current taste in her mouth.

When she'd jumped back in time with Emma, Caroline had been in her trailer watching an inane show on television. Celeste had entered her body like she was waking from a dream, opening her eyes to the sights in front of Caroline before Caroline was shifted into Celeste's body. Celeste had felt the weight of the baby on her lap and had rushed to catch her before Emma rolled away.

Emma had jumped through time with her, but the experience had been hard for her. She lay across Celeste, breathing as if she had been running, even though she hadn't taken her first step. There was something different about her baby, but Celeste didn't wait to analyze it.

Once she'd assumed a host's body, that person's physical form belonged to Celeste. She may not have had green eyes and blonde hair, like Caroline, but while she inhabited her body, Caroline's features were hers. As the tingling receded from her arms and legs, Celeste could feel herself acclimating to Caroline's height and weight.

She stumbled through the house in search of car keys. The first couple of hours in a host's body were disorienting, as she adjusted to their dissimilar biology. The perception of sights and sounds was disconcerting, too, as a host with high cortisol levels from prolonged anxieties could have aggravated senses.

Caroline was no different. After years of domestic abuse, Celeste could feel her host's body respond to the loud pops behind her as the trailer creaked from the wind's assault.

The last time Celeste had been in the trailer, she had been beaten by Caroline's ex-husband, Willie James. Her injuries had landed her in the hospital, and Caroline had joined her, as at the time, the woman had been determined to leave her abuser. Caroline was pregnant, and Willie's constant abuse had put her in fear for her baby's life. Celeste sighed as she realized that Caroline would have gone back to him, but his murderous rampage at the hospital had put an end to a possible reunion.

Celeste hoped he had died from the injuries she had inflicted on him before her last host, Hailey, had died, but part of her knew he was still alive, breathing air that he should be denied.

Celeste had touched her lower abdomen. It was a little swollen, but she hadn't felt as though Caroline's baby had remained in her body. It was just as well. Caroline and her unborn child could enjoy a break as they napped inside Celeste's body. Dr. Maze, Celeste's employer and her grandfather, would monitor them while Celeste... Did what?

She had wanted to find David, but would he believe her outlandish claim? And what would he think of Emma's sudden appearance?

The moment Celeste had truly looked into her daughter's cerulean eyes, she had noticed the golden flecks in them and accepted the truth. Emma was David's daughter, even though her boyfriend, Zam, had been raising her as his own.

Celeste had rubbed her eyes with her thumb and forefinger. *Poor Zam!* He must miss them. He was used to Celeste's absences, as her missions carried her away for months at a time, but he had been close to Emma every day.

The house had reeked of motor oil and unwashed dishes. Celeste had remembered the smell from her first visit, and she had tried to focus her mind on looking for transportation instead of watching roaches as they darted away from the vibrations of her footsteps. Caroline wasn't a great housekeeper, but maybe she'd change now that Willie was gone.

Celeste recalled a truck she had parked beside when she had visited her past host's body. It had been tilted in the driveway, but maybe it was functional.

She had almost lost her breath when she noticed a set of keys in a clear dish on the counter. The fob had the Volkswagen symbol on it, and there was a chip in the corner next to where the key flipped up.

When Celeste had jumped into her host last time, her grandfather had erased her memory. Somehow, the tattoo of her daughter's name had transferred, and Celeste had given the name to David when he'd asked for it. She had built a life in the town, earned a nursing license, and bought a car. Presumably, the same car that the key fob in her hand would open.

A quick check revealed the tattoo on her wrist. She hadn't had time to wonder why it settled on her hosts when she traveled through time, but she had vowed to find out one day.

She grabbed the keys and marched to the door, throwing the blanket over her baby as she stepped outside. The porch was sheltered with a metal awning, so only a few drops of wet wind connected with her face as she stared at her silver Volkswagen.

"How did it get here?" she spoke aloud, and Emma wiggled under the blanket.

Celeste had run out into the rain and had jumped into the car. She clutched Emma close to her and doubted the child's safety in a moving vehicle without a car seat. As if in answer to her prayers, she had glanced in the review mirror and had seen a car seat.

It was set up in its earliest form to accommodate a newborn baby, but upon further examination, Celeste had found a way to adjust the seat to accommodate her baby. Emma had allowed herself to be strapped into the contraption, and Celeste had wondered if she had been in a similar seat when Celeste had been on her last mission. It seemed unlikely, as their home, food, and medical care was within walking distance.

The drive to David's house had been short, but every nerve in her body responded to the stress as she had turned onto the interstate and exited a few roads from his home. When the two-story house came into view, Celeste had felt bile inch up her esophagus and settle in her throat.

She had parked the car next to the hill where she had awoken without a memory. She bolted up the hill, barely closing their car doors after she grabbed Emma, and dashed across the field. Her footsteps matched her pounding heart as she reached the door.

She stared at its old wooden frame and chipped white paint. Not that long ago, she had been a member of the household, and she could open it at will. Now, she was a stranger in a familiar body, holding a baby who had never been inside but had more of a place there than her.

She knocked before she lost her nerve, and the sound echoed in her ears. Celeste couldn't hear the television, so she started to wonder if anyone was home. Just as she turned her head to glance at the driveway, the door opened.

Ag rubbed her eyes and gazed at her from the other side of the door, wearing a rumpled silk nightgown and a matching pair of violet slippers. She tried to cover a yawn.

Celeste realized the time of day as she took in Ag's appearance. Her first thought was to apologize, but she wanted to see David as soon as possible, so she blurted, "Where's David?"

Ag started to answer in a kneejerk response, lifting her thumb in the direction of the stairs, but she stopped herself. She put her hand on her hip, and her eyebrows drew together.

"What is it, Caroline?"

Celeste hadn't thought through her rush to see David, and now she needed to come up with a good reason for her sudden appearance. Caroline was David's ex-wife, and she was unwelcome in the Winsome's home.

"I need to see David," she responded lamely.

Ag crossed her arms. "Go home, Caroline."

Emma peaked her head out from under the blanket and stared at Ag. She muttered some unintelligible baby sounds, and Ag's features softened when she heard Emma's voice.

"This can't be your baby." Ag smiled as she touched Emma's outreached hand.

The baby lunged for Ag, throwing both women off-guard. Despite the situation, they chuckled, as Celeste handed Emma to her aunt.

"What's your name, sweet girl?" Ag asked in a sing-song voice she reserved for small children.

She turned to Celeste and raised her eyebrows, expecting her to answer. Celeste shifted her feet before she told her, "Emma. Her name is Emma."

CHAPTER 2

"David?" Ag called up the stairs uncertainly.

He yelled something back to his sister, but Celeste didn't understand it.

"I think you need to get down here."

There were more muffled sounds. Celeste didn't know what he said, but it was clear David was upset.

Celeste thought she heard a rustle just off the living room, and she imagined Mrs. Winsome was poised just inside her bedroom door with her hands on her walker. She didn't begrudge the elderly woman for listening in, but she wished she'd make her presence known instead of hovering in the eaves of her room.

David's upstairs room door opened, and he bounded down the stairs, his steps livelier than his responses to his sister's calls. "What is—" He stopped when he saw Caroline in the doorway.

He looked at Ag for an explanation, but his confusion only grew as he spotted the baby in her arms. Celeste steeled herself and started with the truth.

"That's Emma," she told him.

"Okay," David said, drawing out the end of the word. "What does that have to do with you showing up here at seven o'clock in the morning?"

Celeste steeled herself against whatever would follow. "Her name is Emma Elizabeth."

Her statement only caused more uncertainty. It took a few moments, but Ag seemed to understand the direction of the conversation.

"You're saying this" —she held up Emma a little higher— "is the product of your missing pregnancy?"

David's eyes narrowed. "Outside. Now," he commanded, pointing to the porch Celeste was already partially on.

Ag waved her on, and Celeste was grateful. She didn't want Emma to be around raised voices.

Once the front door was shut, David's face contorted with rage. "Why the—" He stopped himself, reevaluating his words. "Why are you *really* here, Caroline? I told you the last time that I wouldn't help you anymore."

"What?" His outrage had temporarily distracted her. "No, David. Emma is really yours. I don't want anything."

He issued a dry laugh, rubbing his palms over the stubble on his cheeks. "Yeah, right. Every time I've seen you since you ran out of this house, you've hit me up for money."

Even though he seemed to despise her, Celeste was drawn to David. She loved the man she'd married. He'd divorced Caroline, but Caroline hadn't married him. In her heart, Celeste still felt she was David's wife.

She resisted the urge to touch him, but just barely. Instead, she poured out everything, hardly taking a breath.

"My name is Celeste. I was sent back in time by my grandfather to try to prevent the Great War. He placed me inside Caroline because she was a good host who could be easily placed to alter certain events in the timeline. When I met you, I fell in love with you, and we conceived Emma shortly after we were married. When my grandfather noticed that nothing was shifting in his plan, he pulled me forward into my time frame. I had Emma, and some part of me knew she was yours, even though I thought our baby had stayed inside Caroline's body. I came back inside Hailey Hall's body, and I didn't remember anything until her death caused me to wake up in my time. After my time away, I looked at Emma, and I knew she was yours, so we came back."

David's mouth had dropped during her explanation. "Caroline, I think you need professional help. Are you doing drugs again?"

Celeste started pacing, and she noticed a maroon car next to the Winsome's navy blue SUV. She wondered if it was Marcia's car.

"Who's baby is in there?" he asked calmly. It was clear he was placating her. "Did one of your friends let you borrow her to try to get some drug money?"

"I don't do drugs," Celeste said, glaring at him. "I'm tired of living a lie. I love you, David. We were married, and we had that beautiful baby in there."

Ag eased open the door. Emma wasn't with her, but Celeste was unconcerned.

"Not to interrupt, but you could always get a DNA test."

"I don't need a DNA test!" David yelled. "Has everyone gone crazy? Don't you remember when she *lost"* —he put up air quotes— "the baby?"

"I know," Ag said, moving onto the porch and closing the door. "It's just—"

She looked at Celeste and Celeste understood. Ag had seen the resemblance in Emma's eyes.

CHAPTER 3

Celeste drove back to the trailer, grateful that she was finished explaining herself. Emma gurgled from the backseat, happily studying a plastic bowl Celeste had found in the floorboard. It wasn't a great toy, but it kept the baby entertained as they traveled the short distance back to their accommodations.

Celeste felt almost completely defeated. After she'd told him the truth, David had assumed she was crazy or on drugs. She had spent almost fifteen minutes trying to convince him that she had used Caroline and Hailey as hosts by telling him private tidbits of their time together, but each secret revelation had caused him to become more horrified.

"I saw you in the store last week," he'd said. "You looked like you were ready to give birth. Did you trade that baby for the one in my house?"

Celeste had stared at him. She'd set the time to several days after Hailey Hall's death. Caroline was only around five months pregnant at that time. Could Caroline have gotten bigger after Willie James was no longer a threat? It seemed likely, but it would have happened over months.

She had shoved her sleeve up her arm, revealing the tattoo of Emma's name. "How do you explain this?"

David had looked at the tattoo, but he'd dismissed it. "So, you got the same tattoo as Hailey." His upper lip had lifted. "It only proves that you're sick. The woman is dead. Let her rest in peace."

Celeste had taken in David's rigid stance and blazing blue eyes. She had been more truthful with him than she had been with any person, even herself, but David hadn't believed a single part of her story.

At that point, Celeste had known she had to tread carefully. One wrong word and she'd be in jail, Emma would end up in foster care, and who knew if her grandfather could save them.

A spider had climbed the white siding beside her as Celeste had prepared her lie. "Okay. You caught me. I miscarried, and it's been really stressful for me. One of my friends lets me watch her baby for a little extra money. Most times, staying busy keeps my mind off things, but I was up last night thinking about my lost pregnancies."

David's hand had touched her elbow and he had pulled her to him. He had rocked her back and forth in their embrace, and Celeste had remembered the first time he had held her that way. She'd landed in Caroline's body, and he'd talked her into leaving the emergency room with him. That night, she had been sleeping on the Winsome's couch and cried out from a bad dream. Celeste couldn't remember the dream, but she thought it might have been fueled by the abuse her host had suffered. David had pulled her into an embrace before she was fully awake and rocked her until she drifted into a peaceful slumber.

"I love you, David."

He had broken away from her quickly, firmly distancing himself from her. "There was a time when I would have given anything to hear you say that."

He ran his hands through his raven hair. It was much shorter than it was when Hailey Hall had lived with the Winsomes.

"I'm over you," he had told her. "You destroyed me, and you couldn't even tell me the truth about our baby until now."

Caroline had never admitted to carrying David's baby, and why should she have told him she did, when Caroline had no evidence a pregnancy had existed besides an ultrasound picture? In so many words, Celeste had told him what he had wanted to know, but it was a lie. Their daughter had been inside the house, playing with her aunt and grandmother.

Celeste had opened her mouth to say something. It was a small fact to give her original story more credence, but she didn't have the chance to speak.

The door had pushed open, tentatively at first, and a young woman stepped out. David's features had warmed, and he had smiled at the woman.

"Mindy?" Celeste had said before she could stop herself.

Celeste had remembered Mindy switching shifts with David because of her husband's multiple sclerosis. Her husband was alive, so were she and David having an affair?

Mindy batted her incredibly long eyelashes at Celeste. "Do I know you?"

Celeste regretted her mistake. Hailey had met Mindy when she was using Emma's name, and Celeste doubted Caroline and Mindy traveled in the same circles.

She had said, "It's a small town."

Mindy seemed to have accepted her explanation. Her blonde hair had shimmered as she had thrown it over her shoulder. Her arms had crossed over a sexy blue dress that she obviously had worn the previous night. Celeste's stomach had dropped as Mindy kissed David, and he had put his strong arms around her.

When they had broken apart, David glanced over at Celeste and back at Mindy. The couple had giggled as if they'd been caught.

David had pushed his fingers through Mindy's, and without taking his eyes off her, he had told Caroline, "Caroline may know you, but I don't think she knows you're going to be my wife by the end of the year."

Celeste had seen the small diamond ring on the hand David held, and her world had fallen apart.

Chapter 4

Celeste waited until she was in her car with Emma before she let her tears flow. Thankful that her baby couldn't see her from her car seat, Celeste cried. She turned on the radio and settled on a classic rock station. She hoped it would block any sounds she made as she sobbed.

David moved fast, but how was he already engaged to Mindy?

Questions swirled around her mind, and Celeste couldn't find easy answers to any of them. She decided to go back to the trailer and make a new plan.

When she pulled into the driveway, a woman met her at her car. She opened Celeste's door and spoke to her with familiarity. Celeste assumed she was one of Caroline's close neighbors, and as they spoke, two boys ran out of the neighboring trailer, with sun-kissed skin and dark hair.

"I said to wait until after lunch!" the woman yelled at them and shook her head at Celeste. "They want to feed the chickens as soon as they roll out of bed, but Randy has them on a schedule." She picked at chipped pink nail polish before she folded her arms over an ample bosom. "You'll know what it's like soon enough."

Emma let out a gurgle from the backseat, and Celeste turned around to get the baby out of her constraints. When she adjusted in her seat the woman stared at her.

"What happened?" she gasped, pointing at Caroline's middle and looking around her to see if a newborn was in the car. "I knew you were close to delivering, but you said you'd let me drive you to the hospital when you went into labor. Is that why you didn't answer your phone?"

Celeste thought quickly. "This is my first child, Emma. I went to the hospital, had the baby, and gave him up for adoption."

The woman's mouth dropped open, revealing a few spaces where teeth should have been. "I talked to you at ten o'clock last night. How'd it happen so fast?"

Celeste remembered her time as a nurse. "I signed out against medical advice so I could pick up Emma."

The woman ran a hand through her dark, oily hair. "But what about Harvey? You were so excited about becoming his mommy."

Celeste struggled with the best way to answer the woman's questions. She was close to Caroline, so Emma's sudden appearance coupled with the pregnancy's disappearance must have been hard for her.

Celeste hung her head as she started her performance. She thought back to the ring on Mindy's finger and willed tears to form. When she remembered the joy that crossed David's face at the sight of his fiancé, it wasn't hard to start crying.

"I just couldn't keep the baby," she blubbered. "What if Willie busted out of jail and came looking for us? He could kill him."

"Oh, honey," the woman responded. "That man wouldn't hurt you or his baby."

Celeste was unnerved by her response. *Did she sympathize with Willie after the horrible things he'd done?*

"I didn't think he'd hurt those people in the hospital, but he did," Celeste reminded her.

The woman put a thin hand on her arm, choosing to focus on the missing baby. "You've had a hard life, but I thought Harvey was gonna turn it around."

Emma clapped her hands together, commanding their attention. The woman smiled at the baby.

"I'm glad you got your daughter back." She studied Emma for a moment. "She has your nose." After she had spoken some baby gibberish to Emma, the woman commented, "I'm a little hurt that you never told me about her."

"It was too upsetting," Celeste covered. "I don't think I'll be able to talk about my other baby again."

The woman sighed. "Well, what's done is done. There's no sense in me rubbin' your nose in it." She patted her arm before turning toward the sound of feet running over to them.

The boys raced to their mother, nearly knocking her over. They looked a lot like her, with button noses and round, brown eyes.

Emma laughed at their exuberance, and one of the boys held her when she reached for him.

"Jonas is good with babies," his mother said and appraised the other boy. "Jayden, not so much."

Celeste was glad their mother had mentioned their names, but there was no way to tell them apart. She looked for differences in height or skin tone, but everything on each boy seemed like a mirror of the other one.

Celeste reach for Emma, and Jonas returned her.

"When are you gonna bring that baby over for a cookout?"

Celeste smiled without giving her a commitment, choosing to slip into a dialect that might be more similar to Caroline's usual speech pattern. "I'm a little tired. I'm gonna go inside and sleep for a while."

The woman nodded. "Of course you're tired. Go inside and sleep. Do you want us to take care of Emma while you take a nap?"

Celeste shook her head. To soften any potential blow to the trust Caroline might have in the woman, Celeste added, "Is it okay if I call you when I wake up?"

The woman nodded. "You'll probably have ten missed calls from me."

"I'm sorry." She assumed the woman was Caroline's good friend, and she didn't want to jeopardize the relationship. Her host would need all her connections in order to make better decisions.

Once she was inside the trailer, Celeste slid down the door. The smell of dirt and machine oil rushed up to meet her.

Celeste was unprepared for the time into which she'd jumped, but there were still a few small things she could control.

Celeste surveyed her work. She had cleaned the hallway, living room, and kitchen, and the trailer smelled a little better. The cockroaches ran from her, and she hoped Caroline had enough money for an exterminator.

The neighbor had hinted that Caroline had a phone, but Celeste's attempts to find it were unsuccessful. She spent a lot of time cleaning and arranging the drawers in the kitchen and bathroom, but Caroline must have placed it in another part of the house.

Emma lay on her blanket taking easy breaths. She had fallen asleep midway through the living room cleansing, and Celeste had transferred her to the couch, placing pillows around her.

"I must have really upset your schedule," she said to her sleeping child.

She thought about Zam and wondered when he'd missed them. Had he slept through the night and walked into Emma's room to discover she was missing? Had he assumed Celeste had taken her to the market or to see her grandfather at the facility?

She put the thoughts of her boyfriend out of her mind and continued looking for Caroline's phone. She had avoided the bedroom at the end of the hall as she knew it had been the one Willie and Caroline had shared.

She picked up the disinfectant and bucket full of clean water and headed to the room. She had no intention of sleeping there, but it needed to be cleaned.

As soon as she entered the room, she smelled Willie's scent. Caroline must have sought to preserve his aroma, as there were bottles of a musky discount store cologne arranged across a dresser. Celeste cleared the trash in the room, and she added the cologne to her bag. Her host could buy more when she returned to her body.

She dropped one of the bottles, and when she bent to pick it up, she noticed a black cord coming out of an outlet by the bed. When she studied it, she found a fully charged phone attached to one end.

Celeste hit the side button, and the phone illuminated, revealing a display with a photo of an ultrasound. The date and time stared back at her from the upper half of the phone. Celeste dropped the phone and gasped.

CHAPTER 5

"It's October first," she said aloud.

The phone had slipped from her hands when she'd discovered the date, and she picked it back up to confirm what she already knew. Somehow, instead of days, Celeste had jumped months after Hailey Hall's death.

She had set the correct date, but machines, like humans, were as fallible as the human hands that constructed them. Celeste had calibrated the machine, and unless her grandfather had adjusted the algorithm, she should have ended up in time to go to Hailey's funeral. As the thought crossed her mind, she knew it was true. Her grandfather had foreseen her deflection and adjusted the time on the machine. All he would have had to do was hit a few buttons and Celeste would never have known.

Why did he let her go then? Why not keep her there and prepare her for a new mission? The answer was obvious: he wanted her there for his own reasons.

Unfortunately, Celeste had no idea what he wanted in the current time frame. Everything seemed to be stable, and if her last mission had been successful, the Great War should be nonexistent in all time frames.

Celeste decided she wouldn't be part of her grandfather's scheme. She'd go through the motions of an average life until he got tired of it and zapped Emma and her home.

Celeste tried all the combinations of numbers she could come up with in her head, but the passcode on Caroline's phone thwarted her. She sat with the phone, trying to unlock it until Emma woke up.

Celeste was pleased to find a washer and dryer in a long closet in the hallway. She had thrown away the oil-soaked rags in the hallway, but she set to work washing Emma's outfit and blanket with a load of Caroline's shirts.

Celeste found a box of rice in the kitchen cabinet, and she fixed it to share with her baby. Emma took a couple of bites and pulled at Celeste's shirt. Caroline's breasts had flowed with milk for Emma since Celeste had arrived. At first, she thought her milk had transferred through the time jump, but when she evaluated the idea more, it seemed more likely that Caroline's body was responding to a baby she had carried and the absence of an almost full-term pregnancy.

Celeste perused the cabinets, but she didn't find anything else besides a can of expired beans. Caroline was thin, but she had been close to delivering her baby. What had she eaten?

Celeste had avoided going through Caroline's tattered brown purse, but she realized the necessity for it when she thought about the meals she'd need to prepare in the next few days. She grabbed it from the kitchen counter and looked through the contents.

Caroline's purse was like a go bag she kept in case she needed to leave quickly. The anxiety Celeste had talked about with the neighbor may not have been far-fetched. A toothbrush kit, travel-sized deodorant, and pictures were sealed inside a sandwich bag, along with another set of keys and a wallet.

The other set of keys may have belonged to Willie, and Caroline's wallet contained social security cards, insurance cards, and driver's licenses for Willie and her.

What was Caroline doing with his driver's license?

First of all, it was a shock that the State of Tennessee had granted Willie James the right to drive a motor vehicle. Secondly, the license seemed like something Willie would have been carrying on him when he ruthlessly killed the nurses in the hospital and gave Hailey the wounds that had ended her life.

She lifted the plastic card and studied it. In the picture, Willie stared at the camera as if he were angry. Celeste remembered the look and shuddered. He was the man who had brutally beaten both of her hosts from this time period. Celeste felt a hint of an old injury in Caroline's hip every time she walked too quickly or bent at her knees.

She almost added the license to the garbage bag, but her eyes fell on Willie's birthday. She plugged it into the phone and the lock screen disappeared, revealing a nauseating picture of Caroline kissing Willie.

Celeste unsheathed a card she thought helped Caroline get free food, and she called the number, writing down the amount. She couldn't find cash or a debit card in her wallet, and Emma wondered how Caroline was paying for rent, electricity, and gasoline.

Celeste changed the phone's password to Emma's birthday and took a quick picture of her daughter. She made the picture her new screensaver but kept the lock screen image. It would serve as a gentle reminder for her to pray for the safety of the baby Caroline had been carrying.

Celeste reviewed Caroline's recent calls and found the neighbor's name at the top of the list: Marlene. She was glad to solve that mystery.

It seemed as though they were close friends, as they spoke daily and for extended periods of time. Celeste thought it might have to do with her pregnancy. Caroline had asked Marlene to go with her to the hospital when she delivered her baby, so Caroline may have viewed her as an experienced birthing coach. After all, the woman had delivered twins, and Celeste didn't know if she might have other children.

Most of the other numbers were from an obstetrician's office, and some of the calls didn't have a name assigned to them. Celeste thought about dialing a few of them but decided against it. Instead, she wrote down the numbers before they disappeared from the call history. One number repeated eight times. Celeste put it at the top of her list.

Celeste dived into Caroline's text messages, but her texts were as cluttered as the trailer had been before Celeste had started cleaning it. Marlene's name was at the top, and seven missed messages asked about Caroline's well-being. The second number didn't have a contact name. It only said "hey", and it had been typed three days ago. Caroline had sent the message, and any replies or previous messages hadn't been forthcoming or had been erased.

Celeste couldn't find other pertinent messages as she scrolled through waves of spammy texts. Why didn't Caroline erase them? Celeste thought back to the number of dish soap caps and empty toothpaste containers she had thrown away, and she understood the answer.

Emma commanded her attention, so Celeste put away the phone and ran a warm bath. She only filled the tub a fourth of the way and bathed with her baby, keeping Emma from trying to stand up on the slippery surface.

Celeste surveyed her host in the mirror. Caroline's green eyes were more vibrant with Celeste in her body. She didn't know if that spoke more about her higher intelligence or her happiness. She guessed the latter. Caroline had taken care of her teeth, so with the proper nutrition, and a good hair trim, Caroline could have been an attractive woman.

She covered Emma in a fluffy blanket as she searched for something comfortable to wear. Caroline had several sets of cat pajamas, and Celeste picked the one with the least vibrant colors.

Emma's clothes and blanket were still damp, so she pulled her baby closer to her and decided to stay in the warmest room in the trailer. Celeste counted her lucky stars that there were thin towels she could make into diapers for Emma.

As she looked through Caroline's underwear drawer, she found a wad of bills and counted out almost one hundred dollars. It wasn't much, but it would help with diapers, clothes for Emma, gasoline, and maybe a hair trim.

Celeste wasn't vain, but she knew the importance of looking nice for a job interview. She was certain that she'd have to start working soon, and she hoped to make her host look her best.

After their bath, Celeste and Emma played in the living room. Emma's clothes and blanket finished drying, and it was warm and comforting to wrap Emma in her blanket while the residual heat enveloped their skin.

Celeste didn't want to lie down on the bed Caroline and Willie had shared. She was pretty certain that she'd feel the same even after the bed sheets were washed. It was bad enough that Celeste had to stay in the home of a violent murderer, but she couldn't expect to have good dreams in a bed where he had slept.

She put pillows on the floor to catch Emma if she rolled away and curled up with the baby on the couch. It was more spacious than she realized, and the events of the day left her mind as she drifted into an easy sleep.

CHAPTER 6

Celeste juggled Emma in her arms as the baby lunged for a stack of plastic rings on the shelf. The toy teetered and fell.

One of the kind ladies Emma remembered from her previous trips to CHIPS picked up the toy and handed it to Emma. The baby promptly put it in her mouth.

"That's where everything seems to go these days," Celeste commented. She laughed until she looked up and saw the hard look on the woman's face.

Stella had been kind to her when Celeste had created her new identity, unknowingly using her baby's name as her own. After she had been told her true identity was Hailey Hall, Stella had been overjoyed when Celeste visited the store to make a donation to further the store's purpose in aiding domestic violence victims.

Her face didn't change as she nodded. Stella didn't even offer a platitude or a playful comment to Emma before she turned around and approached the lady at the counter. Celeste could hear them whispering as she looked over the items in the store, and she was convinced it was about her.

Some people were opposed to mothers who shopped with their children, so perhaps they didn't approve of Emma's presence in the store. It went against what she thought about Stella, who was a children's Sunday school teacher at the First Baptist Church across the street. Celeste hadn't been in the store with a child before, though, so the prejudice could have existed without her knowledge.

Celeste had already collected three outfits for Emma and a nice dress for her in case she went to a job interview. She let Emma keep the toy, and she approached the counter.

Celeste hadn't met the woman who tallied up the cost of her items, but she could sense hostility in her actions as the woman slammed the clothes into a plastic bag. She paid her, and the woman slapped her change into her hand. Finally, Celeste couldn't take the passive-aggressive behavior any longer.

"What's your problem? I brought my baby in here, and we supported your cause by buying clothes and a toy." Celeste held up her bag of purchases to prove her point.

Stella hadn't moved far away when Celeste approached the counter, and she was next to the other woman in seconds. She put a trembling hand on the other woman's shoulder.

"What are you doing here, Caroline?" Stella asked. Her voice was shaking with poorly controlled anger and two blossoms of pink had appeared on her cheeks. "I thought we told you to stay out."

Celeste realized it had nothing to do with her, her baby, or Hailey Hall. Caroline had done something to upset the women.

"What did she do?" Celeste asked before she could fully process that the women thought she was Caroline.

Stella glanced briefly at Emma. "Your baby" —she scoffed— "or the child you say is your baby is welcome here. You are not."

Celeste was glad the women thought she had meant Emma when she'd asked what Caroline had done. She tried another approach.

"I don't know what you're talking about."

The other woman almost climbed over the counter in her rage. Her hands fisted, and a blue-green vein bounced over her eye.

Stella tried to calm her. "It's okay, Shelly," she soothed, patting her back, but the woman didn't listen to her.

"What do you think you're playing at?" She yelled at Celeste.

Emma cowered into her mother's neck.

"You come in here and act like you didn't put all of us in danger! We welcomed you into the shelter, made friends with you, and helped you. How did you repay us?"

She cocked her head as if waiting for a reply, but Celeste knew better than to respond. Anything but silence from her could send Shelly over the edge, and Celeste had to think about Emma's safety.

"You called *him*!"

The emphasis put on the last word could only mean one person. Caroline had called Willie James to pick her up from the domestic violence shelter.

When she was searching for her identity, Celeste learned that the CHIPS store supported a domestic violence shelter in the area. The location of the shelter was private, so no one's enraged partner could endanger their life or the lives of the other women and children there. Caroline had broken the most important rule.

Celeste lost her ill feelings and wanted nothing more than to leave and never return to the store as Caroline Fletcher. "I'm sorry," she said, apologizing for her host.

"You're *sorry*!" Shelly shouted. "So, you're sorry that, instead of meeting your piece-of-garbage husband somewhere else, you told him to knock on the door?"

By trying to remedy the pain Caroline had caused, Celeste had ignited a wildfire in Shelly's temper. The woman inhaled sharply, and tears glazed her eyes.

"Did you ever stop to think that your knight-in-shining-armor would tell his wife-beating buddies, and they'd raid the house for their wives and children, too?" Shelly threw up her hands, and Stella flinched. "You were there. You saw Norman drag me out by my hair and Ralph punch Maria in the stomach until she lost—"

"That's enough," Stella said firmly. "For whatever Caroline's done, the baby shouldn't be made to suffer for it." She turned to Celeste. "You have your stuff." She nodded to the items in the bag. "Now go. And I think it'd be best if you never came back."

Celeste thought about apologizing again, but she opted to leave while Stella had Shelly under control. Celeste had nothing to do with Caroline's offense, but the weight of her host's actions followed her out the door and haunted her thoughts.

CHAPTER 7

Celeste had no difficulty in the store until she had to pick out diapers. In her time frame, children wore cloth diapers, but in her current time, only paper ones were available at the grocery store. Emma's size eluded her, even though she was the child's mother. She wondered if Zam would know the correct size Emma wore, and hastily dismissed her thought.

Zam was tucked away in her other life, possibly waiting for her to come home. Celeste thought about how it would feel to go back to Zam, sleep in his bed, and raise Emma with him. The idea left her feeling hollow, incomplete, and resentful.

Just as she settled on a pack of diapers for Emma, she heard someone talking.

"You hurt him," the voice said.

Celeste turned around and came face-to-face with Mrs. Winsome. At first, she tried to give a greeting of familiarity, but Mrs. Winsome cut her off with her sharp tongue.

"Why did you break his heart and send him back to me?"

Celeste didn't have an answer to her question. It was the second time in an hour that she felt the need to apologize for her host's behavior. Caroline had left the Winsome home, and Celeste understood Mrs. Winsome's insinuations.

"I'm sorry," Celeste replied shakily, adjusting Emma on her hip.

The elderly lady had on an umber jacket that contrasted with her long, tawny skirt. Her tightly rolled hair had no adornments and seemed strict over her wrinkled face. Mrs. Winsome's cold, brown eyes narrowed, and she shifted her weight on her cherry wood cane. One gnarled finger pointed at Celeste as she spoke.

"All you blonde women are the same. You take good men away from their families and then throw them back when you're done with them."

Celeste smiled uneasily. Caroline was blonde, and she had left David, but something about the accusal didn't feel right. It was almost like Mrs. Winsome thought she was someone else.

A smile that looked cool and calculating spread across Mrs. Winsome's mouth, turning the slash of her lips into an expression that didn't match her eyes.

"You knew who he was the whole time, and you took him from me," she spat. "But he came home. He came home to his wife."

Celeste was certain Mrs. Winsome wasn't referring to David's failed relationship with Caroline, and she was worried about the best way to proceed. She shifted Emma again, hoping the sight of the baby would be enough to stop Mrs. Winsome's misplaced words, but she doubted Mrs. Winsome would allow her to walk away. Thankfully, Ag saved her from the decision.

"Mama! Thank heavens I found you!"

Mrs. Winsome blinked like a switch had flipped in her mind. She was slow to react, but when she did, she seemed more like herself.

"I wasn't lost, Agony. I was just here talking to—" She seemed to notice her son's former wife for the first time— "the gold digger."

It was a new designation that Celeste thought stemmed from Caroline's attempts to manipulate David's feelings for money. Celeste held up her hand.

"I don't want anything."

Mrs. Winsome opened her mouth to speak, and Ag tried to stop her. "Mama, let's go. There's a sale on corned beef."

Mrs. Winsome continued to stare at her ex-daughter-in-law. Celeste braced herself for a verbal assault, and Emma gurgled happily, reaching for Ag.

"She has my husband's eyes." Mrs. Winsome blinked and shook her head. "She has my David's eyes."

Ag tried again to get her mother's attention. "I saw Mrs. Bailey in the cabbage, and I think her next stop is the corned beef."

"She's a snake in the grass," Mrs. Winsome mumbled as she followed her daughter down the aisle.

Ag cast an apologetic look at Celeste and turned back to her mother before David's ex-wife caught the older woman's eye again.

Celeste decided to end her shopping trip early and sped down the aisle. She slowed down at the end, but she crashed into another buggy as it rounded the corner too quickly.

Celeste was thankful that Emma preferred to be carried over riding in the cart, and she balanced her as she helped pick up the items that were thrown from the other person's cart. She apologized several times before she recognized the woman's easygoing answer.

Mindy bent over and helped place several cans of beans into the cart. Her exuberant boys jumped around the women.

"Cameron did it!" Her older son yelled.

Celeste thought he looked about eight years old, with a snaggle-toothed grin and dishwater blond hair cut into a fade. The other boy was almost school-aged, with long, brown locks and freckles splattered across his nose and cheeks.

"Dalton's a liar!" Cameron accused, grabbing his brother's arm in a vice. The other boy stared at him as he tightened his grip.

The show of force halted when Mindy told them to stop. They helped clean up the rest of the food that had spilled out of the cart.

"I'm sorry," Celeste told her again.

Mindy surprised her with her kindness. "It probably wasn't you. I let my boys drive the cart, and they were a little too wild."

Celeste caught herself staring at Mindy's wide blue eyes and shimmering blonde hair. Every time she swung it, the light from the store cast a glow to it that reminded Celeste of a golden wheat field. Mindy was about three inches shorter than Celeste's host and had a naturally thin physique, and the shape of her calves in her leggings revealed a penchant for exercise.

"I'm Mindy," she said, holding out her hand.

Celeste took it and shook it the way Sheriff Murphy had taught her. She was surprised Mindy returned the shake with the same firmness.

"I met you at David's house," Celeste told her.

"I know," Mindy replied. "I didn't like the way David introduced us. He has a kind heart, but he lashes out when his feelings are hurt."

Celeste realized there was a lot of truth to Mindy's words. Every time David had fought with her, his feelings had been injured.

Celeste struggled with what to say next. Finally, her eyes landed on Mindy's ring.

"Congratulations," she told her, pointing to the engagement ring.

"Oh." Mindy glanced at her hand. "Thank you. It was a little fast, but David and I had a whirlwind romance." She seemed to struggle to say something more. "You guys got married quickly, too, right?"

Celeste thought back on her relationship with David. "We might have been together a month when he proposed."

The women stood together, shifting their weight from one foot to another. She tried to think of any valid excuse to politely remove herself from the situation.

"David sleeps over at our house a lot," Cameron volunteered.

Mindy blushed, and Celeste laughed at the boy's presumptuousness. "When your mother marries him, you'll be moving into his house, and then you'll see him every day."

The boys looked at their mother questioningly.

"Actually, David will be moving in with us," Mindy told her. "We have a four-bedroom house, and the kids are used to the elementary school in our district."

Celeste nodded her head. She had assumed Mindy and her children would move into the Winsome's home, but it wasn't practical. The boys would have to share a room, and Mrs. Winsome's knick-knacks would be in constant peril from the daring moves of two rambunctious boys.

Celeste tried to talk politely with the object of David's affection, but she couldn't come up with a lot to say. She kept getting distracted by Mindy's sweet voice and the gentle curve of her arms as she moved them while she spoke. How could Celeste have compared to Mindy as herself or any of her hosts?

Cameron ran around the buggy, almost knocking Celeste over. Emma laughed at him, but Mindy was less forgiving. She asked him to apologize to Celeste after she scolded him for putting Emma in danger.

"I should probably get them home and make dinner before there's a riot," Mindy said.

As the women waved goodbye, Mindy added, "She has your nose." She pointed to Emma. "But I can't place her chin."

Celeste knew exactly why the origin of Emma's chin stumped Mindy. Celeste had looked at it every day for over two days. It was hers.

Chapter 8

As she drove back to the trailer, questions rolled around in Celeste's mind, tumbling over each other like clothes in a dryer. Unlike clothes, though, they couldn't be organized.

First of all, who did Mrs. Winsome mistake her for? At first, Celeste thought she was talking about Caroline's sudden disappearance from David's life, but Caroline seemed to remind her of a woman who had deeply wronged her. When she had lived with the Winsomes as Caroline, Mrs. Winsome had treated her kindly, but she had never warmed to her as well as she had when she lived with them while Hailey Hall was her host. When she was married to David, she had thought of the elderly woman as a guarded person, but maybe Mrs. Winsome hadn't liked her because of a personal reason.

Secondly, why was Mindy so nice to her? She had every reason to hate the woman she thought was Caroline, but she treated her with kindness.

David was an open person, and if they were getting married, then Celeste was sure that he'd shared his experiences. Celeste had to admit, it didn't help her case that she had shown up at his door claiming that he was Emma's father.

Mindy could be a good person, who practiced Christian values, but Celeste thought there was something more to her goodwill. Could she see her fiancé's ex-wife as a threat and seek to endear herself to her?

Thirdly, why was Celeste so upset that Emma had Caroline's nose? Biologically speaking, Caroline and David were the baby's parents. Celeste had only been the vehicle that transported her to another time. Once there, Celeste had carried Emma in her womb and given birth to her, but she hadn't contributed to her DNA. She had been more like a surrogate mother, and she hadn't been surprised when Emma liked to be held with her head over her heart, but she couldn't imagine Emma having one of her physical characteristics. But she did.

Celeste had long eyelashes, ivory skin, and thin lips. Emma possessed the same features. Any of the characteristics could be argued away as a coincidence if it weren't for the indented chin and small birthmark on her left shoulder. Celeste's father had told her that it had reminded him of a constellation, so he had named her after the stars. Emma had the same pattern on her left shoulder.

When Celeste saw it, she convinced herself that her eggs had transferred with her. It was a silly notion, but she used Emma's birthmark as proof. Over Emma's newborn period, she had talked herself out of the idea, instead believing that she and Zam were Emma's biological parents. But that was back when the baby's eyes were new and hadn't shown signs of golden flecks in the irises.

It was one thing for Emma to have her smile, as that was learned, but Caroline's egg had given Emma half of her traits. The egg was from *her* body. Or was it?

Celeste shook her head once to clear the path for a reasonable deduction. If Emma was David's daughter, Caroline was her mother. *But what about her birthmark?*

Celeste decided it was a coincidence. One of her friends, Timberly, lost her father when she was three. Her mother remarried when Timberly was five, and the people who didn't know their family said that she looked like her stepfather. Celeste couldn't see it, but she was close to the family. Their neighbors thought they looked similar because they both had brown eyes and dark hair. An identical birthmark was a different story, though.

Celeste's musings were halted as she pulled into the trailer park. Jonas and Jayden ran around in circles, tagging each other with sticks. When she parked the car, they dropped their weapons, and Jonas helped Celeste get Emma out of the car.

Jayden climbed up his porch steps and flicked chipping paint off the wood. Jonas asked if he could go inside, and Celeste told him to ask his mother. Jayden overheard them, ran inside their brown and yellow trailer, received an affirmative answer, and bolted over to where Celeste and Jonas waited with Emma clapping her hands.

Celeste opened the door, and trapped heat rushed over them. The sun had been out all day, and it had warmed the trailer.

The boys helped her take her groceries to the kitchen table. The plastic bags rustled against each other as they were laid side-by-side. The twins looked around the room in amazement.

"You cleaned," Jonas remarked.

"And it seems nice," Jayden said. "I mean, it still smells like a garage, but it smells like a clean garage."

Jonas batted his brother's arm. "That's not nice. You know what mom would say."

Jayden rolled his eyes and mocked his mother's words, even though his voice and actions betrayed a sullen preteen more than a thirty-something mother. "If you don't watch your mouth, people won't like you."

Celeste smiled. "I'm glad you felt comfortable enough to speak your mind." She admired the job she'd done in the kitchen and thought about the work she still had to do. "It was terribly dirty."

The boys exchanged a glance. Celeste hardly caught the understanding that passed between them.

"What is it?" she asked, moving her eyes from one boy to the other.

Jayden finally answered her. "You talk funny."

Celeste's eyebrows shot up. Part of her had known to model her neighbors' speech, but she had relaxed around the boys, and they had noticed the difference.

Celeste thought fast. "Did you know my father was a senator?"

The boys shook their heads.

"I was raised in a house where people spoke differently."

"Willie wouldn't let you talk that way, would he?" Jonas asked timidly.

Celeste thought about what he had said and realized it would have been true. Willie wouldn't have let Caroline speak more properly than him; his ego couldn't have taken it.

She shook her head. "But he's not here anymore."

She thought it'd be the end of the conversation, but Jayden said, "If Rowdy breaks him out, he'll be back soon."

Celeste couldn't determine the boys' loyalty. On one hand, they may have seen the result of the beatings he had given Caroline, but on the other hand, domestic violence could be commonplace to them.

Celeste decided on a diplomatic response. "That's true."

Emma broke the silence that followed by reaching for an applesauce packet poking out of the bag. Celeste gave it to her, opening the propeller top.

A knock sounded on the door, and Jayden rushed off to answer it. He came back into the kitchen with his mother.

Marlene appraised the kitchen and living room. "You cleaned all this after having a baby?"

Celeste reminded herself that Marlene thought she had given birth the previous day. The burst of energy was uncommon for someone who had been through the hardships of labor and delivery.

Drawing on her experience with Emma, she said, "My labor only lasted a couple of hours, and he was delivered quickly." Marlene gave her the same look the boys had before they told her she spoke differently, so she added, "After he was born, I thought them nurses were gonna rip me open when they pushed on my belly, though."

Her comment seemed to relax Marlene, and the woman chuckled. "Girl, don't I know it! They tell you that you need to have your uterus massaged" —she put up air quotes— "but that's not like any massage I've ever had."

Marlene pointed to Jonas. "With that one, they only had to do it twice. Everything seemed to settle where it needed to go, but with Jayden, they had to bring another nurse in to hold me down while they did it."

Celeste made a mental note of what Marlene had said. The boys weren't twins, but they seemed to have been born close together.

Celeste recognized her cue to contribute to the conversation. "It's their job, and I know it's supposed to help, but I wish they wouldn't push down on your stomach like they're tryin' to poke through the other side."

It must have been the right thing to say because Marlene laughed and helped her put food in the cabinets.

"I'm glad to see you aren't fretting over your weight anymore," Marlene said, holding up a box of sugary cereal. "I thought you'd feed yourself better after they took him away, but I'm glad you're doing it now."

Marlene had said "took him away" as if Willie had been ripped from a law-abiding life instead of arrested for killing innocent people. Celeste took a deep breath and tried to remember that Marlene may have gotten her information from Caroline.

"It was time," Celeste said, unwilling to carry on a conversation about Caroline's ex-husband in front of the children.

Marlene nodded. She glanced over at Emma. "How old is that one?"

That was a conundrum since the seasons in the two time frames were different. Emma was born in the summer, but it was autumn in their current time. If she stayed true to her birthday, Emma would either be four months old or over a year. Neither one matched her development. Celeste decided to give her daughter's age and make the calculations for an aligning birthdate later. "Emma's eight months old."

Marlene had been turned around, putting canned corn and beans into the cabinets. When she heard Emma's age, her head whipped around.

"You know you shouldn't give one of those packets to one that young." She pointed at the potential hazard, the propeller cap on the table.

Celeste swiped it up and deposited it into the trash can. She was struck by a sudden idea.

"Do you know anywhere that's hiring?"

"You're gettin' a job?" Marlene seemed puzzled. "Section 8 covers your rent and electricity, and you get food stamps—"

"They don't call 'em food stamps anymore, Mom," Jayden said.

Marlene was undeterred by her son's interruption, waving away his correction with her hand. "You already have WIC, and you can get AFDC."

Celeste was shocked by all the government's programs. She assumed Caroline had lived off the government's generosity for most of her adult life, and Celeste had studied the ones she thought Caroline was on. She chanced a question about a program she didn't know a lot about. "What is AFDC?"

"It stands for Aid for Dependent Children," Marlene informed her. "You can get it at the DHS office."

Celeste's caseworker had been at the Department of Human Services when she didn't know her identity. It was within walking distance of the trailer park.

The boys had put Emma on the floor between them and were taking turns hiding their eyes with their hands. Emma laughed hysterically every time they revealed themselves.

"Anyway," Marlene continued. "You just go down to the DHS office and tell your caseworker that Willie's in jail, and you need AFDC."

Celeste had no intention of going through with it, but it would seem out of character for Caroline to be disinterested in free money, so she said, "That's all I have to do."

Marlene put a hand on her round hip and her dark eyebrows drew together as she stared in a different direction. "Let's see. The boys were two and three when Randy had to do his time for grand theft auto. I had to take out AFDC, and my caseworker asked for their birth certificates and shot records."

Marlene nodded to the baby, who was standing between her new friends clapping her hands and waiting for them to copy her. "Has she had her shots?"

Emma had been vaccinated for polio and measles, as well as several other old and new diseases. The problem was going to be falsifying her birth certificate.

She had been silent for too long, and Marlene assumed Emma was unvaccinated. "You can get a letter from her doctor—"

Celeste held up her hand. "Emma's been vaccinated, but I can't get her records without a computer."

She thought Marlene was going to tell her to go to the public library, and Celeste was ready with her response. She was going to tell the woman that the information was too private to go across a public server, but in reality, Celeste didn't want to risk getting caught falsifying records.

"Randy has the laptop he uses for work," she offered. "And our printer is old, but it gets the job done." Marlene patted her hand. "We'll help you get some extra money."

Celeste wasn't going to go to the DHS office with Emma's records, but she realized the importance of having them. Before she had left for her last mission, her grandfather had requested a copy of Emma's birth certificate in case something happened to her in the transfer.

Emma squealed, and the women looked down at her. Jayden held the red plastic ring from Emma's ring set out at a distance. She reached for it and toddled a step.

"Wow!" Marlene cried. "She just walked!"

It was only one step, but Celeste was amazed, too, especially when Emma took another step.

"Are you sure she's only eight months old?" Marlene asked.

"Don't babies usually walk around this time?" Celeste asked. She was unfamiliar with developmental milestones.

"I guess there are some that do," Marlene conceded, but she seemed skeptical of her own words.

"You're a baby genius!" Jonas declared, and Jayden punched him on the arm.

Celeste agreed that Emma was smart, but she'd thought her baby was making average progress. In fact, her grandfather never noted exemplary leaps on Emma's developmental charts, so Celeste assumed her baby achieved her milestones around the same time as other children her age.

Marlene had said some children could walk at eight months old, and even though Celeste believed her, her daughter's steps seemed early. Celeste tried not to let herself dwell on it, but a possibility for Emma's new skill pushed forward in her mind, and she didn't like what it might mean.

CHAPTER 9

Celeste finished typing and printed the documents. She had worked quickly, but it had taken extra time to find a birth certificate in the state in which Emma was born. It took a moment for her to remember the name of the state, as the states were separated into continental zones in her time frame. The Great War had divided the countries of the world and one thing had united them.

Celeste had chosen a busy time of day to walk over to Marlene's trailer. The boys had just gotten off the school bus and Randy was due to come home any minute. With the demands of her household, Marlene was too busy to watch what Celeste was doing when Randy walked in the door and handed Celeste his laptop.

Celeste pulled the forged birth certificate and shot records off the printer. "Well, that's done," she commented, tucking Caroline's birth certificate under the papers in her hand. Caroline's birth certificate was easy to find, and she copied the state seal from it to use on Emma's birth certificate. She hoped no one looked too long at the seal, as the date and year of Caroline's birth had been added in sloppy script.

"Did'ja get what cha needed?" Randy asked amicably.

He had stretched out in his denim work suit, leaning against the back of their small couch. He rubbed his small, dark eyes and wiped a hand down his oily face.

"Yes, thank you."

He looked up at her. "Well, aren't you a proper lady now."

"She can talk like a senator now that Willie's gone," Jayden commented.

"What're you talkin' about, boy?" Marlene said.

Jonas nudged his brother. "She's not a senator. Her father was the senator."

"Are you talkin' to him again?" Marlene asked with her hands on her hips. "He was puttin' his nose into your business last time."

"I'm not talkin' to him," Celeste reassured her, scaling back into their dialect.

Randy had moved to take off his boots, and he peeled off one sock at a time. "Willie will be back soon enough, and you need to be ready to bolt when he does."

Randy's confidence in Willie's return rattled her. Marlene misunderstood the fear in her eyes and rushed to put a thin arm around her.

"Don't worry, honey. Everything will be alright. Rowdy has a fool-proof plan that will get your husband back to you."

Celeste tried to smile, but it convinced no one.

"She's probably scared about what he's gonna do when she tells him she gave away his son," Randy said without looking up. He examined his thick, yellow toenails, and he ripped off the tops.

"Enough about that," Marlene said, staring at her husband until it was clear that he wasn't going to speak again.

She turned her attention back to Celeste. "Now you'll be all set for your appointment with DHS."

"I haven't made an appointment yet."

Marlene patted her shoulder before letting her go and traveling into the kitchen. "I did it for you."

Celeste was upset with Marlene for overstepping the boundaries of their friendship, but she tried not to show it. Instead, she gathered Emma in her arms and turned to leave.

"Why're ya goin' to DHS?' Randy asked.

Celeste opened her mouth to speak, but Marlene answered him, telling him in around ninety seconds.

"Oh, I remember that mess," Randy said. "They came to the jail to swab my cheek."

"Why did they do that?" Celeste asked.

"It's for DNA," Marlene explained. "You see, when Jonas was born, I was still a minor, so Randy was afraid he'd get in trouble if he signed the birth certificate."

Celeste nodded along as if she understood, even though it raised a few more questions.

"By the time Jayden made his appearance, I was an adult, and we were married, so all I had to do was put his name on the form they gave me."

They went on to explain something that sounded like a subset of laws in the state that differed or went beyond the laws of the country. Celeste was glad to have one set of rules she followed in her time. If Emma had been born under the laws of the state, Zam wouldn't have been recognized as her father until he signed an acknowledgment of her.

They were wrapping up their explanation by the time Celeste drifted back into the conversation.

"So, they swabbed my cheek, and eight weeks later I got a letter that told me the percentage chance that Jonas was my son."

"Percentage?"

Marlene flicked him with a dish towel. "Yeah, he forgot to mention that it was a ninety-nine percent match."

"It was a little less than that, but yeah."

Marlene flicked him again. "As if there was ever any doubt."

A sly smile spread across his lips. "Well, there was that other percent..."

That earned him a wagging finger from his wife. "Now, you better take that back!"

Jonas had looked up from the show he and Jayden had been watching. "Am I your son?"

Randy's face was instantly serious. "You are my son, and I don't need a piece of paper to prove it."

Marlene turned to Celeste. "You'll just tell them to test Willie's DNA, and he won't have to pay child support since he's in jail. After he gets out, you guys will be on the run, so it won't matter."

Celeste put her faith in the ability of the wardens to keep Willie in prison and placed the idea of his homecoming far from her mind.

Deciding to keep the appointment Marlene had made for her, she asked about the day and time. Celeste formed a plan, and a visit to the DHS office seemed to be the perfect place to put it in motion.

Chapter 10

Celeste sat in the small waiting room of the DHS office with Emma on her lap.

Books lined the wall within reaching distance of any curious child. The flat rug was marked by years of use with juice stains and remnants of gum that had been rubbed into its fibers. A blue table and two rainbow chairs were stationed over the rug, and Emma used them to balance herself over to the books.

Celeste watched her, still in disbelief that her baby could move around so easily. Under her mother's gaze, Emma returned, placing the book in Celeste's lap and lifting her hands to indicate that she wanted to be picked up.

Even with the change in time, Celeste's best guess was that her daughter had recently turned nine months old. The season of the time in which she left had drifted into the coldest part of the year, but fall had just started in her current timeline, so Emma's birthday had to be shifted. Emma's new birthday was around the first of the year, and she hoped it matched her developmental milestones.

The book Emma had chosen was a sweet story about a little boy who was struggling with his emotions and the animals who tried to tell him how to deal with it. Emma listened to the book without amusement, almost appearing somber as Celeste read aloud in the otherwise empty waiting room.

"Caroline Fletcher?" an unamused voice called out.

Celeste jumped up with Emma in her arms and shifted the toddler to her other hip. She replaced the book and quickly followed the woman into an ice cube tray of cubicles. The woman motioned for her to sit in one of the two chairs in front of her desk as she took her place in front of a monitor.

Without introduction, the woman started typing, never glancing over at the woman she thought was Caroline and her baby. Celeste thought about offering the papers in her hand, but she surmised that it was better to be patient. Soft music from another cubicle drifted through the air, and a country music singer talked about his lover's sad, blue eyes.

"You were pregnant the last time you were here."

The statement wasn't meant as a question, but it was obvious that the woman wanted an explanation. Celeste had prepared her story and she hoped it worked.

"Yeah, I lost him."

"You were almost full term," the woman said. She stopped typing and leveled her gaze. "Didn't the doctors characterize him as stillborn?"

Celeste sensed a hole in her elaborate story. She agreed quickly, hoping it wasn't the wrong move. She hung her head, seeming sad over her loss, not knowing if Caroline had lost Harvey when she was transferred into Celeste's body.

The woman's voice softened. "I'll need to see documentation of it, okay?"

Celeste nodded, chastising herself for forgetting such a large detail. Of course they'd need to know what happened to the baby.

"Who do you have with you?" she asked.

Unlike the other women who had met her daughter, Emma held no charm over the woman. She seemed to regard her as another client. Emma kept her body across Celeste's chest, lying her head on her shoulder.

"This is Emma," Celeste answered with a smile.

"I saw on your renewed application that you're filing for AFDC. Is she your child?"

"Yes," Celeste answered, handing her a birth certificate. The woman looked over it.

"Why am I just learning about the baby now?"

The nameplate on her desk read Rebecca Masters. She seemed familiar with Caroline, so Celeste assumed she had been her case worker for some time. Celeste's mind raced to find a suitable reason for Emma's sudden appearance and berated herself for her total lack of preparation. She had been over her story several times, but she had fallen asleep after calming Emma the previous night, so she hadn't looked for possible pitfalls.

"Willie wouldn't let me talk about her," Celeste finally answered.

The woman's lips pressed into a thin line before she spoke. "You'd think he'd want the extra benefits another dependent could provide."

Celeste nodded. It was agony to wait for the woman's next question, but she didn't want to overexplain her lie.

The woman stared at Celeste for another moment before she resumed typing. Celeste looked around the cubicle as the sounds of gentle strokes of the keyboard joined the chorus of the other computers in the room.

A diffuser issued a warm scent of cinnamon and nutmeg and reminded Celeste of the celebrations of the season. Leaves in reds and oranges had been laced along the top part of the cubicle, but they seemed to be part of the general decor of the room instead of Rebecca Masters' personal contributions. One picture stood on her desk next to her nameplate. In it, an older man and woman celebrated their fiftieth wedding anniversary.

"My parents," Rebecca Masters said, nodding to the picture. "They made it fifty-three years before lung cancer took my dad."

"I'm sorry, Mrs. Masters," came Celeste's automatic reply.

The other woman almost jolted in surprise. "I've known you for over a decade Caroline, and you've always called me Rebecca." She let out a sigh. "Did I do something to offend you?"

"No," Celeste answered quickly. "I'm just practicing for job interviews."

Rebecca looked completely stupefied. She reshuffled her features and stared back at her computer. It did nothing to camouflage her reaction, as once her fingers were on the keyboard, they were immobile.

"Where do you plan to interview?"

Celeste had very little experience when it came to locating a job. Her grandfather had guaranteed her a career when she completed her studies, and David had guided her into a position at the hospital when she didn't have an identity.

"I was hoping you could help me. I don't know where to start."

The woman nodded as if she'd expected the answer. "We have some programs that can help you. What are your skills?"

"I'm interested in nursing," Celeste tried. She was experienced in engineering and computer programming, but she wanted a job that would put her closer to David.

"They're hiring janitorial staff at the nursing home," Rebecca suggested.

Celeste pretended to mull it over, even though she would have accepted the idea if it had been an opening at the hospital. "I'd prefer to work with people."

"You'll need to take classes in order to be a certified nursing assistant. Are you ready for that type of responsibility?"

Celeste had prepared for that question. She assumed the people who had handled Caroline's case had seen her lack of desire for employment.

"Willie kept me tied down for years, but now that he's gone, I don't have to worry about whether he's going to let me out of the door or even out of the bed from one day to the next."

Rebecca pursed her lips as if she were keeping herself from saying something she'd regret. She opened them to help satisfy her client's request. "The next set of CNA classes starts on Monday. Is that too soon for you?"

Celeste had the perfect opportunity to tell Rebecca that it wouldn't give her enough time to locate childcare, but she wanted to impress her with a positive effort. It would further the bigger plan she had in mind.

They ironed out the details, and Celeste thought she saw a change in the way Rebecca treated her. She hadn't been unprofessional before Celeste had mentioned a job, but she almost seemed more invested in Celeste's case. Celeste would attend twelve weeks of classes, and then they'd discuss her placement. Celeste wondered how she'd wait for a job at the hospital if one wasn't available, especially since she wanted to earn Rebecca's respect.

Rebecca returned to typing briskly. "Well, that takes care of one requirement of AFDC." She looked back over the birth certificate. "Do you have Emma's shot record?"

Celeste handed her the forged paper.

"She goes to the same pediatric office as my niece. Isn't Dr. May amazing?"

Even though her phone came with internet access, Celeste hadn't looked at the list of doctors on the pediatric website. She didn't even remember the one she had selected when she'd chosen the doctor she placed on Emma's records.

"Yes," she replied, and she was happy when Rebecca was satisfied with her answer.

"Do you have your social security cards with you?"

Celeste shook her head. She didn't recognize the term, and Marlene hadn't mentioned social security cards when they'd spoken about her appointment.

"I'll need them to finish your case," Rebecca told her. "I have yours on file, but I need to see it again when you bring me the baby's card."

Celeste said nothing.

"Be sure you get them to me by the end of the week."

Rebecca took a deep breath. "Now for the hard part." She looked at Celeste as if she were trying to read her, her gray-green eyes darting left and right. "Is Willie James Emma's father?"

This is the part Celeste had spent most of the previous day rehearsing. She was glad Emma had fallen asleep on her shoulder. Her baby may have been too young to remember anything she said, but Celeste felt more comfortable lying without her daughter watching her.

"I don't know."

"I thought that might be the case." Rebecca didn't quite smile, but something like victory tugged at the corners of her mouth.

"Do I need to order two DNA tests?"

Celeste hung her head. She replied affirmatively without looking up.

"Can you list the names of the alleged fathers and their last known addresses?"

Rebecca made it sound like the men were accused of a crime. Even if she could move past Willie and David's criminal-like treatment, Celeste was disconcerted with the way it poked at her legitimacy in determining the timing of her sexual partners.

She remembered the Winsome's address, and she gave it to her. She had found a letter from Willie to Caroline, and she handed the envelope to Rebecca.

The caseworker surveyed the hearts and declarations of love on it and wiped her face clean of an expression. Celeste felt the need to explain, even though she knew it was best to remain quiet.

"He sends me letters because of the baby."

Rebecca didn't say anything, and Celeste stopped talking.

She talked to her about ways to redeem her benefits, and the increase in her food allowance on her benefit card, but Celeste was only half listening. Her true reason for the visit was almost fulfilled.

"When will the DNA results come back?"

"It depends on when the jail allots a time for the test," Rebecca told her.

"Jail?"

Rebecca pushed the envelope over to her, pointing to the left corner. "He's in the local jail. He'll probably stay there until he's tried and convicted." She slid the envelope back to the stack of papers Celeste had given her. "It's a short distance to travel for the families of the victims to see justice for their loved ones."

Celeste didn't utter a sound. Her body went cold with the knowledge that Willie James was that close to her.

Rebecca noticed her changed pallor. "Didn't you read the letter?"

Celeste could only shake her head as bile climbed up her throat.

Rebecca's voice softened, and for the first time, she seemed genuinely concerned for the woman in front of her. "He really scared you this time, didn't he?" She didn't wait for Celeste's affirmation.

"Okay, I'm not supposed to tell you this, but my husband is an officer. Sometimes, they're a little short-staffed, so he works with the inmates. The jail is secure, and there's no way Willie is getting out. After his trial, he'll be transferred to a state penitentiary, and you'll never have to see him again."

Rebecca put the papers in a file. "As far as the DNA test goes, his DNA has been on file since his first violent crime, but he'll still have his cheek swabbed. They like to be certain, I suppose."

She gave Celeste directions to a facility in a nearby county. "You and Emma will have your cheeks swabbed, and they'll send the results to me. You'll get a letter with the results of the tests after I receive all of them."

She raised her eyebrows, peering seriously over the brown-rimmed frames. "David Winsome will probably get a lawyer. You can expect another court date in your future if Emma is his."

"Why?" The question was out of her mouth before she thought about it.

"I imagine he'll want visitation rights," Rebecca replied. "And with your history, he may even ask the court for full custody."

CHAPTER 11

Celeste wasted no time. She drove to the DNA testing facility right away, with Emma kicking her feet in the backseat to the beat of the music as it pushed through her tired speakers. The building was in Gray, an area just outside of Johnson City that seemed to have everything from grocery stores to restaurants to call centers and museums on one road. The ride took over half an hour, so Celeste had plenty of time to think about the directions in which her decisions were going.

Celeste was a little worried over a potential custody battle, but she was certain she could turn Caroline's character around before David received his DNA results. She looked in the rearview mirror at the baby that had stolen her heart. She couldn't imagine one moment without her, but Emma deserved to know her father, even if it meant Celeste had to make some sacrifices.

She passed the exit for the DMV. Erwin didn't have their own office, so Lewis had taken her to get her learner's permit there when they were dating. Like so much else during that time, their relationship crept up on her unaware and surprised her. It was almost like she was a passenger in her life, allowing things to happen to her and around her, but never raising an objection to alter the course. Not anymore. Celeste was determined to be proactive. Each decision she made was to bring her family back together, and if she couldn't be part of that family, at least Emma would know her father, aunt, and grandmother.

Celeste worried that they would be waiting a considerable amount of time, but the woman who checked her in took her paperwork, gave her a form to fill out and sign, and led her through an alcove and into a larger room. Small beakers and bright lights gave the appearance of a clinical room, and the technician moved quickly.

First, she swabbed Emma's cheek with something that looked like a cotton-tipped dowel. At the start, Emma wasn't a willing participant, and the technician asked Celeste if she'd hold the baby's arms. Celeste was a new parent, and she was a little nervous, but her embarrassment played second to the need to rationalize the situation with Emma.

In her time, babies were soothed with words, and stronger actions were reserved for steering children away from danger. Celeste realized the situation was new to her daughter, the process had been overwhelming, and Emma was hungry.

Taking out a bag of yogurt treats, Celeste sang a song to Emma that her father used to sing to her. A stab of sadness tried to worm its way into the lyrics when Celeste realized that her father was Emma's grandfather, but she would never meet him.

The distraction allowed the technician to insert the swab into Emma's open mouth. Celeste thought she jerked it around too quickly, but she was unaccustomed to the practice, so she didn't know what it took to get a good sample.

After the swab was removed, Celeste handed the bag of yogurt treats to Emma. The baby dived a hand into the bag, spilling a lot of them on the seat around her. Celeste took the bag back, cleaned up the mess, and fed the remaining ones to her baby as the technician took a sample from her.

The woman asked her to open her mouth, and the technician repeated the process she had gone through with Emma. The toddler giggled when the cotton swab jerked around Celeste's mouth.

"Did you think that was funny?" Celeste asked the baby while the technician secured their samples.

Emma stared back at her, smiling with strawberry goo on her sporadic teeth. Celeste took a picture of her, hoping to savor each moment with her daughter at any time.

CHAPTER 12

Marlene sat on her deck when Celeste pulled into the driveway. Jonas and Jayden were still at school, and Marlene was enjoying the warm fall day while she smoked a cigarette. When Celeste got out and waved to her, Marlene crushed the cigarette on the steps and placed the filter into a tin coffee can at the base of the stairs.

She had pulled her curly brown hair into a mid-ponytail, but her face and neck showed signs of perspiration when she approached them. A bit of mascara and black eyeliner had smudged from the heat, but Celeste could tell Marlene had made an effort with her appearance.

She complimented her, and Marlene said, "Yeah, I usually dress up a little to go to the doctor."

Marlene asked her about the appointment at DHS, and Celeste filled her in. She stopped her when Celeste mentioned work.

"But they're givin' you everything you need! Why're you gonna work?"

"It's something I feel like I have to do," Celeste answered. "First, I have to take some classes, but then I'll be ready to start a job as a CNA."

"Once you start makin' money, they'll take your benefits away," Marlene cautioned.

Celeste patted the woman's arm, following her over to sit on Celeste's covered back deck. Once on her feet, Emma explored the back porch, moving from overturned flowerpots to an abandoned cigarette pack Celeste assumed had been Willie's. Celeste snatched it up just before the baby's fingers touched the cellophane.

"What are you going to do about Emma while you're takin' those classes?" Marlene asked.

Celeste had already given it a considerable amount of thought. "I wondered if you'd watch her for me."

Marlene's eyes lit up. "I'd love to take care of her! With the boys at school, it's pretty lonely for me while Randy works all day.

Her eyebrows drew together as if she'd just remembered something. "What about Wednesdays?"

Celeste didn't know what Marlene meant, but Caroline would have been familiar with her neighbor's schedule. She decided on a vague response. "I don't know."

"I can't take her with me." Marlene stared at her, expecting her to come up with a solution.

"I'll figure it out." Celeste smiled and changed the subject.

Emma dived a hand into a flowerpot, pulling out a handful of dirt. She studied the dirt, and while the women waited for her to stick it into her mouth, she threw it onto the boards of the deck. Celeste was unaffected by the mess. Her father had encouraged her to play by using anything around her. The time he gave her for exploration led to her interest in engineering.

"She's a very smart baby," Marlene remarked.

Celeste agreed.

"I bet her doctor goes crazy when you tell him what all she can do."

Celeste smiled in agreement, hoping the woman didn't speak more on the subject of a doctor. Celeste planned to start Emma's regular visits to a pediatrician soon, but she had to wait for their next available appointment.

It was nice to sit with Marlene in the early afternoon, watching leaves fall lazily from the trees and feeling the humid-free solar touch in the air. Sometimes, they spoke of her expectations of class or something cute the boys had done, but there were moments of tranquility the women spent gazing at Emma playing in the dirt.

"I wish he wouldn't have broken the other one," Marlene remarked.

Celeste didn't respond. She could only assume she meant that the painted terra cotta flowerpot had once been part of a pair. Willie James must have destroyed the other one.

"I won't say a lot in front of Randy because" —she waved her hand in the air — "you know."

Celeste had no idea what Marlene meant, but she assumed it had to do with some sort of comradery Randy and Willie shared.

"It bothered me when he threw it," Marlene went on. "The boys didn't do anything to him. Sure" —she shrugged — "they may have been a little loud. But how were they supposed to know he'd still be sleepin' at two o'clock in the day?"

Marlene's eyes glazed over, and she wiped her face as a tear betrayed her emotions.

"I'm sorry," Celeste offered.

Her neighbor waved away her apology. "You know how he was better than anyone. He was a good guy until he felt like he was being disrespected."

Celeste resisted the urge to roll her eyes. Two little boys playing outside in the middle of the day was hardly disrespectful.

"I was shocked when he threw the pot at Jayden," Marlene said. "I begged Randy to do somethin', but he just stood there. I think he's a little scared of him."

"I know how he feels," Celeste said before she realized she'd spoken.

Whatever mood had caused Marlene to speak ill of Willie James lifted. She patted Celeste's leg. "Now I know you love your husband, so I'll quit goin' on about it. It missed Jayden, so no harm was done."

Celeste disagreed. It sounded like a lot of harm had been done. She thought Willie James had only abused Caroline and lashed out at people who tried to keep her from him, but he had been a tumor, infecting and darkening all the goodness around him.

CHAPTER 13

Celeste almost turned around three times on her way to the Winsome's home. She had spotted the family's blue SUV in the parking lot of the hospital before she made her trip. She didn't want to run into David by accident, and if he was at work, that meant that he'd be there until evening.

The gravel crunched under her wheels as she turned into the driveway. Emma had fallen asleep during the ride, so Celeste carried her with her head lying on her shoulder.

Her knock was answered within moments, and Ag stood at the door. Since she had started dating Marcia, her appearance had changed. She wore brighter colors and applied makeup to enhance her round eyes and high cheekbones. She had dressed up, but she appeared haggard, as if she was already exhausted from a full day when it was only just after noon.

Ag didn't invite her inside. Both women were a little surprised by the unexpected visit.

"Can I speak with you?" Celeste asked.

Ag sighed. "If it's about money, I'm not giving you any, and I don't want you to play on my brother's heart to try to get some."

Celeste had expected her response. Ag protected her brother and their family.

"I don't want any money. I just want to talk to you about Emma."

Ag's face hardened.

"If it's the religious folk, tell 'em I got plenty of Jesus in my life," Mrs. Winsome called from the living room.

Ag closed her eyes, embarrassed. "It's just Caroline."

A sudden crash sounded from the kitchen, and Ag bolted into the house. She left the door open, and Celeste listened from the eaves.

"Get off me," Mrs. Winsome shouted. "I can get another cup of coffee if I want one."

"I know, Mama," Ag replied in a lower voice. "The cup was just slippery."

"That's right," the older woman agreed, instantly soothed.

"It's almost time for your show. Can I bring you a cup of coffee after I find a less slippery mug?"

Celeste heard the familiar sound of Mrs. Winsome's cane as she shuffled into the living room. "What're ya doin' standin' in the door? Get in here and bring me that baby."

Celeste was shocked by Mrs. Winsome's invitation. She stepped timidly into the house. Mrs. Winsome sat in her chair and held her arms out. The baby transferred easily into the older woman's lap, and she held her.

Ag appeared with a cup of coffee, standing over her mother like a worried parent. "Are you sure you can hold her, Mama?"

"I am perfectly capable of holding an infant, Agony," Mrs. Winsome responded curtly.

"She's a beautiful baby," Ag remarked. "How old is she now?"

Celeste wondered if Ag was attempting to put a timeline to her pregnancy and the baby's age, so she gave her the age that coincided with Emma's new birth certificate.

"Does she have a stork mark?" Mrs. Winsome asked.

Celeste looked at Ag questioningly.

"It's a red birthmark at the nape of the neck."

Mrs. Winsome rolled Emma over and looked at her neck. She moved some hair aside, and a vestibular birthmark presented itself under a mass of blonde hair.

"All my children had stork marks," Mrs. Winsome commented.

"Did they?" Celeste said, more as a means of continuing the conversation than out of interest.

"They were all born with blue eyes and black hair, but their hair fell out and turned blond."

Celeste glanced at Ag, and Ag told her, "It turned brown when I was a teenager."

Celeste assumed David's hair had done the same. A memory of running her hand through his dark hair surfaced and she pushed it away. She wasn't there for David yet.

Ag drifted into the kitchen, and Celeste followed her, leaving Emma sleeping on Mrs. Winsome's lap. The music from her soap opera swelled until it led into the first scene of the show.

Ag glanced into the room and nodded in satisfaction. "She'll be busy for a while."

The house was mostly unchanged since Celeste had lived there. As she looked around, though, she spotted small differences, like the dust on the furniture or the extra dishes in the sink. It was like the family had less time to complete certain household tasks. Was David neglecting his duties to the family, or was something deeper going on?

Celeste picked up dishes and carried them to Ag. As the woman washed them, Celeste wiped down the furniture with polish, careful to breeze through the wood in the living room when Mrs. Winsome was immersed in her program. She would have been appalled to learn a guest was cleaning her home.

When she finished, she found Ag at the kitchen table with her head in her hands. "Thank you."

Celeste returned the polish to its place with the chemicals under the sink. "You're welcome."

"I didn't mean for you to clean the house," Ag said, lifting her head to look at Celeste. "I have to get things done when Mama's occupied."

Celeste waited for Ag to go on. It seemed like she needed someone to listen to her.

"David's at Mindy's a lot, and she can't stay here with the boys, so..." She trailed off. "It gets hard to handle Mama, do the housework, and work."

"I'll help if you'll let me."

Ag sighed heavily, and Celeste thought she'd ruined her chances to gain her favor, but then Ag's expression fell into acceptance. She stood and motioned for Celeste to go with her. The pair passed Mrs. Winsome, walking directly in front of her chair, but the elderly woman hardly recognized the movement.

Celeste hadn't been inside Mrs. Winsome's room when she had lived there. As she looked around at the lady's most treasured dove trinkets and pictures, she was hit by the woman's smell of anti-inflammatory rub and day-old hosiery.

Ag pointed to a sticky note by Mrs. Winsome's bed. Eleanor Martin Winsome was scratched onto it in curly script.

Once Ag had shown her that note, Celeste's eyes crawled over six or seven other yellow sticky papers. One at the closet read *favorite shoes* over an empty place, and another note at the dresser said *Don't let Agony give you warm milk.*

Two of the notes baffled her. One of them had a set of numbers and letters. It had been attached to the wall and seemed to have no point of reference. The other note was affixed to a black-and-white picture of five people at a table in a classroom or library. Piles of books had been loaded onto the table, and most of them were studiously bent over their work, but one boy stared off into the distance. Mrs. Winsome looked up in time for the photo to be snapped. She seemed young, maybe in her late teens or early twenties. The note above it read: DOVE.

"It's gotten pretty bad," Ag told Celeste in a whisper.

"I'm so sorry," Celeste responded when she realized Ag was talking about her mother's aphasia. "Have you taken her to the doctor?"

Ag nodded. "She fought me the whole way, and she hasn't been back since they diagnosed her."

"Dementia," Celeste guessed.

Ag didn't respond. It seemed that she couldn't get past the tears welling up in her eyes.

Celeste embraced her. Ag didn't return the gesture, but she allowed the affection.

"What can I do to help?" Celeste asked, echoing the words David had said to her so many times.

Ag shrugged her shoulders and wiped her eyes. "There's nothing you can do."

Mrs. Winsome's show was ending, so they snuck past her again. In the kitchen, Celeste resumed their conversation.

"What if I came by once in a while and helped you clean?" Celeste offered. "Maybe I could keep your mother occupied so you could work."

Ag shook her head. "David wouldn't like it."

"I'd come when he was at work."

Ag took a deep breath and rubbed her tired eyes. "I should show some solidarity here. You left David for your abusive ex-husband, and you've only been back to ask for money." Her mouth formed a thin line. "If that's what this is about, you should know that we don't have any money. I put everything I earn into keeping up this house."

"What about David? Doesn't he help?"

Momentarily distracted, Ag waved away the question. "He has a life to live. He pays his portion of the utilities and buys groceries. He doesn't need to worry about taxes and—"

"What's broken?" Celeste could tell there was a large expense somewhere.

"It's the electricity," Ag said. "I went to school with the man who came out, so he didn't charge me to assess it, but he said it'd cost thousands of dollars. It's faulty, and it has to be completely reworked."

"I don't expect to be paid," Celeste put a hand on Ag's shoulder. "You could help me, though."

"Here it comes." Ag buried her head in her hands. "David's gonna kill me for letting you in."

Mrs. Winsome had invited Celeste inside, but she wasn't going to argue the point. Celeste had initially visited to give the family a warning about the DNA test, but she couldn't find a way to bring up the subject without ruining the warmth Ag had shown her. She decided on a different tactic.

"I start CNA classes on Monday. Most of the time, my neighbor can watch Emma, but she can't do it on Wednesdays. Could you take care of her so I can go to class?"

Ag looked up quickly. "You're going to school?"

Celeste resisted the urge to show her exasperation. She had to remember that she wasn't Caroline, but everyone was used to Caroline's actions.

"When you were married to David, you were good at fixing things." The statement was made like an accusation, and it hung in the air. Finally, she added, "Are you going into nursing to get closer to David?"

Celeste didn't want to answer her question. She looked away, shaking her head and letting out a long breath. "I'll find someone else to watch Emma."

Ag's expression cleared. "No. I'll take care of her." She blushed after speaking so quickly. "I'm sorry for saying anything, but David's my brother. I only want to protect him."

"You won't have to protect him from me," Celeste assured her.

Mrs. Winsome was napping when the baby stirred. She woke with a start, hugging the baby closer to her.

"Babies are so comfortable," she said.

"I know," Celeste agreed.

She and Ag had worked out all the arrangements for the coming weeks. Ag would care for Emma on Wednesdays, and Celeste would help her with housework and managing Mrs. Winsome during the afternoons when David was at work.

Ag had made Celeste a cup of tea and talked with her before going into her room to get some work done. Celeste was happy to start fulfilling her end of the bargain immediately.

Momentarily disoriented, Mrs. Winsome looked around. "Where's Agony?"

"She's in her room." Celeste rose and moved to gather Emma from the older woman's arms. "I can go get her."

"We'll be just fine," Mrs. Winsome replied, pulling the baby against her.

Celeste didn't know if she was refusing Ag's attention or the exchange of Emma. She sat back down.

"Why are you here?"

Celeste answered honestly. "I came here to warn you guys that the state is going to order a DNA test from David."

"He's not going to like that."

Celeste dropped her head. "I know."

"Did you tell Agony?"

"I didn't have the chance to tell her. I asked her to keep Emma while I went to school."

Mrs. Winsome shifted in her seat. "It's best that you don't tell her. She'll let her brother know, and then you won't have enough time."

Celeste couldn't hide her bewilderment. "Enough time for what?"

The older woman gave her a knowing look.

"Are you awake, Mama?" Ag called from her room.

"I've been in here starving for the past five minutes," Mrs. Winsome said. "You left me in here with a baby, a bipolar woman, and no food."

Papers rustled as Ag got up to fix supper for her mother. She came into the living room moments later with a bowl of soup beans and a standing tray table.

Once she'd set the table and food in front of Mrs. Winsome, Ag stood with her hands on her hips. "You shouldn't say that about Caroline."

Mrs. Winsome's eyebrows pressed together as she stared back at her daughter. "What would you call it then? She loved your brother, but then she left him and said she couldn't remember him. Now, she's back, and she says Emma is his child."

"That's not bipolar. That's..." Ag trailed off in search of a diplomatic word.

"It's okay," Celeste accepted. "I deserve it."

Mrs. Winsome pointed at her. "See! The bipolar woman gets it!"

Ag sighed, completely defeated. "Can't you just call her Caroline?"

The older lady's lips crawled up into a smile. "Now what would be the fun in that?"

Emma rolled over in Mrs. Winsome's lap and looked around for her mother. When she spotted her, she reached out her arms, opening and closing her hands.

"I should leave before David gets back," Celeste reasoned, picking up Emma.

"Don't come back without that baby!" Mrs. Winsome said as Ag walked them to the door.

As the women said their goodbyes, Mrs. Winsome added, "David's a fool if he can't see himself in that baby's eyes."

CHAPTER 14

The pain was intense. It pulled at her hips and tore at her back.

Celeste tried to wake up, but something held her eyes closed. She was forced to deal with the torture in total darkness.

Beeping machines and clanking metal sounded in her ears. She could feel the presence of others, but they didn't speak to her or communicate verbally amongst themselves.

As soon as the suffering lessened, leaving a raw feeling in her lower abdomen, a new wave would begin. Celeste tried to count the minutes, but she lost track of them.

She could feel a bed beneath her, but her wrists were restrained, making it impossible to explore her immediate surroundings. Her ankles were tied to objects raised a little higher than her hips. She shook them, and a hand touched her ankle. It was large, masculine, and warm.

The periods of distress were longer than her reprieves, but she finally made it through the worst. Afterward, she lay there panting as small cries filled the air.

Celeste woke inside Caroline's body. Emma lay next to her, breathing in steady puffs.

She was no longer tied up, if she had been in the first place. She stretched her arms in front of her, and there was no presence of bruising or other markings.

She touched her stomach, and it wasn't tender or swollen. She felt the firm muscles that had hardly been stretched by pregnancy.

Her grandfather had the power to call her back at any time, but after he hadn't zapped her back within a day, she thought he would leave her suspended forever in the past. He had found a reason to buzz her into the future, and luckily, he had sent her back to the past.

Even though it seemed like a dream, she realized that Dr. Maze had popped her back to her time, but the jump had only been temporary. He had brought her back with one purpose in mind: to deliver Caroline's baby.

Chapter 15

The weeks rushed away from her. Celeste established an easy routine that involved waking, playing, and eating with Emma, rushing her over to Marlene's house, completing her school day, picking up Emma, helping Ag, and hurrying through short evenings with her baby. Emma went to sleep early in the night, giving Celeste time to complete her work before falling into an exhausted heap beside her baby.

Her classes were easy since she'd already completed the same material when Hailey Hall was her host. She learned a few new things, and some of the instructor's stories and examples were eye-opening, but most of the work was the same.

It wasn't easy to leave Emma each day, but Celeste knew they needed money to afford clothes and diapers. She had no intention of accepting the AFDC after the DNA results showed David that Emma was truly his daughter. Celeste was willing to work for the things she needed, and she wanted to move to an income bracket where she would be dependent on herself instead of the government. She wanted to be financially independent three months after she started her job.

Celeste wanted to work at the hospital, but no openings were available when she scanned the online job listings. It seemed her hope of getting closer to David while he was at work wasn't going to happen.

She never ran into him when she dropped off or picked up Emma on Wednesdays. If David suspected Emma had been there, Celeste didn't hear about it. She assumed he was too wrapped up in his relationship with Mindy to care.

Celeste tried to tell herself that the focus of her trip was to bring David and Emma together. Emma deserved to know her biological father, and David needed to know the baby he had mourned was alive. It was hard, though, to see his engagement photograph on the local web-based announcements. He and Mindy looked perfect together, and Celeste decided she wouldn't interfere with their happiness. Still, in her heart, she belonged to David, even if he had moved on with someone else.

Ag and Mrs. Winsome were careful not to mention David. They made loose references to him, but they protected her feelings.

The ladies were attentive caregivers. They doted on Emma, talking to and playing with her. Ag made organic meals for her, following Celeste's choice to focus on a plant-based diet, and there was hardly a time when Emma wasn't napping in Mrs. Winsome's arms when Celeste arrived on Wednesdays.

Emma was fond of Marlene, but she delighted in her time with Ag and Mrs. Winsome.

Celeste was unclear on their feelings about whether the baby belonged to David, but despite Emma's parentage, they treated her like family. Emma called Ag "Auntie Ag" in her cute, broken words, but she couldn't say Mrs. Winsome's name.

One day, as Emma sat on the rug playing with her stacking rings, Mrs. Winsome announced, "My name's too hard for that baby to say. She can call me her nana."

Ag and Celeste exchanged a shocked glance.

Ag picked Emma up and took her to the older woman. Mrs. Winsome accepted her, turning Emma around to face her. Celeste wondered if the elderly lady saw David when she looked into Emma's eyes.

"Nana," she said, pointing to herself.

Emma, who had been trying to call her something for weeks, said, "Ins."

"Nana," Mrs. Winsome repeated.

The baby's jagged tooth grin dismissed her word. She pointed to Mrs. Winsome and said, "Ins."

It was the part of Mrs. Winsome's name she could say, and she was proud of herself, scrunching her nose as she cackled.

"Nana," Ag tried.

Mrs. Winsome waved away her attempt. "That baby can call me whatever she wants."

Before she knew it, it was Halloween.

Pumpkins and fall wreaths dotted her neighbors' porches and smiling jack-o-lanterns stared at her from Marlene's deck as she climbed the stairs to drop off Emma.

Jonas and Jayden were finishing up their toasted pastries. Jayden wiped strawberry jam on his mouth, completing the look of his vampire costume. Jonas laughed, and almost spilled his apple juice on the black cowboy hat he'd laid next to his breakfast.

"Don't get anything on my hat," his father warned. "My brother got that for me."

"Where's the baby's costume?" Marlene asked.

Celeste shook her head. "I didn't get her one. She's just an infant."

Marlene rolled her eyes. "How's she supposed to go trick-or-treatin' without a costume?"

Celeste was genuinely shocked. She didn't know children were supposed to trick-or-treat at such a young age. Emma wasn't even old enough to have a costume preference.

"She probably couldn't afford it," Randy commented.

Celeste had swallowed her pride and asked her neighbors if she could borrow enough money for gasoline to make it to and from class. They had given her what they could afford, but Celeste was still short on the amount she had calculated she'd need to finish her course.

Marlene tapped her chin. "I think I still have Jayden's dog costume from when he was Emma's age. Do you want me to wash it while you're at school?"

"Sure," Celeste replied. Emma had been pointing to dogs when she saw them, so the idea of dressing her up as a puppy was cute.

"Haven't you gotten your money from AFDC yet?" Marlene asked.

"No," Celeste replied. "They haven't sent back the DNA results yet."

Marlene zipped up Jayden's backpack and hung it on the back of his chair. "You'll get the money long before those tests come back. Maybe they're waiting to send it on the first of the month."

Celeste shrugged her shoulders, unwilling to discuss her true intentions with her neighbors.

"I need to try to find a way to make money before my classes end," Celeste said.

Randy spoke through a mouthful of eggs. "You didn't need extra money before."

Marlene glared at him. "She also didn't have a baby. Babies cost money."

Randy looked at Jonas and Jayden, who had grabbed more toaster pastries. "Don't I know it."

Emma was precious in the basset hound costume. The brown and white material felt new to Celeste, and she assumed it was because Jayden had only worn the outfit once.

Celeste drove to the Winsome's house, and they fawned over Emma in her costume. Emma hid her face in her mother's neck, unaccustomed to so many people gushing over her at one time.

"Are you gonna take that baby trick-or-treating?" Mrs. Winsome asked.

Celeste looked at Emma. "She's a little young for it, but I think my neighbor wants me to go with her when she takes her boys."

"That sounds like fun," Ag said. "It's not really about taking Emma for candy as much as it's about getting yourselves involved in the community."

Celeste could understand Ag's reasoning. Other people needed to see her doing well with her daughter. It would help her if there was a custody battle with David as well as the view others in the area had of her.

Celeste was surprised that Mrs. Winsome and Ag hadn't mentioned a letter requesting David's DNA. Perhaps it had arrived but had remained unopened as David hurried to go to Mindy's house.

"You better go ahead and get started," Mrs. Winsome told her.

Celeste looked at Ag. "Don't you need me today?"

Ag shook her head. "It's a holiday. Take Emma out and have some fun."

Celeste waved at the women and reached for the door. Gravel crunched in the driveway and her heart dropped into her stomach. A look behind her revealed her shock reflected in Ag's face. Mrs. Winsome remained unaffected.

Celeste and Ag remained frozen until David opened the door.

<h1 style="text-align:center">CHAPTER 16</h1>

"Hey," David spoke uncomfortably.

"Hey," Celeste and Ag echoed.

"Well, there's enough *hey* in this room to feed a horse," Mrs. Winsome said.

Emma gurgled and reached for David. He looked at her, deciding what he wanted to do. "I have to wash my hands."

Ag's face hardened as he passed her. He washed his hands at the kitchen sink, but instead of picking up Emma, he stood across the room.

"I was just leaving," Celeste said, hating herself for leaving Ag to explain their agreement.

"That's something you do well," David retorted.

A threw her hands up. "David!"

Celeste waved the hand that wasn't holding Emma. "That's okay." She was disappointed when she heard the crack in her voice.

She rushed out and hurried to put Emma in her car seat. Before she turned around, she smelled the musky notes of David's cologne.

"What were you doing here?"

Celeste didn't trust herself to speak. She'd tried not to cry until the Winsome's home was in her review mirror, but her traitorous tears had flowed down her face as Emma tried to wipe them away.

"Are you trying to get more money out of my family?"

Celeste was exhausted by his charges. She turned her flaming, tear-streaked face to him, shutting Emma's door. She whispered her words, but she hoped they stung far worse than the injury she'd received from his accusation.

"Who do you think you are?" Once she started, her words flowed freely. "Why do you get to judge me? You don't even help your sister with your mother anymore. You're too consumed with your girlfriend to care that your mother's memory is getting worse, and your sister is buried in responsibility!"

Sometime in the middle of her tirade, David's expression changed. He lost his haughty expression and his crossed arms seemed like a means to protect him against his ex-wife's words.

"My family is none of your business." His tone had lost its bite.

"I'm trying to help your sister," Celeste told him. "I watch over your mother so Ag can work, and she takes care of Emma so I can go to school."

David scowled. "That sounds about right. You'd never do anything without getting something in return."

Celeste was incensed. "What do you mean? I never asked you for anything when we were together. I worked and contributed to the family!"

David glanced away angrily. "Fine. You worked for a year of your life, but that doesn't take away what you've done since then." He jerked his thumb at Emma, who was playing with a musical phone, oblivious to their argument. "What are you doing with that baby?"

Celeste remembered her lie, and she decided to wait until the DNA test results were sent to him before she revealed the truth. "I guess that's my business." She crossed her arms to mimic his stance and dared him to challenge her.

"Stay away from my family, or I'll call the sheriff," he threatened before he walked away.

He'd issued a similar warning to her before, and she hadn't listened then either.

Chapter 17

Celeste was still fuming when she pulled in front of the trailer, but the sight of Jonas and Jayden passing a football calmed her mind. There was something so innocent in the gentle way they threw the ball that reminded her of a time she'd shared with her father.

She'd had a hard day at school, and her father had sensed it when she'd dropped her school bag at the door. He'd offered to help her with her assignments, and when she'd declined, he'd taken her outside to pass a football.

Before they'd started, he'd said, "I remember how hard my father was on me. I know classes with him are difficult, but you'll never have a better science and history teacher."

Celeste didn't tell her father about the way her grandfather berated her when she missed a problem. She was sure he knew anyway.

They had thrown the football in the yard for an immeasurable amount of time. They seemed to connect every pass after the first few tries, so they established a rhythm until her father's contact slipped, and he had to rush back inside to put it back in.

Celeste had thought his eyes had been beautiful. They reminded her of the sky and the lush grass, but he was insecure about their opposite colors.

Emma whined in her seat, demanding Celeste's attention. She pulled out of her memories, thankful she had periods of reflection.

The last time she'd time hopped, she had longed for memories of a family she couldn't recall.

Marlene came out of her trailer as Celeste took Emma out of the car. "Are you ready?"

Marlene and her children dragged Celeste and Emma to every trailer in the park. The boys had given Emma a pillowcase, and she dutifully held it out when candy was offered.

Everyone spoke to Celeste as if they knew her, and she tried to keep up with their conversations. Without realizing it, Marlene rescued Celeste from attempting to answer questions when she talked over her.

Celeste thought they were finished with their outing when they came back to Marlene's trailer. The boys dumped their candy out in piles and encouraged Celeste to do the same with Emma's bag.

Randy was freshly showered and shaved. "Whose car are we takin'?"

"We can't take just one car," Marlene told him. "There are too many of us."

Marlene had insinuated that Celeste and Emma were going wherever they planned to go, and her heart sank. She had hoped to spend the rest of the evening with Emma, quietly dodging trick-or-treaters since she hadn't had enough money to buy candy for the occasion.

The group drove to downtown Erwin. The main street was lined with a plethora of costumed children, who were eager to fill their bags with sweet treats. Owners stood outside their businesses with bags of candy.

Jonas skipped to the beginning of the line and started speaking with a boy around his age. They seemed familiar with one another, so Celeste assumed that they attended the same school. Jayden hung back a little, swiping extra candy when no one was watching. When she noticed what he was doing, Celeste nudged Marlene, and she told Randy.

At first, Celeste regretted her interference, as Randy grabbed Jayden's arm and dragged him out of the line. She relaxed when he squatted and talked to the boy instead of whipping him. Jayden returned with red-rimmed eyes after giving back the candy he had stolen.

At the end of the road, Celeste saw Stella and Shelly handing out candy in front of CHIPS. As they neared their station, Celeste feigned a problem with Emma and crossed the street.

Marlene caught her staring at the ladies when she rejoined them. "It was a long time ago."

Celeste assumed she knew about the incident. "They still remember it."

Marlene shook her head. "What happened with that woman wasn't your fault. She made a vow, and she should have honored it."

Celeste concluded that she was talking about the woman whose husband had struck her until she'd lost her baby. She disagreed strongly with Marlene, but she couldn't raise an argument in front of the children, so she remained quiet. It didn't keep her from thinking about it, though, and she believed strongly in Caroline's guilt.

She liked Marlene, but she wished she could change some of her views. Marlene lived in a progressive time, and Celeste wondered what made her think a woman should stay in an abusive relationship. Celeste may only have been one person, but she was determined to alter the mindset of her neighbor for the better.

After they'd gone down the other side of the street, Celeste was certain that their evening was over. The sun had just slipped behind the mountains, and the temperature dropped at least ten degrees. Celeste slid Emma's arms through a purple jacket Mrs. Winsome had gotten for her.

"Can we go down Elm Street?" Jonas begged, grabbing his mother's hand and bouncing it up and down.

Marlene pulled her hand away. "It's up to your father. He's worked all day, and he has to go back in tomorrow."

"I haven't had supper yet," he said by way of an answer.

"But you can have supper anytime," Jayden told him. "It's only Halloween once a year."

The boys begged until their parents relented. Celeste tagged along, thinking about the time when Emma would pull her along to snag extra candy. Halloween was celebrated similarly in her time frame, but she didn't know if Emma would ever celebrate it in the time frame in which she was born.

Although Elm Street was named long before certain iconic horror movies made it famous, it lived up to its spooky reference. Aside from the owners of the homes who gave out candy, several property owners chose to dress up.

One stop had a theme from a popular tale about an ice queen, and Emma was thrilled when a snowman danced around them. She reached out to him, but he held up his twiggy arms, indicating that he couldn't support her weight. Celeste was silently thankful to whoever was inside the costume. She never would have been able to pull Emma away from the stranger.

Three houses away, artificial smoke filled the air and the buzzing of chainsaws ripped through the noise of the crowd. Marlene and Randy shared a glance.

"It's their favorite part about Halloween," Marlene said, watching her boys jump up and down in anticipation as their group neared the smoke.

Randy ran a hand across his balding head. "It's mine, too, if I'm bein' honest."

As they neared, Celeste smelled the dry ice and lights flashed through the smoke. Suspenseful movie music sounded from speakers in the windows two-story house. It seemed no different than the homes around it until you took in the spectacle in front of it. The yard was littered with classic main characters from famous horror movies. Some of their namesakes could control your dreams while others chased after the people in their movies with the intent to kill them. None of them spoke, not even the witch who stirred a pot of candy and fake eyeballs.

It was eerie when they didn't cackle or speak, but Celeste thought they were great at playing their parts. A man in a hockey mask stayed uncomfortably close to Randy, dogging his steps until they walked off the property, and a man with long man-made claws cocked his head at the children as they left. Emma laughed at a clown with a red balloon, and Celeste waved him away kindly when he wordlessly offered it to her.

"They always put on a good show," Marlene commented when they walked out of the smoke.

Randy chuckled over his close encounter with a serial killer. "Yeah, they know how to be creepy."

More houses were in the Halloween spirit, and Celeste marveled over the piano that played by itself. She understood the simple mechanics that made it possible, but she wanted to take it apart and look at it. She reminded herself that nursing allowed her that opportunity with the human body. It wasn't exactly the same, but it would be very close if she were a nurse in an operating room.

A colonial cottage blasted creepy sounds from a speaker on the porch and the windows were covered with mummies and skeletons. Ghosts made from suckers and tissue were tied to the branches of the dogwood beside the front walk. Emma tried to grab them as they walked by.

Jayden had already knocked on the door, and he was bouncing on his heels. Celeste was certain he'd eaten a handful of candy every five minutes since they'd started their adventure.

Celeste climbed the steps as the door opened.

"What do we have here?" a familiar voice asked.

Marlene turned to Celeste. Her eyes conveyed a similar feeling, but it was too late to run.

David's attention was on Jayden, but it moved to the rest of the group, and his jovial face fell. Two boys hopped into view, and he passed the candy bowl to them, excusing himself.

"Dalton!" Jayden yelled, high-fiving a boy dressed as a werewolf.

They started talking, but blood marched through Celeste's ears, so she couldn't make out their words. Mindy joined them, picking up Cameron in his dragon costume and engaging Randy in conversation, as he was the only adult who hadn't recognized David.

Mindy noticed Celeste and crossed her porch. She surprised everyone by embracing her.

"Caroline," she spoke. "It's so good to see you."

Celeste was less than thrilled, but she was grateful for David's fiancé's goodwill. She could have made the situation much more awkward.

Randy stared at them. "Do you two know each other?"

She opened her mouth, but Jayden answered for her. "She's going to marry Caroline's ex-husband."

Randy startled. "That was Davis?"

"David," Marlene corrected.

Mindy took Celeste's hand. To her horror, she led her inside, motioning for the rest of the group to follow them.

"Wow-ee," Randy said as he crossed the threshold. The house was immaculate with high ceilings and polished oak floors. Cinnamon smells escaped a diffuser that pumped scented steam into the foyer.

The living room was spacious and led into a tidy kitchen. Mindy sat down on a tan, suede sofa and everyone else chose their seats. Mindy had placed herself uncomfortably close to Celeste, but Cameron tickled Emma, so it was simultaneously awkward and relieving as the two played. It was strange to be in the situation, but the happy children took the edge off Celeste's embarrassment.

"She's so cute in her puppy dog outfit," Mindy said. "Where did you find it?"

Marlene mistook her question and sought to defend her friend from the imagined slight. "She bought it at a store with her own money."

Celeste wished she could crawl under Mindy's beautiful home. Mindy seemed unphased.

"It's absolutely adorable." She leaned in confidentially. "I had a mommy fail. Dalton wanted to be a vampire, but I couldn't have the costume shipped in time. I waited too long to order it."

"I'm sorry," came Celeste's automatic response.

"I think he may like the werewolf costume better," she said. "He told me there were some rumors of werewolves in Lost Cove."

Celeste looked around for Dalton, but he had taken Jayden away from the group. Two thumps upstairs announced their location.

"Where's Lost Cove?" Celeste asked.

Randy was staring at the eighty-inch television. It wasn't on, but he seemed fascinated by its size. "It's an abandoned place between Erwin and the North Carolina line."

"It's in North Carolina," his wife clarified.

Randy held up his hand, ending the debate. "It was abandoned decades ago, and it's haunted."

Jonas nodded solemnly. "My friend's dad hikes up there, and he says it's really spooky."

"Tis' the season for spooky stuff!" Mindy exclaimed with a smile. Noticing Randy sizing up her television, she asked, "Do you want to watch a movie?"

"We should be going," Marlene said. "It's going to get too cold to have the baby out if we don't get a move on."

Randy nodded in his wife's direction and stood. Jonas ran to the steps and called for his brother.

Celeste moved to stand, but Mindy placed a hand on her arm. "Could I ask you something?"

Celeste smiled at her. She hoped it seemed genuine.

Mindy sighed, looking down at Cameron. "David and I don't get a lot of time together when it's just the two of us, and I heard you were helping Ag watch over his mother, so I thought you might be open to the idea of watching the boys once a week so we could go out."

Celeste was horrified. She tried to keep a passive look on her face, but she doubted she succeeded.

Mindy wanted her to watch her children while she went out with the love of Celeste's life. She was asking her to sit in her beautiful house where he slept beside her almost every night. It was almost too much.

She tried on her brightest smile. "I'm really busy."

"I'll pay you," Mindy added hastily.

A glance at Marlene showed a similarly shocked face, but Randy was having a hard time keeping his laughter at bay.

"You said you needed some extra gas money," he reminded her, and his wife batted his arm.

"It's settled then!" Mindy clapped her hands together. "You can come over at seven o'clock this Friday. We probably won't stay out past ten."

Celeste left the house after Mindy hugged her again. As she walked out into the crisp night air, she marveled at how Halloween could be a terrifying night for adults, too. Oftentimes, in an unsuspecting way.

CHAPTER 18

"What?" Ag exclaimed. She clapped her hands over her mouth. "She asked you, David's ex-wife, to watch her children while they go out?"

Celeste nodded. Truth be told, she still felt like David's wife, as she hadn't been the one who divorced him.

Ag shook her head, her brown curls bobbing around her ears. Since Celeste had been helping her, Ag's complexion had improved, her brown eyes expressed more energy, and the bags under them had disappeared. A rosy glow accompanied her smiles, instead of a simple shrug in her cheeks, and Ag appeared more able to handle a small crisis, like her mother's refusal to drink warm milk before bed or a glitch in the power turning off the pot cooking their supper. The latter had been more of a disaster, as Mrs. Winsome's supper had been late, and she was upset that she had to eat a peanut butter sandwich instead of the roast she had expected.

"You aren't going to do it, are you?"

Celeste looked at Emma, who was chewing one of her plastic rings. "She's really sweet and persuasive."

"You can't be serious," Ag responded. She shot out of the kitchen chair. She paced the room once, reminding Celeste of David before she leaned her back against the counter. "It's not good for you."

"She's so nice, though," Celeste said. "I couldn't say no to her."

Ag lifted her eyebrows. "Why not? I love my brother, and Mindy's nice, but you have no business watching her children while they go out. I know her husband's death was hard on her, but she has my brother now, so she needs to stop inconveniencing everyone she meets."

Celeste decoded more in Ag's statement than a reasonable conversation about Caroline's well-being. To Celeste's knowledge, Mindy hadn't inconvenienced anyone else. Ag seemed angry with Mindy, and maybe a little jealous of her, too.

"You don't like Mindy, do you?"

Ag rolled her eyes. "What's not to like about her," she deadpanned. "She's so sugary sweet that anyone would love her." She fluttered her eyelashes, mocking her soon-to-be sister-in-law.

Celeste pounced on her feelings. "Is she fake?"

Ag slipped back into her chair and leaned in conspiratorially. "No one is that nice."

Celeste giggled, and Emma smiled up at her, trailing a line of drool from the red ring to her lip.

"Your father was that nice," Mrs. Winsome called from the living room.

Ag and Celeste had assumed the older woman had been absorbed in her television program. Ag's face dropped like they had been caught for more than gossiping about David's girlfriend.

"Mindy and her boys go to our church, and she has always been a sweet girl."

Ag buried her head in her hands. "You're right, Mama."

Celeste wasn't Mrs. Winsome's daughter, but she felt as if her words were meant for her, too. Not only should Celeste be ashamed for talking against Mindy, but she hadn't been to church since she'd jumped into the time frame with Emma.

As if she had known Celeste would read her statement as an admonishment, Mrs. Winsome added, "That baby needs to be in church."

"Yes, Mrs. Winsome," Celeste said.

The elderly lady appeared in the doorway, balancing her cherry wood cane on the linoleum. She lifted it and pointed to Ag and Celeste before she settled it back on the floor. "You two chickens are sittin' in here cluckin' about a woman who stole your man."

"He's my *brother*, not my man," Ag interrupted, throwing air quotes around the last word.

"He's the man of this house," Mrs. Winsome shot back. She stared at Ag to be sure her daughter had nothing else to say before she spoke again. "I want David back at home just as much as you, but we can't cast stones at his pretty girlfriend in hopes that we knock her down. At some point, he'll hear us, and he'll stand in front of her. And all we'll do then is hit him. I won't throw rocks at my son, and I know you don't want to either."

Mrs. Winsome had made a good point. If David knew they disapproved of his relationship with Mindy, it would draw him closer to her, but if they seemed indifferent to it, he would have no reason to defend his choice.

It wasn't lost on Celeste that Mrs. Winsome had said "you" as she was speaking to them. She had been talking to both of them, even though she was supposed to think of Caroline as an outsider. It was apparent that Mrs. Winsome had grown used to Celeste in Caroline's body, and she had warmed back up to her as easily as she had when David had brought her home the first time.

Her grandfather, the calculating Dr. Maze, had given Celeste a list of things to do and discuss to win over the Winsome family. She had dutifully memorized it and applied it to her actions.

When Celeste had originally entered Caroline's body and met David, she acted demure and helpless, awakening his urge to care for her. When he told her that she could stay at his family's home, it was more than she'd hoped for, and she'd jumped at the chance, accepting his proposal with hope in her eyes. She had befriended Ag with her knowledge of art history, and she'd remained quiet around Mrs. Winsome, allowing the lady to warm up to her in her own time. Her careful actions were upheaved when she started falling in love with David.

At first, she had been attracted to his blue eyes and dark hair. At the time, it was a little longer, falling in his face when he moved too quickly. But after a couple of days, Celeste noticed that his chivalry never stopped. He opened doors for her and adjusted her blanket to keep her warmer when he left for work each morning. And he listened to her. Instead of nodding along, waiting for his chance to speak, he faced her fully and waited for her to complete her thoughts. He helped her explore her feelings, and when she revealed that she was developing feelings for him, he helped her explore those, too.

A blush had crept up her neck as she thought of her first months with David, and she extinguished it quickly by standing up with Emma. "I think I should go," she announced.

"I made you uncomfortable," Mrs. Winsome observed.

Celeste tried to hold her stare, but she dropped her eyes. "You're right. Mindy has been good to me, and I love David, so I want him to be happy. I'll watch the boys for them to have some time together."

"Now, I didn't say you should watch her children," Mrs. Winsome cut in. "I just don't want you bad-mouthin' Mindy in this house. She's a good, Christian girl, and she lost her husband not long ago."

"Seems like she got over it pretty fast," Ag jeered.

Her mother rounded on her, but Ag held her hands up. "That was the last time, I promise."

Mrs. Winsome nodded, satisfied that she'd doused her daughter's fire.

"Ins!" Emma said, holding her arms out to Mrs. Winsome and ending their conversation.

CHAPTER 19

Celeste's phone rang, shaking her awake with its vibrations. The screen showed the number she had placed at the top of her list of numbers she had discovered on Caroline's phone when she'd originally opened it.

"Who is this?" she answered.

"Braeden," a surprised voice answered. "Didn't you recognize my number?"

"I was asleep," she covered. "How are you?"

"I'm okay." He drew out the last word as if he were uncertain about how to respond. "How are you?"

"I was asleep," she repeated.

"I'm sorry," Braeden said. "You're usually up all night."

"People without class in the morning can afford to do that." She wasn't watching her tone, and she found that she didn't mind. She wanted Braeden to get to the point of his phone call. Her interest was piqued, as she was curious as to why he was communicating with Caroline.

"How's the baby?" he asked.

"Fine," she said, assuming he meant Emma but realizing immediately after she spoke that he was asking about the child Caroline had been carrying.

"When do you think he'll be born?"

Celeste repeated the same lie she'd voiced to everyone else. When she finished speaking, the line was silent.

"Braeden?"

When he spoke, his voice dripped with anger. "You gave away my son?"

"What?" Celeste sat straight up, catching Emma before she rolled off the couch. She balanced the baby on the pillows on the floor and ran to the back bedroom as Braeden yelled at her. As Hailey Hall, Braeden had only spoken to her in a brotherly fashion, always positive and encouraging, but he yelled at Caroline, screaming insults and questioning his intelligence for dealing with her.

Celeste understood part of the situation before she could contribute to the conversation again. "Caroline was supposed to give the baby to you."

She had slipped, seeming to reference herself by name. Braeden missed it as he continued to berate her.

"I'm getting the car back tomorrow!" he threatened. "You didn't hold up your end of the deal!"

Emma sounded her distress at being left alone. Braeden stopped talking, listening to Emma's cries.

"You kept the baby," he accused. His voice dropped so low Celeste almost couldn't make out what he said. "You *will* keep our agreement. I'm going to wake up my wife soon, and she's going to have a baby there to meet her."

An hour later, Celeste had a better grip on the situation.

Two weeks before she had reentered Caroline's body, Macey Hall, Braeden's wife, had been involved in a car accident. Due to her brain injuries, she had been placed in a medically-induced coma. She had resisted waking when they tried to revive her, but Celeste thought Braeden may have prevented it somehow. Celeste assumed she'd lost the baby, and Braeden was attempting to replace the child before Macey resumed consciousness.

Braeden Hall was part of her grandfather's plan, but Celeste wasn't there on one of her grandfather's missions. She decided to wait until Braeden took the car and confront him with better knowledge about the agreement he made with Caroline.

A year ago, her grandfather had revealed that Braeden had a son, but she knew it wasn't Harvey Fletcher. Had he had another child later or had her grandfather orchestrated another glitch in the timeline with disastrous results?

Chapter 20

Celeste had every intention of contacting Mindy and canceling her obligation, but the thought of asking Ag, or worse, David, for her phone number made her more apprehensive than the plans Mindy had made for them. She had no choice but to go through with it.

Marlene spotted her on her way out her door on Friday. She called her over, extinguishing a half-smoked cigarette before Celeste approached her with the baby.

"What're you doin'?" she asked.

Celeste stared back at her. Marlene knew where she was headed, and Celeste didn't want to offer an excuse for it.

"It's not right," her neighbor said. "Apart from the fact that you shouldn't be watchin' your ex-husband's girlfriend's children for them to have a date night, Willie wouldn't like it."

Celeste was incensed at the mention of Willie James. She tried to remember that she was supposed to mirror Caroline's actions and bit her tongue.

"I guess you can't cancel now," Marlene said. "Do you want me to go with you?"

Celeste rolled the idea around in her mind. It might be nice to have a friend go with her. Marlene could help steel her nerves as she faced David and his fiancé before a romantic night out. It wasn't practical, though. Randy liked to drink on the weekends, and even though Jonas and Jayden could probably take care of themselves,

Celeste didn't want to feel responsible if something terrible happened in their mother's absence.

"No," she answered, looking at Emma. "I've got my little helper with me. We should be fine."

Marlene threw up her hands. "Suit yourself. Text me if it gets too sticky, and I'll think of a way to get you out of there."

Mindy welcomed her inside with a flurry of hugs and questions. She asked her about her day, if she could get her anything to eat or drink, and if she could turn on a particular show for Emma.

"She's too young for television," Celeste related, choosing to answer her last question first.

Mindy paused in the doorway of the living room. "You're right. It's been so long since I've had children that age that I forgot."

Mindy led her to the same sofa they had shared on Halloween. "If you and Emma don't need anything, I'm going to get ready."

Celeste thought Mindy's look had been complete. Her perfectly straight blonde hair shimmered under the light and her soft eyeshadow and mascara were perfect, bringing out the almond shape of her blue eyes.

She heard the boys playing upstairs and debated whether she was expected to attend to them right away. She decided that her responsibility wouldn't begin until David and Mindy left, so she seated herself next to Emma. Emma pulled at Celeste's shirt, but Celeste gave her a dissolving wheat treat, hoping that it would keep her from nursing around her father. David was convinced that Emma belonged to someone else, so he'd be appalled if he found his ex-wife feeding the baby.

David was the first one down the stairs. He walked into the living room without seeing Celeste and stepped up to the mirror over the mantle. He was clean-shaven, and his musky cologne traveled to Celeste. He had chosen a pair of dark slacks and a pastel teal shirt.

He straightened his hair in the mirror, and Celeste thought about how much shorter he kept it since their marriage had ended.

Emma let out a squawk, and David startled. "I didn't know you were there."

"I just got here."

Emma reached out her arms for him. "Da," she yelled.

David glared at Celeste, but Mindy chose that moment to glide into the room, looking even more beautiful in her six-inch heels and navy-blue dress. It only brushed her mid-thighs, showing off her creamy legs.

David was distracted by her beauty, and Celeste's breath caught in her throat. She tried to put it out of her mind that Mindy was her competition, thinking her recent mission was only to unite David with his daughter, but she had to admit, Mindy outshone her, whether Celeste was in her host or her true form.

"She's so sweet," Mindy cooed, motioning to Emma.

"I don't want her to call me that," David huffed, color rising in his cheeks.

Celeste's heart dropped, and Mindy looked shocked.

"David, you shouldn't be upset with the baby, no matter how you feel about Caroline." She glanced at Celeste and flashed a reassuring smile. "Besides, it sounds like she was trying to say your name."

"David?"

Mindy nodded, guiding him over to the sofa where Emma still had her arms outstretched. "Pick her up," she encouraged.

David stared at her, trying to silently communicate his unwillingness to comply. Mindy stared back, pushing her idea.

David relented, picking the baby up and balancing her on his hip. Emma hugged him, and he patted her back, bouncing her as he took her to the mirror.

Emma looked at him and placed her hand on his cheek. "Da."

He pointed at the mirror. "There's a pretty girl in there."

Emma looked where he indicated, and her smile widened.

Celeste's breath was almost taken away as she watched David's first interaction with his daughter. He had fumbled her, at first, but he held her close, and his lips stretched into a grin that reached his eyes. He laughed, and it was the same sound she heard in her dreams almost every night as she visited the time they'd shared in her sleep.

"It makes me want to have another one," Mindy admitted, jolting Celeste out of her happy thoughts. "He'd be such a good dad. Look at how great he is with her."

Celeste smiled, pushing her tears away. Of course Mindy would see the scene that way. She had no idea that Emma was truly David's child.

"Are you ready?" Mindy asked.

David called for Dalton and Cameron, and the boys bounded down the steps.

"I left money for you in an envelope on the counter," Mindy told her. "Dalton has my bank card. He can use it to order a pizza, but that's all." As she spoke her eyes narrowed on her son.

Dalton rolled his eyes. "I won't order any skins while you're gone."

"What are skins?" Celeste asked.

"They're suits of clothes for his video game avatar," David explained, bouncing Emma.

Celeste had studied video games briefly, convinced she knew enough about virtual reality to play one if she had the opportunity. The terminology was different for each time frame, though, and in her era, avatars were called aviators, as they guided their users to different planes and playing fields.

"I can show you how to play," Dalton offered. "I'm Dragon Lover 8. The eight is because I'm eight years old."

They shared a good-natured laugh at his words.

David handed Emma back to Celeste, grabbing Mindy's coat off the rack and putting it on her. Celeste recognized his tenderness and longed for the days he had treated her with love.

It was difficult to watch. Caroline had abandoned their marriage, but Celeste would have stayed in David's arms forever. Instead of continuing her time with the man she loved, she held their daughter and watched as he left with the beautiful woman he planned to marry.

The evening passed quickly. Cameron's bedtime crept up on them, so after the pizza was delivered and they ate it, he had to brush his teeth and go to bed. Celeste supervised his teeth brushing and tucked him into bed.

"Mommy doesn't read me a story anymore," Cameron complained, sticking out his lower lip.

Celeste recognized the manipulation, but Dalton cut in. "She reads to you on the nights David's not here."

Cameron shook his head and looked away. "I guess she won't read to me ever again when they're married."

Celeste found herself trying to defend Mindy. "Things might be a little different now, but soon David and your mom will settle into their life together. She'll spend more time with you after that."

"Not if she has another baby," Cameron said, rubbing a chubby hand under his nose. "She talks about your baby all the time."

"She wants a girl," Dalton revealed.

Celeste tried to find a way to make them feel better. "I'm sure she's happy with her two wonderful boys."

"Not since daddy died," Dalton continued. "She went out and got a new husband, and now she wants a new baby."

Celeste decided the conversation was going in the wrong direction. "Why don't you show me all the skins you have for your avatar."

Cameron slept peacefully upstairs while Dalton showed her how to play a shooting game. Emma was asleep on her lap before the first round, and even though she was only an infant, Celeste was glad her baby wasn't exposed to the realistic gore.

True to her word, Mindy and David came back around ten o'clock.

"Emma's asleep," Mindy observed. "You can stay here tonight if you want. There's no sense in getting her out in the cold night air."

David stiffened, and Celeste spoke quickly. "It's okay. We need to get home."

"You could leave her here for the night," Mindy offered. "I'll get up with her if she wakes up."

David's eyebrows climbed up his forehead, and Celeste rushed to find a reasonable excuse. Mindy had trusted her with her sons. It would be impolite to tell her she didn't want her to look after Emma.

"We have to go to an appointment early tomorrow morning," Celeste lied, realizing the necessity of it.

"Okay," David said, rescuing Celeste from saying more by picking Emma up and wrapping her in her coat.

"Did you find your money?" Mindy asked.

Celeste patted the unopened envelope in her pocket.

"I hope it's enough," she said, pulling Celeste in for an uncomfortable hug.

"I'm sure it will be more than enough."

"You didn't open it?" Mindy asked, appearing crestfallen.

"I didn't have time," Celeste replied with a laugh. "I was busy learning about skins and drop zones."

Mindy smiled, and David opened the door. He wanted to hasten her exit, and Celeste was grateful for his help.

Mindy and Celeste exchanged numbers. She promised to send her a message about another date night.

David walked her to the car and fastened Emma into the seat. He stared at her a little longer than Celeste had expected, and she stood in the cold without moving while he took in the baby's features.

He noticed her watching him, and he retreated quickly. "She really is a beautiful baby." He walked away without saying another word.

Celeste got into the car and pulled out the envelope. Curiosity got the best of her, and she ripped it open. She expected a twenty to fall out, but she gasped when she saw a hundred-dollar bill in the security of its folds.

A yellow sticky note held a message for her: *I hope this is enough to keep you in our lives. I see your struggles, and I believe in you.*

During the drive home, Celeste's tears glided down her cheeks. She let go of any hope of winning David back, and she released him in her heart to be with a woman who was beautiful inside and out.

Chapter 21

Braeden showed up with a tow truck on Saturday night.

She heard the cranking of machinery just before her phone rang. She answered it as she threw on her coat and made sure Emma was sleeping peacefully.

"They're repossessing your car," Marlene informed her.

Celeste didn't want to explain her situation, so she replied, "I know. I'm on my way out there now."

"Do you want us to come out with you?" she asked, including her husband.

"No," Celeste responded. "I'll take care of it."

She ran outside, waving her arms. The man who cranked her vehicle up looked from her to Braeden.

"I'll be right back," he told the other man, who threw up a hand and climbed back into his heated tow truck.

"I told you I'd pick up the car," Braeden reminded her.

"I know," Celeste said. "But you didn't have to hire a tow truck. I would have given the keys to you."

Braeden looked much different than she remembered him. It might have been a combination of his sister's death and his wife's accident, but the events had left their mark on him.

His natural dish-water blond hair was cut close to his scalp and his blue eyes had grown cold. His olive-green button-up looked a little too large for him, adding weight to Celeste's theory. The reddish-purple scar on his jaw confirmed it. Braeden had been in the wreck with Macey.

He tapped his foot and narrowed his eyes. "Are you going to say something to stop me?"

"I doubt it," Celeste responded.

He shook his head. "You have some nerve, you know? You came to me, offering" —he looked her up and down disparagingly— "yourself. I gave you another option, and you spit it back out at me."

Celeste felt her stomach roll. In another life, Braeden had been her brother, so the thought of Caroline trying to seduce him made her feel sick.

"I can't give you a baby I don't have," Celeste said when she recovered. "I should never have agreed to it in the first place."

He gave a snort of derision and his nostrils flared. "You're a piece of trash. Macey would never have believed your son was ours."

Celeste allowed Braeden's slight, reminding herself that he was talking about Caroline, not her. She felt angry for Harvey, though, as he had grown up in Braeden's time frame and amassed a fortune. His accomplishments would have made any parent proud.

"What are you going to do with the car?"

Braeden glared at Celeste. "It's mine, so I'll do whatever I want with it."

"Can I buy it from you?" she asked him.

The question took him off guard. He paced, running a hand over his head. Suddenly, he stopped and laughed. "I don't know why I even considered it. You don't have a job."

"I'll have one soon," Celeste countered. "I'm taking CNA classes."

She watched the memory of his sister take hold of him. When Hailey had been Celeste's host, she had worked as a CNA.

"You really know how to manipulate people," he said. "You acted like you knew my sister so well when you went to her funeral, but David told me your game." He put his head in his hand. "I should have listened to him."

Celeste took out the hundred-dollar bill from her pocket and handed it to Braeden. "It's all I have, besides a twenty for gas and diapers, but you can consider it a down payment."

Braden looked at the money like he couldn't process its worth. "But we had an agreement."

Celeste softened her tone. "Look, I'm sorry Macey lost the—"

"She didn't lose him!" Braeden thundered. He stared at her in disbelief. "You really are a piece of work."

Celeste searched for something to say, but she came up short.

He crumpled the bill into his fist. "Consider us done! Any arrangement we made is over. You can keep the car, but I never want to see you again. If you call me, I'll report it stolen, and you'll go to jail. Do you understand me?"

Celeste nodded.

The tow truck driver climbed out of his truck as Braeden walked back. Braeden tossed him the crumpled money. "Put the car back down. Let's get out of here."

Once the man caught a glimpse of the amount of money Braeden had tossed him, his eyes widened, and he worked quickly to place the car back in the driveway.

After Emma went to sleep, Celeste loaded very specific searches into her web browser. It didn't take long to find out the reason Braeden had been so upset when she'd said his wife had lost the baby.

Macey had delivered a premature infant, and he had stayed in the neonatal intensive care unit of the hospital until he was stolen. All the hospital staff had been shocked, as the infants were monitored at all times. The police checked the homes and contacts of everyone who had access to the unit, but they couldn't find the baby. They reviewed the footage from the night of the disappearance, but it showed nothing. It was like the baby had disappeared.

Celeste looked at the blue eye and green eye of the missing child, marveling at the anomaly. She thought she knew exactly where he had gone and who had taken him.

CHAPTER 22

On a frigid day in the late fall, Celeste took a break from her duties at the Winsome house and stepped out on the front porch. The wind battled her clothes, so she pulled her jacket around tighter.

It had been eight weeks since Celeste had visited the DHS office and she hadn't received a letter. She decided to call her case worker.

Rebecca answered on the third ring.

Celeste asked her about the status of her case, expecting Rebecca to site problems within the DHS office. Instead, she told Celeste that she had closed her AFDC case.

"Why?" Celeste asked.

"You never brought by Emma's social security card," she reminded her. "I sent you a letter about it."

No mailboxes stood outside the trailers and bringing her case worker the social security card had slipped Celeste's mind. She stated that she hadn't received the letter.

"I told you to bring it to me before the end of the cycle, and it ended" —she paused, and her chair squeaked as if she had moved to look at a calendar— "about six weeks ago."

Celeste needed the DNA test to confirm David was Emma's father. After she had watched them together, she owed it to both of them. She decided her best route was to act desperate for the money the AFDC would provide, even though she had no intention of using it.

"Is there anything I can do?"

Rebecca's voice was cooler. "It's all in the letter I sent you, but you'll have to reapply for assistance."

"I don't know when I could come for another appointment. I have classes and I help a lady with her mother in the afternoons."

After a brief pause, Rebecca answered, her tone friendlier. "You're still going to classes?"

"Yes," Celeste answered. "I'm over halfway to earning my certification."

"Can you swing by the office and fill out an application?" Rebecca asked. "I'll arrange a phone interview when I receive it."

Celeste's spirits lifted. She told her case worker that she would drop by the office soon.

"But I won't do anything until I get a copy of Emma's social security card," she warned.

"I'll bring it with me," Celeste promised.

Celeste was filled with purpose when she hung up the phone. She swept the kitchen floor and vacuumed the living room.

Mrs. Winsome was irritated by the loud noise of the vacuum, and she used it as an excuse to go to the bathroom. Ag wandered into the living room, and Celeste was surprised by the scratches on her face.

"What happened?" Celeste tried to survey the damage.

Color rose in Ag's cheeks as she touched the marks. "It's nothing."

The Winsomes didn't own a cat, and Ag usually didn't come in contact with other people. Celeste guessed who had scratched her.

"Did Marcia do this?"

Ag hadn't talked about her girlfriend in the weeks Celeste had helped her, and Celeste was afraid to befriend David's sister on social media because of their dubious history. She wondered if they'd fought.

"No," Ag said quickly, irritation clear on her features. "Marcia wouldn't have hurt me. But I haven't seen her in months." She motioned to the house with her hand. "Marcia doesn't deserve this stress."

She'd kept her voice just above a whisper, and when Mrs. Winsome went past her to return to her chair, she retreated into her room. After checking on Emma and seeing her playing happily on the kitchen floor, Celeste followed Ag into her bedroom.

Ag typed on her laptop; the keys clicked rapidly against her short nails. Celeste waited on her to stop, but the woman seemed determined to avoid the issue.

"Who marked your face, Ag?" she asked, even though she already knew the answer.

Ag closed her laptop and sat it beside her on the bed. She didn't invite Celeste to join her.

"It was Mama," she confessed without looking up. "Can you leave me alone now?"

"No," Celeste spoke firmly, taking a seat next to Ag on her bed. "What happened?"

Ag sighed, and Celeste was reminded that she was no longer the person Ag had trusted with her secrets. She had welcomed Celeste with open arms when she had married David and when Hailey Hall had been her host, but Caroline had ruined any possibility of an innocent relationship with David's sister when she had left him for her ex-husband.

Ag picked up her laptop and put it back on her lap. "I'm trying not to be mean to you, Caroline, but it's none of your business."

Celeste disagreed. "I'm here five days a week to help you, and you look after Emma for me on Wednesdays. If there's something going on, I have every right to know."

Ag sighed heavily, and a tear of resignation slipped down her cheek. "You're right. You have the right to know if you or Emma are in danger, and I can honestly say I don't know."

Celeste waited for more. She'd learned that Ag's long pauses were usually followed by intimate details, so she stayed silent while the other woman gathered her thoughts.

"I was so tired," she started, looking at one of the pictures of Paris that lined her floor. "I wanted to go to bed, but Mama kept insisting that Daddy was on his way home. She wanted to wait up for him."

She looked at Celeste. "You see, David didn't live here when Daddy died. He stayed at Ashley's place with her, so when David started staying over at Mindy's house, I guess my mother's brain flipped back to that time." She glanced away. "Or at least it did that night."

Celeste wanted to put her arm around Ag or hug her, but while she was inside Caroline's body, her actions would be unwelcome. She sat rigidly and hoped she could find a way to help.

"I brought her a glass of warm milk, but she screamed at me and slung it across the room. I tried to reason with her. I showed her Daddy's obituary, and she clawed my face." She touched the marks her mother had left. "She called me a demon."

"Oh my gosh, Ag," Celeste gasped. "I'm so sorry."

"It's fine," Ag dismissed, wiping away a couple of tears that had fallen on the angry red gashes. "She didn't remember doing it the next morning, so it was like it never happened."

"Have you told David about it?"

She shrugged. "What's there to tell? Mama had a lapse in her memory, but she's fine now. There's nothing he can do."

Celeste decided to bring up the most difficult subject. "What if it happens again? What if it happens all the time?" She swallowed audibly. "What if you need to consider alternate care for your mother?"

"My mother is eighty-two years old, Caroline. She's lived in this house most of her life, and I can't take her out of it."

Celeste nodded as if she accepted Ag's answer, but she didn't agree with it. When she had occupied Hailey Hall's body, she had worked with a lot of dementia patients. Sadly, they never improved. There were good days, and there were days that were so terrible that they almost erased the good ones from your mind. It was a time-steeler, and in Celeste's opinion, it was one of the worst ways to die.

Ag was still convinced that her mother's condition would improve. It would take some time, and interference from David before she accepted it. Eventually, Mrs. Winsome was going to need more experienced care, and Ag was going to have to let her mother receive it.

"I think you should talk to David," Celeste encouraged. "Just to let him know what's going on."

Ag stiffened. "I can handle it." She glared at Celeste, surprising her. "Would you be saying the same thing to David about me if I was living with a girlfriend?"

"Yes," Celeste said solidly. "You'd deserve to know in case there was anything you wanted to say to your mother before the situation worsened."

Ag's features softened. "You're right." She put her head in her hand, massaging her temples. "Of course you're right. I need to tell him."

"Agony!" Mrs. Winsome called. Celeste was unaccustomed to the shrillness in her voice.

Ag bolted off her bed, and Celeste followed. Emma was still happily playing on the floor with her plastic rings, and she'd added an empty coffee can to her collection of toys. Ag had rinsed it out and sat it in an unlocked cabinet within the baby's reach. She'd accumulated several pots and pans and some plastic containers to the collection, too. Emma gnawed on the lid of a container as Mrs. Winsome pointed to her.

"You need to get that away from the baby," she advised Ag.

"It's okay, Mama," Ag chuckled. "It's—"

"Laura shouldn't be playing with it," Mrs. Winsome barked.

Ag was speechless, but time seemed to stop until she recovered. Ag had shared her story about the baby she had given up with Celeste when she was inside Caroline and Hailey, so she didn't have to feign ignorance.

"How do you know about Laura?" Ag asked her mother.

Mrs. Winsome's eyes narrowed. "Everyone knew. Sam Bailey knew, too, but he didn't say much of anything since you'd jilted him, and the baby was a girl."

Ag grabbed a chair and sat. She stared into space as if the information had caused a glitch in her brain.

"You need to get that away from Laura," Mrs. Winsome repeated. "She doesn't need the caffeine."

Celeste pried the can out of Emma's hands and replaced it with her sippy cup. Emma gulped down the last of the apple juice and banged on a pot with the cup.

Celeste was in an awkward position. She didn't know if she should help, and if she did, how she could best assist Ag and Mrs. Winsome.

Mrs. Winsome retreated to the living room, satisfied that the baby wasn't eating coffee out of the can. Ag focused on the calendar in the far corner of the room. The number of wildlife, like deer and foxes, witnessed by her mother was tallied each day. Occasionally, Ag shook her head as if she were arguing with her thoughts.

Celeste placed her hand on Ag's shoulder. There was no use asking how she could help. She had no way of repairing the feelings that were damaged by others.

After a moment, Celeste started preparing Mrs. Winsome's evening meal. Ag joined her, retrieving potato salad from the refrigerator and adding it to the corned beef sandwich on Mrs. Winsome's plate.

"Can I take it to her?" Celeste asked. Had she asked if Ag wanted her to take it, Ag would have insisted that she should take her mother's dinner to her.

Ag nodded, still lost in her jumbled thoughts.

"Where's that baby?" Mrs. Winsome bellowed when Celeste brought her the food on a tray.

"She's in the kitchen," Celeste responded brightly, glad that Mrs. Winsome had left the world she'd slipped into.

"Is it time for her nap? I like holding her while she sleeps."

"I think I'm leaving soon," Celeste responded. "She'll probably start her nap in the car."

"That's a pity. She looks so much like her daddy when he slept on my lap."

Celeste's breath caught in her throat. She walked back into the kitchen, doing her best to camouflage any emotion.

Emma helped Ag replace the pots and pans. She tried to lift a heavy silver pot, and Ag asked if she could help, supporting most of the weight, but giving Emma full credit for putting it back in place.

Keys jingled in the front door and the women froze, looking at each other.

David gave a casual greeting to his mother and walked into the kitchen. His gaze moved from his ex-wife to his sister. "What's going on?" His voice was nasally, and he sniffed after he spoke.

"I've asked Caroline to keep helping me with some chores around the house," Ag said.

David took out his wallet. "How much are you paying her?" He threw out a couple of twenties on the table.

Celeste was horrified. "I'm not receiving any money."

David stared at her. "You need to get the baby out of here. I have the flu."

Ag picked up Emma and handed her to Celeste.

Celeste gathered Emma's toys and sippy cup, throwing everything into her bag. She left the money on the table.

David followed her out the door, but he kept his distance. He waited until she buckled Emma into her car seat and closed the door before he spoke again.

"Isn't Mindy giving you enough money?" he asked. He turned his head to cough.

"I never asked your girlfriend for anything," Celeste shot back. "In fact, why don't you tell her I'm unavailable this week!"

"Will do." He crossed his arms over his chest. "And my family can't watch that baby for you."

Celeste felt tears prick her eyes. She knew Caroline had hurt David, but she wasn't Caroline, and his animosity stung her.

"Why are you so mean to me?"

David shook his head. "Are you serious? After everything you—"

"What have I done lately?" Celeste asked him. When he stood with his eyebrows raised, she continued. "I have been kind to you"—she threw up a finger, noting her points— "I've been good to your family" — another finger followed the first— "I've watched your girlfriend's children so that the two of you could spend more time together, and I haven't asked you for money." She held up four fingers but put them away quickly when she placed her hands on her hips.

"I realize that I hurt you, David," she said, taking the blame for another woman's actions. "But you never let me rise above it. Everyone has more faith in me than you, and you were supposed to have loved me."

He stood with his arms crossed, and when he didn't respond, Celeste realized that he had nothing to say. She got in her car and drove away, happy to leave him behind.

CHAPTER 23

Ag caught the flu, so she wasn't able to watch Emma for Celeste to attend her classes that Wednesday. Celeste explained the situation, but her instructor warned her that the absence would count against her.

As she wouldn't be helping Ag with Mrs. Winsome, Celeste was free all day. It was unseasonably warm, so she took Emma to a playground in the center of town.

It was vacant, except for a young mother and her son. He was a couple of years older than Emma, and he led her across the bridge and slid down the curving slide with her.

His mother followed him, making sure that he was careful with the baby. After they sat playing in the mulch, the young mother relaxed, joining Celeste on the bench.

"He's really great with Emma," Celeste remarked.

"I've been talking to him about babies," the woman said, patting her stomach. "He's excited to have a new baby brother or sister on the way."

Celeste looked at the woman's midsection. She saw only traces of a possible pregnancy. "How far along are you?"

"I'm almost eight weeks," the woman responded.

Celeste thought back to that time in her life. She had been so worried that Zam would realize she'd been pregnant before she'd returned to him, but he'd never questioned her. He was completely in love with her, and he'd been a good father to Emma in her absence. She felt a pang of guilt over taking Emma away from him.

After they left the playground, Celeste drove to Johnson City to the social security office. She claimed she never received a card for her daughter, and she showed them her birth certificate. The lady behind the counter regarded her with drooping eyes, fogged from the cold medicine Celeste spied peeking out of the bag next to her. She looked over the certificate and sent Celeste to the cubicle of a man who smiled apologetically as he looked over the certificate.

"Do you have the original?" he asked. "It has the red seal."

"I probably have it at home," Celeste replied.

"I'll need it to process your request. Emma isn't showing up in our system." He stroked the keys, and his color lightened. It was clear that he was as ill as the receptionist. "I've added her to our system, but I'll need the official birth certificate before I can—"

He bolted up, holding a hand to his mouth, and darted out of sight. Celeste didn't hear him regurgitating, but she was certain that was the reason he'd left so quickly. After twenty minutes, a lady appeared. Her dark hair was pulled up on her head over a face of pale foundation and bright red lipstick.

"Jeffery's going to be out the rest of the day," she informed Celeste. "Can you come back next week?"

Celeste sighed. "I have class, and I help a family in the afternoons."

The woman's lips pressed into a thin line. "Well, to be honest, I don't know if next week would be any better. This flu season has taken its toll on our office."

She moved past Celeste and Emma and took Jeffery's seat. She noticed Celeste's shock when she touched the sick man's keyboard without sanitizing it.

"I was out until yesterday with the flu," she explained.

Regardless, Celeste would have wiped down the keyboard, but she didn't say anything about the other woman's choices. The woman typed quickly and excused herself. When she returned, she held a social security card with Emma's name on it.

Celeste was pleasantly surprised. "Thank you so much."

The woman smiled. "Jefefry already had it typed up and ready to go, so I only pushed a couple of buttons."

On the way to the car, Celeste marveled at her luck. Any number of things could have prevented Celeste from obtaining Emma's social security card, but Jeffery had been overcome with sickness just before he added the note about Emma's original birth certificate.

Celeste decided to drive to the DHS office right away. Emma fell asleep during the ride, but her eyes popped open when Celeste turned off the car.

Celeste was surprised when Rebecca ushered her to her cubicle to complete the application. She'd had a cancellation, due to the recent flu outbreak, and she finished Celeste's request quickly.

Celeste gave her the social security card, and Rebecca left briefly to make a copy of it. Celeste tried to occupy Emma, who was spirited after her short nap in the car.

"Was class canceled today?" she asked casually.

"No," Celeste replied honestly. "I didn't have childcare."

"Employers frown upon that."

Celeste understood Rebecca's concern. She had wondered what she was going to do when she started a full-time job, as her hours might not accommodate the people who were caring for Emma while she was in school.

Rebecca stared at her computer screen, squinting her eyes. "It looks like we received DNA results for you and Emma, but you're going to have to take them again."

"Why?" Celeste was trying to keep a wriggling Emma on her lap, so she was a little distracted.

"The results don't confirm you as Emma's mother." She leaned back in her chair.

Celeste felt the color drain from her face. *Could Emma be her biological child? Could Zam be her father?*

"I mean, it shows that you could be her mother, but it's not as conclusive as the other tests I've seen. It's like you're her half-mother." She laughed when she noticed Celeste battling her toddler for her own hair. "There's nothing half when it comes to that, is there?"

Celeste tried to return her humor, and she finally pried Emma's slobbering hands away. She hoped the distraction made her appear less nervous about the test results.

Rebecca swiveled in her seat and placed her hands on her desk. "You'll just have to take another test."

Rebecca's smile was reassuring, but Celeste had the feeling that she could take a dozen other tests and the results would be the same. Not only was she concerned that she'd been wrong about Emma's paternity, but Celeste considered the possibility that David could use the DNA test against her if he found out Emma was his child. He wouldn't think Emma had another mother, though. Would he?

CHAPTER 24

Celeste accepted the paperwork for the testing facility, but she decided not to go. She'd wait for David's results to arrive, and she'd drop the case. If her maternity was questioned, she'd laugh off the test as a fluke and ask David how many women he'd been sleeping with during their marriage. She hoped it'd be enough to end any debate.

She thought about the possibility that Emma was Zam's daughter, but she dismissed it when she looked at Emma. It wasn't just Emma's physical characteristics that confirmed her suspicion; Celeste could *feel* her belief was right.

Emma fell asleep early, and Emma laid her on the bed. She'd washed the sheets and cleaned and rearranged the room, so it felt less like Willie's bedroom. She still couldn't sleep there. When she was ready to lie down, she'd carry Emma to the couch to sleep with her. The bedroom was a quieter place for Emma to rest until Celeste was ready to sleep, though.

She poured herself a glass of orange juice and sat down with her notebook. The material was familiar to her, but the instructor's style of teaching was different, so she poured over her notes in preparation for a quiz. The instructor liked to give out surprise tests to measure their knowledge, and she had always received perfect marks on them. She didn't want to damage her streak of success.

A gentle rap at the door pulled her out of her thoughts. She wondered if it was Marlene, slipping over for a late-night chat, but when she opened the door, she lost her breath.

David stood on the other side. His hair was oily and disheveled, and his clothes were rumpled as if he had rolled around on the light jeans and white button-up before he threw them on.

"I'm sorry." His voice was nasally, a result of his illness. "I had no right to be mean to you when you're trying to do better." He reached out his hand to her. "Can you forgive me?"

Celeste looked at his hand. It was such a shift, and she was unclear on what to do. David misread her hesitation.

"I probably shouldn't touch you." He withdrew his hand. "My fever broke a couple of hours ago, but I've thought about what you said for the last few days." He ran his fingers through his hair. "The thing is, you were right. I have been mean to you." He looked up sharply, almost causing Celeste to jump from the determination in his eyes. "That stops now."

David expected her to speak, and she fumbled over possible things to say. "Okay" was the only word she could get past her lips.

"Okay," he echoed and nodded as if her acceptance gave them a clean slate.

He turned to go, but he stopped before he made it to the steps. "I never stopped loving you," he said without turning around. Celeste had to strain to hear him, competing with the wind rustling through the last remnants of leaves clinging to the trees. "It was easy to move on when you acted differently, and you didn't seem to care about me." His head dropped. "But now, you act like the woman I fell in love with, and it scares me. I don't want to be close to you again. Not even as friends."

David went down the steps and got into his family's SUV. Celeste closed the door, willing herself not to watch him drive away.

David had come to apologize and left her with conflicting thoughts. Were they on speaking terms, or had his final words dismissed her from his life? Celeste sat with her warring emotions until well after midnight. Finally, she decided it didn't matter. The results of David's DNA test would change everything.

CHAPTER 25

Celeste's instructor handed out a quiz within the first ten minutes of class, and she was glad she had studied. He might have thought she'd perform poorly on the HIPPA portion, as he had gone over the regulations when she was out, but Celeste remembered them from the classes she had taken when Hailey was her host, so she got all the questions right.

She drove back to the trailer triumphantly. She heard raised voices inside Marlene's trailer, and she tried to listen to what was said before she knocked.

Randy came home for lunch, as his shop was only a couple of miles away. Celeste heard his voice towering over Marlene's, but she couldn't make out more than mumblings against the metal of the trailer.

She knocked, and the voices hushed. Marlene threw open the door with a large smile on her face. "You're here early."

"She's always here at this time," Randy said gruffly. He picked up his sandwich and took a bite. He rubbed the crumbs of the bread left on his fingers over his plate.

"Where's Emma?" Celeste asked.

"Jonas and Jayden are playing with her on the back deck," she said, wringing one of her hands. "We've had a stretch of pretty days, they're out since the school's gettin' cleaned cause of the flu, and I want them to soak in all the sunshine they can before winter sets in."

Celeste was glad her daughter hadn't heard whatever disagreement was going on before she knocked. Randy and Marlene had their faults, but they didn't argue in front of the children.

Randy took another bite of his sandwich and Celeste almost gagged. The smell of roast beef had taken over the living room and kitchen, making it impossible to smell anything other than cooked animals.

Caroline's body reacted to meat the same way as Celeste's body. In her time frame, due to poisoning during the Great War, no one ate meat anymore, and the smell of it turned her stomach. Celeste was worried Randy had noticed her repulsion when he threw his sandwich down on his plate, but something else was on his mind.

"Here!" he shouted, handing Celeste folded notebook papers.

Celeste took it automatically. She opened the paper and realized it was a letter. A rollercoaster of emotions was written across the page. Little hearts decorated the margins, and scratchy script jumped out in waves of regular text and booming block letters. At the top, "Care" was scribbled.

"Why did you block Willie's letters?" Randy demanded.

Marlene stood at Celeste's side with her hands on her hips. "Now, don't you get started again!"

He didn't even look at his wife. "The man's in jail, and you won't even provide him with any comfort!"

Celeste would have reasoned with someone else. She would have explained that Willie James had killed a number of innocent people and knowing that he was less than five miles away in a regular jail cell sometimes kept her awake at night. But Randy wasn't a regular person. He had compassion for Willie's situation, and Celeste's excuses would be flicked away like bothersome flies.

"It's too much," Celeste spoke. She couldn't think of anything else to say in the silence, and she could almost feel Randy's anger coming off him.

Randy banged his fist on the table and stood. Marlene held her ground, but Celeste backed up a step. Randy seemed harmless, but he had a temper.

"It's too much to read your man's letters and write him back?" He let out a laugh without humor. "He's in jail because you ran off with some woman, and it's too much for you?"

Caroline had hardly run off with some woman. She had narrowly escaped in the back of Hailey's Volkswagen after Willie James had assaulted both of them.

Randy's fist was still on the table and his fingers were turning red. "You're doin' odd jobs and gettin' ready to make big bucks. It wouldn't hurt for you to put something in his commissary. They don't feed him enough in that jail. One of the nurses was a guard's sister-in-law, so they spit in his food, too. Do you know how hard that is for him?"

Celeste thought Willie deserved rivers of spit in his food, but she said nothing. As far as money was concerned, she'd rather share a fiery sauna with Hitler than send Willie a dime. She didn't speak her feelings aloud. She thought it was best to allow Randy to get out everything he had to say.

"Read that letter!" Randy commanded. "Take your kid and go home. Go home to the place Willie provided you with and think about all the things he's done for you."

Celeste hung her head and tried to appear chastised.

"I have to get back to work," Randy announced brusquely. He pushed a twenty-dollar bill at Marlene. "Make sure that gets to Willie." He eyed Celeste. "Maybe she'll put somethin' with it, and he'll be able to eat or pay down some of his poker debt."

After Randy left, Celeste was still uncomfortable. Marlene wasn't as friendly with her, and she hadn't spoken since her husband walked out the door.

Celeste turned to go, but Marlene stopped her.

"I understand why you can't send him money," she said. "You had to ask us for gas money to get to class, so I doubt you have a lot left over."

Celeste had two twenties stashed under one of the couch cushions, but after she used it for Emma's Christmas present, she'd be broke again. David had been sick, so Mindy wouldn't need her to babysit.

"I'm worried about you, Caroline," Marlene spoke. "You don't write to Willie, and you don't even talk about him. What are you gonna do when Rowdy busts him out?" She pointed down the hall, in the direction of the door to her back deck. "What are you gonna do with that little girl? You know he won't let you take her when you go on the run with him."

Celeste remained silent. It was her best answer when she thought anything she said would make things worse.

Celeste didn't think Willie would ever get out of jail. The community had been horrified by his actions, and he was watched very closely. If he managed to escape, though, Celeste had no plans to leave with him.

Marlene stared at her for a long moment, but when it was clear she wasn't going to speak, Marlene threw up her hand. "Go get Emma. I know you're dying to get over to David's house anyway. Maybe you should be asking him for gas money."

Celeste bit her tongue. It was a low blow. She didn't bother to tell Marlene that David's family was sick, so she was going back to the trailer she could never consider her home. Instead, she walked down the hall and onto the back deck.

The air was turning crisp, but Emma and the boys had on light jackets. Celeste put a hand above her eyes to shield them from the bright sunshine slanting over the yard. A lone bumblebee buzzed up to her, bouncing off her hand and going on its way.

Jonas held Emma's hand as she stomped across leaves and dropped her body onto the ground. She had amazed Celeste with her ability to motor around at a young age. She was able to run, and she wasn't even eleven months old.

Jayden saw her and nudged his brother. Jonas smiled, picking up Emma and walking her to where Celeste stood on the deck. Celeste reached for her daughter, but she almost dropped her when Emma spoke.

"Are you okay, Mommy?"

Chapter 26

Celeste tried all afternoon, but Emma wouldn't repeat herself. She talked to her conversationally and attempted to speak with her directly, but Emma remained tight-lipped. Once, Celeste thought she saw her daughter smile when she begged her to say what she'd said in Marlene's backyard.

Celeste was certain that her daughter wasn't supposed to be speaking that well at her age. Jayden and Jonas had been unaffected by Emma's speech.

"Have you heard her talk before?" Celeste had asked them.

Jayden had shrugged and laughed. Jonas had seemed to struggle with his answer as if he had worried that he would be revealing something he hadn't known was a secret until that moment.

Celeste tried again. "Hello, Emma. How are you?"

Emma climbed off Celeste's lap, ignoring her effort. She found two blocks and banged them together.

Celeste searched through the internet for cases where children spoke at a younger-than-average age. There were many claims of early speech from parents who wrote their own blogs, but the documented cases gave her some comfort. Emma wasn't completely alone in her ability, but it had shocked Celeste.

Her grandfather had kept a close eye on Emma after she was born. He had noted her developments and referred often to her intelligence. *Could her daughter be a genius?*

Celeste sighed and put away her phone. She had a feeling there was something more to Emma's abilities, but she was too tired to investigate it until after she'd had a good night's sleep.

Celeste reheated some of the vegetarian chili she had made the previous night. The day had been warm, but the night was cooler, and the trailer didn't retain the heat from the day for long.

Midway through the meal, Celeste's back and legs started to ache. She tried to sit differently and roll her neck, but the feeling persisted. She drew a bath of warm water, but she couldn't rest in it for long. She got overheated, and Emma kept trying to get in and out of the tub.

The heat she felt from the tub didn't go away, and she concluded that she had a fever. She found some acetaminophen in the bathroom cabinet, but it had expired several years ago.

Celeste was exhausted, and she hoped Emma would fall asleep early so she could lie down. The baby continued to play, though, spurred by some unknown energy bequeathed to her because she understood on some level that her mother couldn't keep up with her.

Emma put a movie in the aged DVD player, and talking toys lit up the screen. She thought Emma was too young for television, but Celeste was starting to see double, and she needed something to entertain her toddler so she could rest.

Celeste fell asleep holding Emma's hand, convinced that if her daughter moved, she would feel it and wake up. Just before her eyes closed, she saw movement in the back corner of the room. Willie James stood up from a squatting position on the floor and smiled down at her.

When she woke up, sirens were blaring.

Chapter 27

Celeste's first thought was about Emma's whereabouts, but the baby sat up on the gurney next to her. Her fingers were around Celeste's wrist as if they were trying to find the best purchase in case someone tried to pull her away.

"Her eyes are open," someone spoke.

"Ma'am?" a man's voice said. "Can you tell me your name?"

"Celeste," she croaked in a half whisper and coughed. Her throat felt like someone had tried to claw their way out of it.

"Okay, Celeste, we're going to take you to the hospital, but the baby can't go with you. Is there someone who can care for her, like family or a neighbor?"

Celeste's mind flickered to Marlene, but after Randy had talked about how Caroline would need to discard Emma to run away with Willie, she no longer trusted her neighbors. What if he coaxed Marlene into taking Emma to child services while she was gone?

"No one," she pushed out. It was getting harder to breathe, but every time she sucked in a lung full of air, she coughed until her eyes felt like they were going to pop out of their sockets.

"Are you sure we can't call someone?" the EMT asked.

Celeste shook her head.

Celeste winked out for a few moments and consciousness revisited her while two men rushed her down a brightly lit hallway. Celeste thought she was in a dream, as the edges of the lights started to blur. Emma was smiling at her, and she told her she loved her.

"What?" one of the men asked.

She hadn't spoken to them, but she was certain they were trying to help her. Maybe they were some of Zam's friends. In fact, one of them looked like Zam, with his dark hair and gray-green eyes.

The gurney swung around, and Celeste's stomach flipped. She felt the warm vomit slide down her chin and thought it was too hot against her already burning chest.

The gurney was wheeled into a room and stopped moving. A nurse with a familiar voice spoke.

"What do you have?"

"Young woman, approximately twenty-five to thirty years old. She phoned 9-1-1 about an intruder, but when the police got there, they found her outside with the baby."

"Caroline," the familiar voice said. "Who can we call to pick up the baby?"

Celeste said the first name that danced across her mind. It appeared in her field of vision as if the name were made of cotton candy clouds. "David."

The woman sucked in a deep breath. "I can't call him, Caroline. You aren't married to him anymore."

The group left briefly, and a lady entered. She had a stronger scent than the other woman, but when Celeste opened her eyes, all she could see was a blob with blonde hair.

She told Celeste a name she forgot as soon as it was spoken. Her hand was cold when it touched Celeste's arm, and she thought she was wearing a mask, as when she spoke, her words were muffled and hard to hear.

The lady wanted her to give the names and phone numbers of people she could call to take care of Emma. Celeste repeated that there was no one, and it was quiet as the woman wrote something. Celeste almost fell asleep to the scratching of her pen.

The door opened and a musky scent filled the room. Usually, she loved David's smell, but in her fevered condition, her stomach rolled.

"Jesus! What happened?"

The woman talked to him as David felt her forehead with the back of his hand. He ran out of the room, and the nurse with a familiar voice returned. They moved around her bed a lot, and Celeste tried to keep herself steady. She didn't want to vomit again from the sudden movement.

"I'm calling child services to come get the baby," the lady said.

Celeste's blood ran cold. How would she get her daughter back? How long would they keep her at the hospital? She wanted to voice her concerns, but she could only issue a low moan.

David's voice cut through Celeste's fear. "I'll take the baby."

"Are you a relative or family friend?"

"I'm her ex-husband."

"David, you know I like you, but you can't save everyone." The lady was firm but kind.

"It's a baby, Rowena," he argued. "My mama and Ag watch the baby for Caroline to go to her classes. Between us, we can handle it."

"Is Ag still sick?"

"No. No one in the house has had a fever since yesterday."

The lady sighed. "I wouldn't do this for anyone else."

Celeste tuned out and drifted. She wasn't as hot as she had been, but the bed sheets were sticky and uncomfortable.

Emma put her chubby arms around Celeste's neck. She tried to hug her, but she couldn't find the strength to lift her arms, so she pressed her face into her infant's hair. The soft strawberry scent was lifted from her, but Celeste didn't hear her daughter crying.

Emma was going to be okay. She was with her father.

Celeste's fever rolled over her. She felt like a furnace was placed under her bed, and she even accused some of the nurses of putting one there, until her chills made her beg them for as many heated blankets as they could pile onto the bed.

Celeste should have recognized the medicine they injected into her, but she didn't care. She felt a little better after the medicine worked its way into her system, but then she'd ease right back into her symptoms. It seemed like she battled the vicious cycle for days.

Her phone rang, and she picked it up. She thought she heard Ag's voice, and she told her that the baby was okay. At some point, Celeste drifted out of the conversation, and one of the nurses hung up the phone when she came in to administer more medicine.

Celeste woke up, and someone was holding her hand. The room was dim, and she couldn't get her eyes to focus, but it looked like David. His head was bowed, and he was praying rapidly. Celeste tried to hear the words he spoke, but she couldn't concentrate on them. It was like she could understand them as they were spoken, but they took flight after they left David's lips.

"I love you," she confided. "It's about time you know it."

The words stopped, and his head moved. She couldn't tell if he was looking at her, but she had his attention.

"I wish he wouldn't have pulled me back," she spoke. "I didn't want to leave you. You made me so happy, and we were perfect for each other."

Tears rolled down her cheeks and into her ears. She swallowed and coughed. Pushing past the gritty burning in her throat, she continued.

"You were the love of my life, and I crossed time for you, but you've moved on." She had to say it, and once it was out, she felt like she could tell him anything.

"Emma was born several generations from now, but she's your daughter. Can't you see it?"

She wasn't privy to his expression, so she kept talking. "I want you to know your daughter, and I want her to know you." She took the straw that was placed in her mouth. She held the cool liquid on her tongue for a moment before the pain of swallowing it followed. If it had been anything other than water, she couldn't have distinguished its flavor.

Before he left, David leaned over her. He caressed her face, running his palm down the side of her cheek.

"I loved you so much," he whispered.

He placed a tender kiss on her forehead, lightly touching her skin with his lips. He left without saying goodbye, and Celeste couldn't help but hope it was intentional.

CHAPTER 28

When Celeste woke with clarity, she didn't know if David had been in her room or if her fevered mind had made him up. After all, she was certain that the guilt she'd felt over leaving Zam had manifested into her fevered visions, as she had thought one of the nurses was him.

She considered calling Ag, but she hesitated. *What if Ag asked for news about her condition?*

She glanced at the large analog clock in front of her bed. The doctor usually made her rounds in another half hour, so Celeste thought she'd wait to hear what she said about her illness before she spoke to Ag.

Celeste tried to get up to use the bathroom, but she had to call a nurse for help. Now that she felt better, it was a little degrading to use the portable toilet placed beside her bed, but she hadn't felt a catheter, so she assumed she'd been using it during her stay.

The process took twenty minutes, as Celeste kept losing her balance and had to lie back down once before she could place herself on the contraption with assistance. She apologized to the nurse, embarrassed that she needed help to perform a basic human function.

The nurse shrugged away her apology. "Honey, after what you've been through, you don't have to apologize for anything."

Celeste wondered just how bad her sickness had been. She recollected bits and pieces, but she knew those would fade away, too, if she didn't make a special effort to remember them.

Dr. Sing breezed into her room with a tablet in her hand. After confirming her name and birthdate, she asked her about the last thing she remembered.

Celeste thought back. "I was exhausted, and Emma, my baby, wasn't ready to go to sleep, so I put in a movie for her. I held her hand while she watched it to make sure she was there."

Dr. Sing watched her with dark eyes. There was a point in time when Celeste could have told her that her red lipstick was smeared, but Celeste had been a different person, and she couldn't use her past familiarity with a person if that person was convinced that they were strangers.

"You didn't take anything to make you feel sleepy?"

Celeste hesitated. Maybe Dr. Sing had known Caroline. She might have examined her during one of the times Willie had abused her or when she'd had an accidental overdose. Caroline had discussed those times with her when they were in the hospital together.

"No," she said firmly. "I looked for some acetaminophen, but the bottle I found had expired."

"Is there any medication you need me to report on your file?" She looked at her tablet and traced her finger down the screen. "It looks like you were taking buprenorphine and clonazepam the last time you were here."

Celeste was familiar enough with the opioid crisis of the time to recognize the drugs some doctors prescribed to transition their patients into sobriety. She hadn't experienced withdrawals from the drugs when she entered Caroline's body, so Caroline had been completely sober.

"I quit taking them," she answered simply.

"When?"

Celeste thought of a reasonable answer. "Five months ago."

Dr. Sing nodded. "I'll note your file."

After her fingers danced across the screen, she turned back to Celeste. "I asked about your drug history because of the 9-1-1 call you made."

Celeste raised her eyebrows.

"You claimed there was an intruder in your home."

Celeste thought back and tried to remember, but she drew a blank. "I'm sorry. I don't think anyone was there."

Dr. Sing stared at her. "The authorities found you outside your residence with the baby."

"I had a fever," Celeste defended, suddenly worried that she'd be declared an unfit mother before David's DNA test concluded what she already knew.

"I know," Dr. Sing responded, and Celeste relaxed a little. "Your fever was 105 degrees when you were admitted. It's possible that the phony call saved your life."

They discussed her illness, and Dr. Sing expressed some surprise at her reaction. Celeste had caught flu type A, and even though Caroline had been vaccinated against it, the disease had nearly killed her. Celeste wondered if, like her pregnancy, Caroline's immunity had carried with her when they had swapped bodies.

Celeste consented to a short examination, opening her mouth for the otoscope and breathing at intervals when the stethoscope was placed on her chest. She described the pain in her throat but explained that most of the irritation was gone.

"You were given an antibiotic," Dr. Sing told her. "Your strep throat culture came back positive, too, so you were treated for it."

"Thank you," Celeste said.

"You had some very capable emergency room nurses," Dr. Sing related.

Celeste remembered why everyone liked Dr. Sing. She gave credit to the other staff members when they did well, even when she could solely accept all the accolades for a patient's recovery.

"I heard David Winsome took your baby home with him," she commented, looking down at the tablet. Dr. Sing was human, and even the most professional people could be lured in by gossip.

"I think he did. I was pretty out of it."

Dr. Sing nodded. "He comes from a good family, and he's a great nurse."

Celeste took the opportunity to ask when she'd be allowed to leave. "I want to get home to my baby as soon as possible."

"Of course," Dr. Sing said. "But you're still weak. I'd like to see you keep down liquids and solids and go to the bathroom on your own. I think you can achieve that in the next few days."

After her time with Emma, she couldn't imagine being separated from her for several more days. She thought of school, and another question sprang to mind.

"How long have I already been here?"

Dr. Sing glanced at her chart. "Three days."

"It's Monday!" Celeste exclaimed, sitting up in bed. Lightheadedness threatened, sending her body back onto the pillows she had propped against the head of her bed. "I have class!"

"I can provide you with an excuse."

Celeste groaned, and a cough rattled her body. "I'm not supposed to miss more than one day."

"Then you may have to take the class again."

Dr. Sing's advice was practical, but it irritated Celeste. It was easy for her to dismiss the effort Celeste was making to move into a more independent state. She could only imagine Rebecca's disappointment when she had to sign her up for classes again. She had hoped to improve the town's view of Caroline, but she seemed to be following the same path as the woman whose body she inhabited.

Celeste called Ag after Dr. Sing left. She answered on the second ring, as she probably recognized the hospital's number.

"Caroline? Are you okay?"

Celeste smiled at her concern. Even after all Caroline had done to David and his family, they were still willing to forgive her.

"I'm going to be fine. How's Emma?"

The sound in the phone shifted as Ag moved outside. "David's been collecting leaves with her."

David wasn't at work, and Celeste was curious about the reason. "I'm glad they're having fun. Did he take the day off?"

"Mindy's covering for him today," Ag replied.

Celeste could have cried at the mention of David's betrothed. It nauseated her that she couldn't just hate Mindy. The woman was way too kind.

"Do you want to talk to Emma?"

Celeste waited for her little girl's voice to reach her ears. "Mommy!" she squealed.

Celeste listened to her jabber for a few minutes, and she told her that she'd see her soon.

"Here Daddy," she said.

Celeste's mind raced with a possible explanation for her child's words. Obviously, the time Emma had spent with David had brought them closer together, but she doubted he'd told Emma to call him anything other than his name.

But that wasn't her biggest concern. *Had David heard her?*

Celeste waited to hear David's voice or to be passed back to Ag, but the line went dead. Someone had hung up.

CHAPTER 29

Celeste stared at the clock in front of her. She willed time to pass quickly, watching the shows that came across the television screen but not really hearing them. Every time she thought she'd made it through a chunk of her day, she'd glance at the round display, and she'd see that she'd only been distracted for a few minutes.

It was difficult to rest when her mind was buzzing. Emma had called David "Daddy". The thought made her stomach do a front and back flip. On one hand, he was her father, so their time together had helped seal their bond. On the other hand, though, David wasn't ready to accept the tale that came with his paternity.

Her grandfather must be laughing at her predicament. Celeste couldn't leave the current time frame without his help, and she was at his mercy as to how long he allowed her to stay. Celeste rationalized that she must not have been upsetting the balance of the timeline, because he hadn't pulled her back. She felt like a fish caught on the end of a lure, waiting to be jerked out of the water.

The nurses flitted in and out of the room, checking her temperature and helping her to the bathroom. Celeste drank as much fluid as her body would allow, but she only created the embarrassing reliance of asking for help to relieve herself.

The nurses had been using a hospital-grade pump to exercise the milk from Caroline's breasts. She didn't know if David had told them she was breastfeeding, but she was thankful to whoever had prevented her from waking with a case of mastitis. She used the pump on her own every couple of hours, and her milk flowed freely, even though Emma's nursing had declined.

The next morning, she took a shower, and a nurse changed the sheets on her bed. She looked at herself in the mirror and noted the damage the illness had taken on Caroline's body. Her skin was deathly pale, and circles ringed her eyes. She trembled as she stood from lack of sustenance, but she had no appetite. The result had caused the bones on her already thin face to appear sharper.

Caroline's hair had gotten longer and fuller, and it hung to the middle of her back. Celeste attributed its growth to prenatal vitamins and pregnancy. Her green eyes were vibrant for someone who had been admitted to the hospital with a raging fever, but her skin had suffered, as it was oily and showing early signs of sun damage.

She lay in her bed and prepared for another boring day in the hospital. Her lunch arrived, but they'd brought her a cheeseburger, even though she'd asked for a vegetarian meal. It was an easy mistake, and the food service attendant would have corrected the issue, but Celeste didn't report it. She wasn't hungry.

A gentle knock sounded at the door, and it eased open. David came into her room smiling with a bag of food and a tray of drinks.

"How's my favorite patient?" he asked.

Celeste's heart didn't skip over his words. He said that to everyone who was admitted to the hospital. However, her stomach flopped when she realized she had on no makeup and was sitting cross-legged in a hospital gown.

She moved into a more flattering position and smiled back at him. "I'm doing much better."

"That's good." He placed the bag in front of her, and the oily scent of the cafeteria's fries wafted up to her.

He lifted the lid on the food tray by her bed. "Cheeseburgers were never your favorite." He winked at her and replaced the lid.

Celeste opened the bag of fries, convinced that David's presence would make her too nervous to eat, but after the first one hit her tongue, she couldn't stop eating them. When she glanced up, David was smiling at her.

"You always loved fries and pizza," he remembered.

She wondered if he recalled that they were two of Hailey's favorite foods, but she didn't ask him. Instead, they talked about Emma.

"I picked her up this little pink riding toy," he told Celeste. "Once she learned how to straddle it, she started riding it all over the house." He laughed, and his merriment reached his eyes. "Everyone has to watch out for their toes, but we taught her a signal for when she sees our legs." He leaned in like he was going to tell Celeste a secret. "Now she yells 'Beep' when she's about to hit us, so at least we have time to tense up before the wheels roll over our feet."

"Oh!" Celeste gasped. "I hope she doesn't hurt your mother's toes!"

David shook his head. "She does a pretty good job of avoiding Mama when she's riding. She'll scoot it up to the side of Mama's chair and stare at her sometimes, but she doesn't go in front of Mama or into her room."

Celeste was glad that her daughter had picked up on the unspoken boundaries of the house. She spoke the question that was really on her mind. "Does she ask for me?"

David put his hand on her arm. "She asks about you, Caroline, but I think she understands that you need to be here."

His eyebrows drew together thoughtfully. "She may grasp it better because she saw how sick you were, and she rode with you to the hospital. She seems well-adjusted though. She knows you're coming back for her."

Celeste didn't know if the reasons David mentioned were the right ones or if Emma's secure attachment to her stemmed from the time she spent as Hailey Hall.

"She gets a little fussy at nights," David mentioned. He looked at her sheepishly. "Well, she did until I put her in bed with me."

Celeste couldn't help the smile that spread across her face. "She's used to sleeping with me now, and I think Zam may have slept with her sometimes while I was gone."

David's face dropped, and the distance between them grew. "Who's Zam? Is that Emma's parent?"

There was no simple answer. Zam thought he was Emma's father, but more than biological ties, he had cared for Emma when Celeste had time jumped into Hailey's body.

She waited too long to reply, and David sighed. "Caroline, you need to let me call that baby's parents. If you're watching her for them, they need to know you're sick. And if they've abandoned her, you need to call child services."

Anger burned Celeste's stomach, rolling fiery acid into her chest. "She's mine," she spat. "Emma is my child."

David shook his head. "I thought we were past this. If Emma were your child, then she'd be *our* baby. You lost our baby, Caroline, and as sweet as that little girl is, she's not ours."

Celeste was on the verge of losing her temper. She tried to distance herself from their conversation and focus on her breathing.

David was unaware of Celeste's rising anger. "And what happened to Willie's baby? You were close to delivering him the last time I saw you, but no one knows where he went."

Suddenly, Celeste's argument with David seemed less important as a realization washed over her. Dr. Sing had told her she had dialed 9-1-1 over an intruder, but Celeste had dismissed the information. Once David brought up Caroline's ex-husband, though, the memory of his snarling face flashed across her mind.

She grabbed David's wrist and squeezed it until he stopped talking and gave her his attention.

"It was Willie!" she insisted, almost losing her breath as she spoke his name. "He was there."

CHAPTER 30

David flew into action. He left the room to call the police, and twenty minutes later, Sheriff Connor Murphy was standing in Celeste's room.

He wasn't an investigator, but he knew the Winsomes well, so he handled every unfortunate event that befell them. Celeste smiled when he stalked into the room, but it was clear that he had sided with David when he and Caroline had divorced, as he regarded Celeste as a stranger.

Celeste almost cried when she thought of all the fun she'd had with Sheriff Murphy when she had occupied her hosts' bodies. He'd meant so much to her that she had named a business after him when she'd returned to her time frame. He'd never know how much his advice had shaped her journey as an adult.

He asked her questions right away. Most of the time, he didn't look up, and Celeste watched his silver head nod along at her words.

"Are you certain you saw Willie James?"

Celeste nodded and gave him her answer when she realized his head was bent over his notes. "Yes."

"Can you describe him?"

Celeste thought back to what he was wearing, and she dug for a deeper description. Caroline was accustomed to staring at his face and tattoos, but Celeste had to work harder to pick out more than his most notable features.

"He's a little taller than me, with brown eyes and hair. He has a sleeve of tattoos" —she cupped her hand over her wrist and moved it up her arm— "on his arm, and a line of facial hair on his jawline." Sheriff Murphy looked up at her, and she remembered an additional detail from the first time she'd met Willie James. "He has a tattoo on his back that reads: 'Only God can judge me'."

"That's true," Sheriff Murphy conceded. "But did you see that when he broke into the trailer?"

Celeste raised her eyebrows. "No."

"What was he wearing?"

David had hovered just inside the door, but he sensed Celeste's discomfort and stood beside her. He didn't touch her, but his presence made her feel like he supported her.

"He had on a pair of basketball shorts and a white A shirt," she said.

"Anything else?"

"No."

Sheriff Murphy closed his notepad and his mustache wagged over his mouth as he pressed his lips together. When he spoke to her, he was firm but not unkind. "Young lady, Willie James is in his cell at the Erwin Jail."

"You caught him!" she cried out, happy that he had already been apprehended.

"No."

Celeste was baffled. If they hadn't caught him, how was Willie James in his cell?

"He's been there since we arrested him," Sheriff Murphy briefed her.

After Celeste looked from David to the sheriff, David finally explained. "I called Sheriff Murphy, and he checked Willie's cell immediately. He was there. They checked the cell for a possible escape route, but it was secure." David sat on the bed facing her. "Caroline, you suffered a lot of abuse from that man, and it's possible that the trauma and your fever caused your mind to manifest an image of your ex-husband."

"Besides, we've had some warm days, but the nights are cold, and people don't go traipsin' about in a pair of basketball shorts and an undershirt," Sheriff Murphy added.

Celeste remembered that the A shirt and the shorts were the clothes Wille had been wearing when he'd assaulted her. She may not have been Caroline, but David's explanation made sense. Her traumatized and fevered mind had placed Willie in the trailer.

Celeste was relieved, but on the tail of her relief, she was embarrassed. She put her hand over her eyes and cried.

"I'm so sorry," she told the men. "I caused all this trouble for nothing."

David's arms locked around her. "Don't apologize. You thought you saw your ex-husband, and you told me to get help. It's more than—"

He stopped speaking, but Celeste could almost hear the rest of his words. She knew it was more than Caroline would have done, but she wasn't Caroline. She was Celeste, and the only thing keeping her from yelling in frustration was David's embrace.

He released her to walk the sheriff down the hall, but when he returned, he slid onto the same place on the bed beside her. He took one of her hands in a friendly gesture, rubbing the inside of her palm with his thumb.

"I've been gone past my lunch break," he told her. "But I don't want to go back to work if you need me."

Celeste could almost remember his touch on the morning she was popped out of Caroline's body and back into her own. He was so close to her that it was almost like they were still married, and she could ask him for anything.

She saw his eyes on her lips seconds before he kissed her. His tongue slid into her mouth and hers danced with it for an immeasurable amount of time. David's hands roamed over her body, but when he squeezed her breast, Celeste winced, and the moment was sucked away.

David was a nurse, and he had known Caroline's body when he and Celeste were married, so he noticed the engorgement. He shot up off the bed.

"I—" He ran a hand through his hair and scrubbed his face. "I'm sorry."

Celeste didn't know what to say. *Should she confess her love? Should she ask if he broke up with Mindy?*

As if he had heard her unspoken question, David's face registered the horror over what he had done. "Mindy!" He threw his hands up. "How could I do this to her?"

He sat in the chair beside Celeste and put his head in his hands. "I have to tell her," he spoke miserably. He shook his head, rolling it across his hands. "How am I going to tell her?"

He jumped up, and remembering that his ex-wife was in the room, he addressed her directly. "I'm sorry. I'll— I'll have Ag call you later."

David left Celeste looking after him as he tormented himself. As he stepped out of her view, Celeste decided her situation wasn't as hopeless as she'd thought, and she held out hope that one day David would know that Emma was his daughter, and they could raise her together.

CHAPTER 31

Ag helped Celeste up the steps. She would have run to her daughter, but she was still weak from her illness, and she didn't want to fall.

The temperature was a little cooler, so Emma was playing indoors at Mrs. Winsome's feet. Celeste had been worried when Ag had left her toddler with the aging woman, but no harm had come to Emma in the Winsome's home.

As she climbed into the SUV, Celeste noticed a car seat in the back. It warmed her heart that one of the Winsomes had purchased a car seat for Emma so she could go on outings with them. It made her presence seem more permanent in their lives.

Emma ran to her mother, surprising Celeste with her speed and balance. It wasn't the first time Celeste had marveled at her developmental leaps.

She tried to pick her up, but she had to settle for holding her on the first step of the stairs. The wood was uncomfortable, but she hardly noticed as she listened to Emma jabber about the block in her hand.

"You bought her plastic blocks?" Celeste remarked.

Ag turned away with a small smile, tossing her keys into the dish by the door. "Actually, the blocks were my brother's. He got them out for her on the first day she was here."

"I bought her a baby doll," Mrs. Winsome volunteered. "Every little girl needs a baby doll."

"Why, Mama?" Ag asked. "I didn't play with my baby dolls, and I was fine."

"Playin' with dolls teaches young ladies to be good mothers. After the way you've lived your life, I'm not surprised that your dolls stayed in your cedar chest. Laura didn't have a chance."

Ag sucked in a breath, cold resentment flashing across her eyes.

Celeste had learned that children who play with dolls often model the behaviors they see instead of the actions they intend to do when they assume adult roles. She could have commented on Ag's lack of interest in her dolls based on her observations between the mother-daughter pair, but she chose to stay out of their argument.

"Emma loves her dolly," Mrs. Winsome cooed when Celeste brought Emma into the living room. They sat on the couch, and Emma stroked her face.

"She didn't show signs of getting sick?" Celeste asked.

"Nope," Ag replied. "David had already given us the flu last week. We caught it pretty fast, but we broke our fevers in a day or two."

Ag's assessment had been generous. She still had a deep cough, and Mrs. Winsome was nasally when she spoke.

"It's amazing that Emma didn't catch it."

"Nursin' babes sometimes don't catch a lot of sicknesses," Mrs. Winsome claimed.

The ladies were quiet as an uncomfortable silence blanketed them. Ag and Mrs. Winsome had watched her breastfeed Emma, but David had told them the child belonged to another mother. It was an awkward subject they wanted to avoid.

Ag was especially embarrassed after her mother's observation. She fumbled for a new conversation, sighing after she'd opened and closed her mouth several times in search of one.

Her mother picked up on it. "Agony, for heaven's sake! I nursed you and your brother, and there were wet nurses in the Bible. There are still women who give milk to other women's baby's now. I watched it on one of my shows." She nodded resolutely as if the information on a soap opera was enough to settle the debate.

Emma tugged at her mother's shirt, possibly aware of the suggestion in the conversation. Celeste accommodated her, as Ag made an excuse to prepare lunch for them.

"I have to take the SUV back to David," Ag announced. "He can take you home later."

Celeste was going to protest that she needed to return to her trailer immediately, but she decided to stay and help Ag with some housework. While she was gone, Celeste cleaned the kitchen and vacuumed the floors. Mrs. Winsome directed her to a drawer in her room that held new outfits for Emma, and Celeste almost cried when she saw the beautiful flower dress hanging in Ag's closet.

"We took her to church with us," Mrs. Winsome told her. "Even Dotty Bailey complimented her little dress."

Emma was starting to become one of the Winsomes. After David realized he was Emma's father, he'd embrace her fully as his own. The idea gave Celeste some comfort. She hadn't been given an official mission for her time jump, but she'd almost completed the most important part of her journey.

The crunch of the gravel indicated that Ag and David had returned. Celeste tried to keep calm when David walked inside with his sister. He didn't look at her before he swiftly climbed the steps to his room. Ag put the leftovers of their lunch into a container for him to take back to work.

"Is he goin' back to that woman's house?" Mrs. Winsome asked her daughter.

"I think so," Ag replied. "Emma won't be here, so..." She trailed off and Mrs. Winsome grunted her understanding. David expected the two of them to care for one another now that Emma was leaving.

A stomp sounded from the floor above them, and a cloud of ceiling dust fell onto the freshly cleaned rug. The women looked at each other.

David's footsteps pounded down the steps. He advanced on Celeste with a paper in his hand. "WHAT IS THIS?" he thundered.

Celeste couldn't make out the wording on the paper he held inches from her face, but she could guess the contents. She didn't even breathe, afraid that David's temper would explode onto her like lava from a volcano.

"David," Ag said cautiously. "What is so bad that you feel the need to yell at Caroline in front of Emma?"

"She's going after me for child support," he barked at her without looking away from Celeste.

Ag took the letter from David and scanned it. "It says you have to submit a DNA sample. You don't have to pay anything."

He rounded on his sister. "Oh yes I do! I have to pay for a lawyer because I am either going to sue her in civil court for damages to my character and emotional well-being, or I'm going to get full custody of that little girl." He turned back to Celeste. "I should have known better. You were playing me all along."

"That's enough yellin' in front of the baby," Mrs. Winsome said forcefully. "I don't care how mad you are at her mother, you won't speak that way in front of the child."

Ag had picked up Emma, and the baby hugged her. Celeste worried about how much tension she felt in the air.

"I need to go," she said.

David shook his head. "You should never have been here in the first place. I wish I would have left you in that hospital room where I found you."

It was one of the most hurtful things he'd ever said to her. He'd rather have lived without the good times they'd shared than experience the doubt the letter cast on his life.

Celeste glared at him as she took Emma from Ag and headed to the door. She didn't have the chance to turn the knob before she stepped on one of the blocks Emma had left on the floor. It caused her to stumble and she landed on her knees.

Tears stung her eyes and pain shot up and down her legs, but she managed to stand. Ag grabbed her elbow and pulled her up.

"Is she okay?" Mrs. Winsome asked.

While she steadied herself, David grabbed a shopping bag from the kitchen. He went into his mother's bedroom. Celeste heard the sound of the wood scraping as he opened the drawer Mrs. Winsome had designated for Emma and threw her clothes into it. He added her doll to the bag, and Emma cried out for it. He gave the doll to his sister, and Ag placed it in Emma's arms.

"I will take you back," he raged. "And then I never want to see you again."

"Let me take her," Ag suggested. "You two don't need to be in a vehicle together right now."

"I started this, and I'm going to finish it," David seethed.

Celeste could feel her anger rising, but she held it back. Emma pushed her head into her neck, not bothering to move her mother's hair as she buried her face.

David stormed out the door with the bag of Emma's clothes in his fist. He slung open the doors on the passenger side of the vehicle and climbed into the driver's seat.

"He may be upset with you, but he's still a gentleman," Ag said, referencing the open car doors.

Celeste disagreed. A more gentlemanly response would have been to have taken her home without a scene.

"He still loves you," Mrs. Winsome croaked from the living room. "A man doesn't get all fired up like that if there's no passion in him.

Celeste thought back to the way he'd kissed her. Any chance she'd had of rekindling a flame with David had been extinguished when he'd read the letter.

Celeste prepared herself to say some final words to Ag and Mrs. Winsome. It wasn't likely she'd see them before David's DNA results were returned.

"Thank you for welcoming Emma into your home while I was sick. I hope when the DNA results come back you understand why I had to do it that way. I hope you'll welcome Emma back into your home when she visits her father."

She left before the women could respond. Emma called for "Auntie Ag" and "Ins" with her hand outstretched, but Celeste didn't look back.

She buckled Emma into the car seat and moved the bag of clothes into the passenger seat so she could sit down. As soon as she was buckled, David backed down the driveway. He didn't go a mile above or below the speed limit, attempting to get them back to the trailer as fast as the law allowed. He didn't turn on the radio, so they were left in uncomfortable silence.

She looked out the window, and tears threatened to fall. She blinked her eyes rapidly, strengthening her resolve to stay strong.

Emma fell asleep, and Celeste worried that David would take the opportunity to berate her. He kept his mouth closed and eyes forward, though, his knuckles white on the steering wheel.

She wasn't relieved when the trailer came into sight. She was glad her car was there, and her door was shut, but Marlene was on her porch smoking a cigarette.

David got out of the car when she did, and he stood with his arms crossed and his jaw clenched while she unbuckled and lifted Emma out of the car seat. Celeste didn't wait for him to say anything. She almost ran for her porch steps, fighting the fatigue that had settled over her body from her recent illness and expired adrenaline spike.

The door was locked when she got to it, preventing her from closing herself off from David. She glanced over at Marlene who was staring at her openly.

"I have your keys in the house," she called over.

Celeste couldn't find her voice, and she was thankful when Marlene stood and slowly made her way into her trailer. Celeste was aware that David hadn't pulled away, but she avoided looking in his direction.

Marlene returned with her keys, and Celeste wondered if the woman had ever walked so slowly. She seemed to take each step on the porch deliberately, and she chose to open the door instead of simply handing the keys over to Celeste.

Once Celeste was inside, she hoped Marlene would leave, but she followed her down the hall to her kitchen. She placed Celeste's keys on the table next to her phone as Celeste returned from laying Emma on the couch.

"I took your keys and put your phone on the table," Marlene said.

"Thank you," Celeste replied tersely. She should have been grateful, but she wanted to be alone.

"Well, I didn't want Randy to go through your messages."

"It's password protected." Celeste realized her mistake as soon as the words spilled out of her mouth. She should have assured her friend that nothing was incriminating about it.

Marlene put a hand on her hip. "What are you playin' at?" She pointed through the trailer in the direction where David had dropped Celeste off. "I thought you were in the hospital, but then he shows up, and it looks like the two of you just had a lover's spat."

"He doesn't love me."

"I hope not," Marlene said. "I thought you were conning him for some money, so I stayed quiet, but he had some passion—"

"We aren't together!" Celeste yelled. "I love him, but he hates me."

With her assertion came the tears, and they poured from her like a waterfall. She dropped to the floor, covering her face with her hands.

"I don't know how you could do Willie like that," Marlene remarked as she stood over her. "He's been good to you."

Celeste didn't acknowledge what she'd said, and seeing no fight in her neighbor, Marlene left. Celeste didn't bother to get up and lock the door.

An hour later, Celeste peeled herself off the floor and walked to the door. She stepped outside, feeling a cool breeze hit her face. David was long gone, but he'd had the last word. Fresh tears stung her eyes as she stared at what he'd left on her porch.

Emma's doll and the bag of clothes were sitting in the car seat the family had purchased for the baby. It was clear that David never expected to see Caroline or Emma again.

CHAPTER 32

Celeste needed a job. She was determined to pull herself out of Caroline's circumstances and make a better life for Emma and her.

The situation with her neighbors was increasingly uncomfortable. Marlene hadn't spoken to her in days, and the boys didn't seem to be allowed to play in the yard that joined their two properties. Celeste wanted to find a way to move out of the trailer, as it had been shared by Caroline and Willie, and she didn't desire to stay in a place where the person who had killed her host had been comfortable.

She had no idea if her grandfather was going to pop her back into his time frame, or if staying in this time was her punishment. She could almost see his lip lift in a smirk as he used the Predictor to determine whether she'd witnessed David's wedding.

She would have given anything to have a glimpse of the events her grandfather saw unfold on his tablet-like device. She had designed a portion of the Predictor, but she doubted she would be as competent at deciphering the information as Dr. Alexander Maze.

She'd been so convinced that she would show Emma to David, and he'd fall into her arms. Celeste had left impulsively, and she could thank herself for the outcome. Maybe if she had caught David just after Hailey Hall's funeral, as she'd planned, she would be with David now. Maybe *she'd* be wearing his ring.

Celeste felt guilty when she thought about Mindy. David's fiancé had been good to her, and she hadn't felt remorseful about her unchecked feelings for David or the kiss she'd shared with him. She loved David, and she felt as though they were still married, as he had divorced Caroline when Celeste's grandfather had popped her back into her time frame.

Celeste scrolled through job offerings, but none of them stood out to her. She tried to find something at the hospital, but nothing seemed to be available.

An ad for a hiring company popped up on her phone. She checked it and found it was local, so she called the number. The representative chewed gum as she spoke, but she assured Celeste that she could find employment for her.

Celeste scheduled an appointment, and then she thought about Emma's care. She didn't want Marlene to babysit for her, and she could no longer ask Ag for help.

She looked through the daycares in the area, and she found one that seemed to be reputable. During a call with the facility, one of the workers explained that they took children on a weekly basis. The only exception was Parent's Night Out when the daycare watched children so that their caregivers could have an evening to themselves.

Celeste doubted the hiring company would allow her to schedule a meeting at seven o'clock on a Friday night, so she ended the call. Perhaps she'd take Emma to that daycare when she had secured a job.

Celeste prepared for her interview with the hiring company, trying not to think of the infant she had to bring along. Emma cooed at Celeste as she pulled her hair into a tight bun.

"This is for our future," Celeste told Emma. "I need you to be a big girl while Mommy talks to some people about a job."

Emma stared back at her, chewing on an orange ring. Celeste wished she had enough money to buy her daughter a proper teething toy, but her dwindling funds would be gone before the end of the next week.

She left without interference, even though she could feel Marlene's eyes on her. Were her neighbors reporting back to Willie James, or had they decided to leave her alone?

Several blocks into her trip, the town opened up for her. She drove past the electric company and down the main road. She glanced up at the First Baptist Church and thought about the services she had enjoyed there. She made a vow to find a church for Emma and her soon.

After the first red light, she noticed a girl crying on the sidewalk. Her dark hair spilled over her hands as she shook with emotion and slid down the outside wall of a consignment shop until she was sitting on the sidewalk.

Celeste hardly registered the scene before she turned on her hazard lights and grabbed Emma out of her car seat. She carried her daughter with her as the girl continued to cry.

"Miss?" Celeste tried. "Are you okay?"

The girl lifted her head, and Celeste took in her hopeful brown eyes and the dash of freckles across her nose. She couldn't have been much older than Jonas.

"I broke it," she said, nodding to a wooden clock at her feet. "Well, my sister broke it, but I dropped it." A fresh sob bubbled up, but Celeste held up her hand.

"Let me look at it."

The girl's eyebrows went up as she regarded Celeste. "What could you do?"

Celeste bent over the clock and examined it. "I used to be good at taking stuff apart and putting it back together." It was true. She had spent her childhood investigating the moving parts of the electronics in her childhood home, from improving the toaster to taking apart her father's electric razor.

As she worked, she learned the girl's name was Kiana, and she filled her in on what happened to the clock. "I was playing ball with my sister," she explained, pausing her story to add, "Even though I know we shouldn't be doing it in the house."

Celeste glanced up encouragingly and placed Emma beside the young girl. Kiana watched over Emma seriously, passing her doll back and forth with her as she spoke to Celeste.

"I threw the ball, and my sister hit it into the dining room. We heard it knock against something, but we thought the ball had hit the table. I found my grandfather's clock on the floor."

Kiana told Celeste that her mother had bought it when her father had died. The clock had a place of honor on the mantle, and she felt as though her father was with her, as his ashes were contained inside the clock.

Celeste handled it a little more gingerly after she learned it contained a person. Kiana held a screwdriver in her hand, and she talked about the way she tried to fix their mistake but gave up quickly and decided she needed to take it to a professional.

Kiana pointed two doors away. "I was taking it there when I dropped it."

The building looked like a pawn shop, and the sign read: *We can fix anything except a broken heart.* Celeste's heart was so deeply fractured that she rolled her eyes.

An old man exited the shop and sauntered over to a green bench on the sidewalk. He flipped out a cigarette from the pocket of his red flannel shirt and lit it with a lighter he fished out of his denim pants.

She took the screwdriver from Kiana and opened the clockface. It wasn't an heirloom, but it had special meaning to the family, so Celeste stared at the clock until its interior design made sense to her. She was at home in the gears and inner workings of the device, and she had it working quickly.

Celeste reviewed the scuff marks on the outside. "I don't know how to fix this, but—"

"Bring it here," a gruff voice called.

The old man had finished his cigarette and watched them from his place on the bench. Kiana took the clock to him, and Celeste scooped up Emma. She moved her car into a parking spot on an adjacent road and jogged back. It had taken her a moment to get Emma in and out of her car seat, but the man was still talking with Kiana when she approached. She followed them inside the shop.

It was dark, and the shelves were filled with dusty items. Celeste expected to see CD players and cases lined with jewelry, but she was a little surprised to notice the displays of centerpieces, books, and trinkets.

"I'm Kerry Shelton," the man said, extending his hand to Celeste. Presumably, he had already introduced himself to Kiana.

He was taller than her with gold-gray hair and a rigid posture. His cold blue eyes betrayed nothing, a result of dealing with the clientele that has passed through his door over the years.

Celeste pumped his hand twice, just as Sheriff Murphy had taught her to do when Hailey Hall had been her host. "I'm Caroline Fletcher."

He nodded and took the clock behind one of the jewelry cases. He buffed it with sandpaper and applied a coat of a shiny substance.

"This should keep your mama from findin' out." He handed it back to Kiana, and she expressed her thanks while trying not to touch the clear coat.

"How much do I owe you?" Kianna asked, digging her hand into her pocket.

Kerry held up his hand. "Free of charge. Besides" —he jerked his thumb at Celeste— "Caroline fixed it. I only cleaned it up a bit."

Kiana looked apologetically at Celeste. "I have to go before my mom gets home. Thank you!" She waved before she bolted out the door.

Celeste remembered her appointment with the hiring agency and wondered how she would explain her lateness. She'd left fifteen minutes early, but she'd spent at least that much time on the sidewalk fixing the clock.

"I guess we need to go, too," Celeste said.

"Where ya headin' to?" He put his elbows on the glass case and clasp his calloused hands together.

"I was going to a job interview. Well, kind of a job interview," she backtracked. "It's a hiring agency."

"Oh." His silver and golden eyebrows shot up. "You've been lookin' for a job?"

Celeste nodded. "I was going to see what the hiring company could offer me, but I don't think I'll make it there soon enough."

He looked at his hands. "No good deed goes unpunished."

"What?" Celeste asked, shifting Emma from one arm to the other.

"It's somethin' my daddy used to say." He blew out a long puff of air. "Can I offer you some work?"

"Work?" Celeste repeated, wondering if she'd heard Kerry correctly.

"Mind you, it won't be much, but I can keep you busy for four days a week."

Celeste didn't know how to respond, so she was grateful that Kerry continued to lead their conversation. She didn't have experience with job offers, but she was certain that they were infrequent unless you had connections.

Kerry continued to speak as if she had already accepted his offer. "I have a nephew in another state." He paused and looked away, telling Celeste more than what she heard when he spoke. "I can visit him once a week, but it takes a couple of hours to get down there and back."

He looked back at her. "If I had someone here that I could trust, I wouldn't have to close the shop for the day."

"What would I be doing?"

He stood up straighter. "You'd be fixin' things. It's a lot like what you did today." He cracked a grin. "'Cept you'd be doin' it for me instead of takin' my business away at my doorstep."

He laughed at Celeste's horrified expression. "I'm only half kiddin'."

Emma let out a giggle and he smiled at her. "You can bring the sprat, too."

Celeste couldn't believe her ears. "I can bring Emma with me? But what if—"

"I have an apartment behind that curtain." He pointed to a dark almost blanket-like curtain to the left of where they stood. "You can let her play in a pen or watch television if a customer needs your attention."

Celeste didn't want to tell Kerry that her daughter was too old for a playpen and too young for television. Instead, she listened to him politely and made plans to arrive at the shop at ten o'clock the following Monday.

By the time Celeste climbed back into her vehicle, the initial shock had worn off. She had a job, and she could take her baby with her. Even better, it was a job where she could use the skills she had developed over her life.

She vowed to work hard for Kerry. He had a secret, or an issue everyone knew about, but he wasn't ready to share it with her, so she wouldn't press him. Heaven knew, she had secrets of her own.

CHAPTER 33

Christmas was a sober affair. Kerry gave her enough of an advance in pay to fill up her gas tank and buy a couple of Christmas presents for Emma.

The baby smiled at her mother as she tore into the packages. She'd rip the paper off one side and examine it, forgetting the gift in front of her. Celeste had to take away the paper to encourage her to rip more off the presents. It took thirty minutes for Emma to unwrap three presents, and the experience had almost drained Celeste.

She made tofu and rice with vegetables, and the two of them ate it at the table. Emma bounced from her plate to Celeste's and ended up in her lap. Once she lost interest in her food, Emma nursed. It gave Celeste time to eat, but it was more difficult when Emma tried to move her hands away from her plate.

Just as she finished with the dishes, there was a knock at the door.

Celeste hurried to answer it without thinking about who could be on the other side. She was shocked when she saw Marlene, Jonas, and Jayden on the porch.

At first, no one spoke. Then Marlene grabbed Celeste's shoulder, bringing her into an embrace. Emma toddled to the door, and Jonas scooped her up.

"I missed you," he said to the baby.

"We haven't missed a Christmas since I've known you," she said, her voice cracking. "I'm not gonna start now."

They talked without discussing the rift that had come between them. Marlene's eyes lit up when she told Celeste about the gift she had for her.

"Run over here with me and I'll give it to you," she said.

Celeste grabbed a jacket for Emma and her, and she thought Marlene seemed a little more anxious when she returned. She wondered why Marlene and the boys hurried her into their living room.

Randy was on the phone when they walked inside, and he held up his finger as he laughed at something on the other end of the line. Celeste relaxed a little when she realized he wasn't going to make her feel uncomfortable.

Her relief was short-lived when he said, "She just got here." He glanced at Celeste. "Here she is."

He handed the phone to Celeste, and she took it automatically. She already knew who was on the line before she put it to her ear.

"Care," he spoke, and Celeste's knees buckled.

Celeste had never been happier to be away from people as she was when she returned to the trailer Caroline and Willie had shared. She put Emma in the living room and went to the kitchen to cry.

She was glad Jonas had been holding Emma when her knees had given out. Marlene had misunderstood her reaction and had helped her to her feet.

Celeste had listened to Willie James, hardly registering his words, but completely horrified by the sound of his voice. The receiver had made it seem like he was right next to her, ready to beat her until she was bruised and bloody.

She must have spoken to him, but she couldn't remember her words. Her goal had been to placate him and get away. Finally, a disembodied voice announced that they had one minute remaining in their conversation.

At the end of the call, Willie mentioned, "They took DNA from me for that baby you have, but we both know she's not mine." Celeste had been silent, but Willie hadn't needed confirmation. "Did you trade our baby for her?" She hadn't taken the bait, and he had given up. "It won't be long, Care. Make sure you're ready to pick up and go. Without that other baby."

Celeste had given the phone back to Randy after the line had gone dead, and he had bragged that he'd paid for two calls from Willie. The first had been for his family, and the second had been for Caroline.

Celeste had expressed her gratitude and had excused herself from their dinner invitations with lies that she'd left her supper in the oven. She'd hurried out the door with rushed hugs and promises to visit and catch up.

She was still shaking from her experience when there was another knock at the door. She approached it hesitantly but decided to take her chances with another visit from her neighbors.

Marlene and her family weren't on the other side. Gifts with white and gold paper and big red bows were stacked on her porch.

Celeste looked for who had dropped them off, but her secret Santa had been too fast for her. She thought she saw a car in the distance, but she couldn't be sure.

The gifts were for Emma, and Celeste opened each of them with her. It took a little longer for Emma to open the stack of presents than it had for her to rip apart her mother's gifts, but Celeste was patient with her. Celeste's curiosity grew with every present she opened. It seemed that the person who had left them had known what Emma liked. From the tights with little pink ballerinas to a big container of plastic blocks, Emma had everything she had enjoyed at the Winsome house.

Who had delivered the presents didn't hit Celeste until Emma opened the last one, but it slammed into her with such force that it almost knocked her over. Part of her knew that Ag had spent enough time with Emma to know the gifts that would make her happy, but only Mrs. Winsome would have given Emma the beautiful, weighted doll in the ornate box.

It seemed as though the Winsomes hadn't given up on Emma.

CHAPTER 34

Celeste enjoyed working for Kerry. He was kind to her, and he made lunch for Emma in his kitchen every day she was in his shop.

He taught her what he knew about jewelry, and she imparted her knowledge about computers. She designed a website for his business in less than a day.

Kerry's crystal blue eyes were kind, but they had seen a lot of winters, and his movements were slow. He stood with pride when he heard the shop bell jingle, even though Celeste could see the toll it took on him in the evenings. He wasn't aware that she watched the bottle of pain medicine in the kitchen dwindle, as he took his prescribed amount throughout the day.

Celeste didn't talk to him about the nephew he mentioned, but she saw the letters. He tried to carry them swiftly to his apartment, but she saw "Bryan" in the top left-hand corner of the envelope. Similar to the ones she'd once received, they were decorated with drawings. Instead of hearts, though, the envelopes on Kerry's kitchen table had eyes, rivers, and the same house next to the water. Celeste thought she'd seen one like it when she and David had been driving one afternoon.

David hadn't spoken to her since he'd dropped her off. She'd seen him in town a couple of times, but he had ignored her. Once, before Christmas, he had been at the store with Mindy and her sons.

Celeste had watched him from afar, noticing the way he had draped his arm over his fiancé and remembering how it felt to be the recipient of his love. Emma had noticed her longing stare and followed it. When she had seen David, she yelled out, "Daddy!"

The entire store hadn't been silenced, with people from every aisle looking at her, but it had felt like it. She had been frozen to her spot, right between the greeting cards and vacuums, and they had been in menswear, looking at shirts that supported the state sports team.

David's eyes had been crinkled in the corners, but they'd lost their mirth, and the emotion had spread down his face until the expression of happiness had disappeared, leaving a hateful stare. Mindy had retained some of her jovialness, but when David had ushered her along, she'd looked back apologetically at Celeste. Dalton had kept his head down, but Cameron had smiled at her and moved his fingers from his eyes to point at her. It had been a gesture that was meant to say "I'm watching you", but Celeste believed the boy's intentions were a little more innocent.

"Hand me that piece," Kerry said, jolting her out of her thoughts.

She gave him a 24-karat necklace with a blue sapphire cut into a teardrop shape. The owner had been a middle-aged woman who had pawned the necklace to buy formula for a sick baby on her hip. She'd told them that the baby needed special formula for his gastrointestinal issues, and he had looked a little ill.

Kerry had given the woman more than he could profit from the sale of the necklace. "That little family needs it more than me," he had told Celeste when the lady had breezed out of the store.

Celeste wondered if he thought the same about Emma and her when he signed Celeste's paychecks every week. Celeste arrived early and stayed late, but she didn't feel like she worked in the traditional sense. Kerry had her sweep and stock shelves with new items, but most of their days were spent in easy conversation.

He held up the necklace to the light before dropping it into a sealable bag. The pawned items had a special room in the building. They waited for their owners for thirty days, and if they weren't redeemed, the items stayed in the room for another thirty days to satisfy state law. After sixty days, Kerry could sell anything that wasn't picked up.

There was an exception. Interest could be paid on the item they pawned, extending their payment window another thirty days. Celeste had noted that a man came in twice to pay interest on his wedding band, and Kerry had handed it back to him when he tried to pay again. When she'd asked if he'd paid off the item, Kerry said, "He's paid me double in interest what I gave him in the first place."

Kerry stood back with his arms crossed. "Not a bad day."

Celeste nodded at the jewelry and crossbow. "Do you want me to make a report?"

He nodded without looking up.

Celeste pressed a few buttons on his aged PC, and the report was generated. She faxed it to the police department, where they would compare the serial numbers and characteristics of the items they received at the shop with their reports of missing property.

"You can go home a little early," Kerry called over.

Celeste glanced at Emma on her blanket. She held the doll Mrs. Winsome had given her and smiled at Celeste with sporadic teeth.

"It might be nice to get an early start on dinner."

The bell jingled, and Celeste's heart sank. Mindy strode into the shop with her sons in tow. As soon as the door closed, the boys took off in opposite directions, Dalton bolted to the case of knives, and Cameron ran to the small selection of toys.

Mindy locked eyes with Celeste and approached her, holding out her arms. Celeste allowed herself to be awkwardly embraced, aware that Kerry's keen eyes were on them.

"I've missed you," Mindy greeted her. "I've begged David to forgive you, but he won't talk to me about it."

"It's okay," Celeste told her.

It was unnerving and a little embarrassing that her ex-husband's fiancé had sought her out at work, and Celeste was unclear about how to proceed. She let Mindy talk and gave the briefest answers.

"Obviously, David doesn't want you to watch the boys anymore, but maybe I could think of another way to help you." She put her hand on Celeste's arm, staring at her genuinely.

"That's not necessary," Celeste insisted.

Mindy's mouth turned down. She didn't believe her, and why should she? From what Mindy knew, David's ex-wife was suing him for child support for a child most people thought belonged to someone else.

She called over her oldest son and gave him the keys to her car. "Bring me the bag in the front seat," she told him.

He obeyed and promptly returned with a shopping bag stuffed with clothes. He tossed it to his mother and ran back to look at the knives.

"I went to the consignment store and picked out a couple of things," Mindy said, handing her the bag. "I hope they fit."

Celeste took the bag and thanked her, wishing Mindy had chosen anywhere else to have given her the clothes. Kerry hadn't moved since Mindy came in, and Celeste knew he was evaluating the scene.

Cameron resurfaced with a dart board. "Can I have it?" he asked his mother.

"I don't know," Mindy said, inspecting the sharp tips on the darts. "I don't want you chasing your brother with it."

Dalton glanced over and sized up the potential weapons. "If Cam gets that, can I have a pocket knife?"

Kerry motioned her to him, and Celeste moved to his side. He spoke low enough that Mindy couldn't hear him as she negotiated with her boys.

"Give them the darts and a knife."

Celeste stared at him for confirmation, and he nodded. She drifted back over to where Mindy stood with an uncertain smile.

"If you're okay with it, Cameron can have the dart set, and Dalton can pick a knife off the bottom shelf."

Mindy stared up at her gratefully. "I could pay you for them."

Celeste shook her head. "It's the least I can do since I can never repay the kindness you've shown me."

Mindy and the boys left in a flurry of appreciation and well wishes. Celeste visibly relaxed when the door closed behind them.

Celeste knew Kerry was going to speak before he opened his mouth, so she waited for it.

"Her husband was a caring man."

Celeste had expected a number of responses to Mindy's visit, but that hadn't been one of them. She looked at him, and he placed a hand behind his back.

"I never really saw much of her, but her husband, Jason, used to come down here a lot. He'd buy her a necklace or ring for every occasion." He rubbed a muscle in his lower back before he continued.

"I never really saw the sense in it. She works at the hospital, so she can't wear more than her wedding band at work."

"Maybe she wore jewelry when she wasn't at work," Celeste suggested.

He inclined his head in the direction in which they'd last seen Mindy. "She wasn't wearing any today."

Celeste wanted to ask him what he meant, but she didn't tell him to speak plainly. As she did with most people, she waited.

"That woman had a good husband who loved her and sought to please her, but as soon as he died, she started seein' another man. She attended to her husband until the day he died, but she hardly waited until the earth covered him before she was sharin' her bed with another man."

Mindy's husband had experienced severe complications with multiple sclerosis, and his health had deteriorated quickly. Celeste had heard about caregivers who were devoted to their loved ones, but after their death, those individuals made strides to live their lives to the fullest. It was almost as if several stages of their grief had been handled while the person was still alive, and they had started to let go of them during their decline.

Mindy had been good to Celeste, and she felt the need to defend her, even though they weren't exactly friends. "Maybe Mindy loved being married so much that she wanted to have that bond again."

Kerry picked skin from under his nail. "Maybe."

Celeste gathered Emma and her things, but Kerry stopped her at the door.

"I'm gonna see my nephew tomorrow," he told her with a note of sadness. "I think you've been here long enough to be a face our customers will recognize."

Celeste hugged him. She wasn't used to showing physical affection to anyone besides Emma, but the action wasn't forced, and she was glad when Kerry returned her embrace.

"Everything will be fine. You enjoy your time with your nephew, and I'll take care of the shop."

She waited for Kerry to rummage in his apartment for an extra key, and she placed it on her keyring before she left. Part of her was disappointed that she hadn't finished her CNA classes, but another part of her was glad it didn't work out so that she could have a job with a good man like Kerry.

It seemed that she was almost meant to find his small pawn shop and work there. She had needed a job, childcare had been an issue, and Kerry had needed someone he could trust to run his shop in his absence. Without knowing it, they had been the answer to each others' prayers.

Chapter 35

Marlene had been speaking to her more frequently since Christmas. It seemed that the news of her new job had renewed her neighbor's faith in her, and she was back in her good graces.

Celeste confided her fears of running the shop by herself, and Marlene tried to build her confidence. When Willie wasn't a topic of conversation, she valued her talks with Marlene.

"You'll do just fine," Marlene assured her. "You'll have your usual customers, and a few people might come in so they can pawn their grandma's broach."

"But what if Emma has a meltdown while I'm talking to a customer?"

Marlene was silent as she weighed Celeste's concerns. "You could leave her with me tomorrow. Jonas and Jayden are out of school for a teacher workday, so I'll have plenty of help."

Celeste considered her offer. She wasn't completely comfortable with leaving Emma, but when she evaluated her reasons, it had more to do with Randy than Marlene and the kids. She decided Randy would have little to no influence over her daughter's care, as he would be at work most of the day.

"Sure," she responded. "I bet Jonas misses her."

"He talks about that baby all the time," Marlene agreed, laughing.

Celeste spent the rest of her evening nervously awaiting her responsibility. When her alarm sounded the next morning, she was surprised to find she was already late.

Celeste jumped out of bed and rushed through her morning routine. She didn't have the time she wanted with Emma before she handed her over to Marlene, but it couldn't be helped.

When she arrived at the shop, she was ten minutes late, and there were two customers at the door. One man was a regular, but a frail woman she didn't recognize stood on the other side of the door.

Celeste opened the door, and the pair filtered inside before she could turn on the lights. The man, Noah, placed a car stereo on the glass counter. Celeste filled out the identifying information quickly, entered it into the computer, and gave him the standard amount of cash Kerry allotted for similar transactions.

The woman looked through the store and left while Celeste was still filling out the paperwork for the car stereo. She threw a hand up as she walked out.

Once Noah was gone, Celeste had the opportunity to go through the routine she usually completed before Kerry opened the door for business. Emma wasn't on her hip, so the process was much faster, and she found herself without customers or work an hour after she got there.

She tried to think of something she could do to help Kerry. His apartment was always in pristine condition, so she couldn't clean it. Some of the products had been on the shelves for some time, though, judging from the dust that had settled on them.

Celeste spent the morning going through the catalog and adding certain things to yard sale websites. She sold a weed eater, a stack of books, and six pieces of jewelry before noon. Most of the people who purchased the items wanted her to meet them for the exchange, but they understood when she explained the items belonged to a business. Before lunch, almost all the people who had made the online purchases had picked up their items, and the man who wanted the weed eater promised to collect it after he got off work.

She had just flipped the sign to closed and set the hands on the return sign for an hour away when Lewis Novack appeared at the door. She flipped the sign back and welcomed him inside.

She smiled at her old friend, but he regarded her differently, though not unkindly. She had met Lewis when she was Hailey Hall, but he had known Caroline for some time, so Celeste had to be careful when she spoke to him.

"I heard you were working here, but I'm surprised you lasted so long."

Celeste was tired of bearing the brunt of the consequences of Caroline's poor choices. It seemed she was destined to live in the shadow of Caroline's past.

She crossed her arms and dropped any show of friendliness. "I've been here for three months."

He looked around the shop and rubbed his clean-shaven chin. "I guess it's easier to keep a job when a man's not beating you half to death every couple of days."

His statement was openly hostile, but he never dropped his cheery expression. He turned his blue eyes back to Celeste, and she wondered if he would have been so rude to her if he would have known how close they had been when Hailey was her host.

"Why are you here, Lewis?" She couldn't hide her exasperation, and his flawlessly-styled blond hair and toned physique weren't as appealing when he was spouting condescension. He wore a beige shirt and olive khakis, so she didn't know if he was there as a customer or a detective until she spied the radio attached to the belt on his pants.

"I need to look at a sapphire necklace you took in yesterday," he said with a sigh.

She retrieved it out of one of the back rooms, and she found him bent over the pocketknives when she returned. He took the bag from her and surveyed the contents.

"Did you take in this pawn?"

She nodded. Kerry had tasked it to her while he gave the woman her money.

He lifted an eyebrow as he looked at her over the bag. "Is she a friend of yours?"

Celeste didn't like his line of questioning. It made her feel like she was on trial.

Maybe she was hungry, and she was probably tired of dealing with everyone's presumptions about her, but his accusation drove her over the edge. "Do you have a problem with me? You've been mean to me since I opened the door."

His jaw clenched. "We've never been able to get along for very long."

"What do you mean? I opened the door, and you started on me."

He laughed without mirth. "I just beat you to the punch this time."

Celeste closed her eyes and let out a long breath. "Look, Lewis, I'm trying to do better, but there are very few people who will let me."

When she opened her eyes, his mood was a shade lighter. "I've given you a million chances to do better, but I'm never going to let you back into my bed. I think David learned the same lesson."

Celeste was stunned. She'd had no idea that Caroline and Lewis had been more than a fling in high school.

"I'm not interested in you," she spit out, the hurt of his words about David still stinging her. "I'm just trying to work and take care of my daughter."

Lewis shook his head. "That's another thing." He held up his hand. "Never mind. I'm not getting into that."

He held up the necklace in the baggie. "This was reported missing, so I'm going to take it with me. I'll send an officer to take your statement. I'd do it, but I don't think I could stand to look at you for as long as it would take to fill out the paperwork."

Celeste was glad he was leaving, but she was angered by how he was doing it.

"I'll see enough of you on Thursday." He shook his head.

"What?" She couldn't hide her curiosity.

His eyebrows went up. "You can't try to skip out on a subpoena."

"I have to go to court?"

"Yeah, we both do. I was the arresting officer, and you..." He trailed off, but Celeste could guess how he was going to finish his sentence.

"I'm not with Willie."

"Whatever," he said. "I'll believe it when I see it. We actually had a bet at the station about if you'd marry him again to get out of giving a true testimony."

"I'll never marry him," she asserted.

Lewis chuckled as he opened the door. "You already did."

CHAPTER 36

Celeste didn't like having her past marriage thrown in her face. She stewed over it all afternoon, and her rage was reawakened when Officer Masters dropped by to take her statement.

He kept a professional attitude, but Celeste could sense his disapproval. She didn't know if it was because of her dealings with his wife, Rebecca, or if he had a negative experience with Caroline, too.

"I'm glad to see you're working," he said after she'd described the lady who had conned Kerry into giving her money for the stolen necklace. "Kerry is a good man. He believes in second chances."

There was something in the tilt of his head or the lightness in his brown eyes that made Celeste feel as though Officer Masters believed in the redemption of his fellow man. His next statement confirmed it.

"Rebecca and I are rooting for you, so stay strong."

After he left, Celeste analyzed his words. *Was he telling her to keep working, or did he mean for her to be strong on Thursday?*

She called the courthouse to see if they had sent her a subpoena for Willie's trial, and they confirmed it. She had to appear at the courthouse at nine o'clock on Thursday morning.

Celeste didn't remember seeing a subpoena when she'd cleaned out the trailer, but Caroline could have placed it in a drawer or thrown it away. Since she knew the date and time that she had to appear in court, she didn't really need it.

The rest of the day flew by. She locked up the shop and drove back to her temporary home. She had been looking at apartments, and one was going to be available in two months. She could afford it, and she was ready to leave Willie's trailer.

Emma played on Marlene's living room floor with Jonas. Celeste enjoyed watching them interact and imagined what it would be like if she were watching Emma play with a younger sibling one day.

Her thoughts fluttered to David and then to Zam. David didn't want anything to do with her, but it wouldn't be difficult for Celeste to win Zam's forgiveness. He wanted to take vows with her, and he believed Emma was his child.

Celeste wiped the thought from her mind. She couldn't be with Zam after she'd crossed time for David. Zam needed to know Emma's paternity just as much as David, and he deserved the chance to be with someone who loved him.

Emma's face lit up when she saw Celeste. "Mommy!" She toddled over to her and hugged her legs.

"She's really smart," Marlene observed, pointing to the blocks she'd stacked with Jonas. "She arranged them by color three different times."

Celeste wasn't as impressed as Marlene expected. "She built them in a pattern." Her neighbor bent down and pointed to several blocks in a row. "What did you call this, Jonas?"

"It's an AB Pattern," Jonas answered, putting the stray blocks into the bag. "Our teacher taught it to us in the first or second grade."

Three sets of blocks demonstrated two colors in an alternating pattern. Marlene held them up for Celeste to inspect.

"This little girl is probably a genius," Marlene commented. "You should call a talk show and have them film her."

Celeste pushed down a smile. In her time, parents worked with their children to increase their intelligence at a young age. In this case, Celeste believed that Emma was acting no differently than children her own age, even if they were from a different time.

"How old is she now?" Marlene asked.

Celeste thought back to the time they'd arrived. She had inhabited Caroline's body for about four months. "She's a little over a year old."

"You didn't invite us to her birthday party," Jonas said, his lip in a pout.

"I—I didn't have one," Celeste sputtered.

Marlene widened her eyes at her son. "Caroline didn't have the money for a party."

It was mostly true. Celeste's grandfather didn't believe in the importance of birthday parties, and he rarely celebrated holidays, so Celeste and her father had private celebrations with cake and pizza.

"We could have one for her," Jonas suggested.

Marlene looked down the hall where the shower had just stopped. Randy would be joining them soon, and it was clear from Marlene's hesitation that he wouldn't approve of their discussion.

"She wouldn't remember it anyway," Celeste said, offering her neighbor an easy way out.

"No," Marlene countered. "But she could look back at the pictures and remember that there were people who loved her and wanted to celebrate her birthday."

Emma reached for Celeste, and she picked her up. She whispered gibberish in her ear and giggled, causing Celeste to laugh.

"She's been telling me secrets all day," Jayden announced as he walked into the room.

"We're gonna have a birthday party for Emma," Jonas told his brother.

Marlene wrung her hands and slipped down the hall. The boys' hearty jokes cover their parents' muffled voices, so Celeste wasn't privy to Randy's reaction.

After a few moments, Marlene appeared with a flushed face and told Celeste to sit down. Randy retrieved a handwritten list from his wife before he left and returned with bags of groceries.

One of the bags held a small cake with a doll on it. It was a depiction of a porcelain doll instead of the quilted one Emma carried, but Celeste appreciated the effort to include something her daughter liked on the cake.

Marlene fixed rib eye steak with mashed potatoes, peas, and biscuits. Emma and Celeste enjoyed the meal, without touching the steak.

"It's okay," Marlene assured her. "We bought the meat on special."

Celeste decline politely. She couldn't tell her that she and Emma were vegetarians, and they came from a time when Slover's disease killed the people who dared to eat meat.

Marlene sliced a piece of the cake for Emma, and the baby made a mess of it. Marlene had the foresight to take off Emma's outfit, but bits of cake covered the table, floor, and Celeste's lap. It took two washes to get the icing out of Emma's hair.

Jonas presented her with a gift, and Celeste's heart melted over his sweetness. Emma opened a learning toy with a sea theme. It announced letters and sea facts depending on the mode.

"He did that on his own," Marlene whispered to Celeste. She nodded at her husband. "He may be hard-headed, but he's a real softie when it comes to children."

Right away, Emma pressed the buttons and mimicked the sounds. Jonas deliberately placed her hands on the buttons, explaining each one, and Emma nodded along like she was following his directions.

"Are you sure she's only a year old?" Marlene joked, winking at Celeste.

Jayden rubbed his hand across Emma's head. "She's smarter than some of the kids in my class."

Celeste glanced sideways at her daughter. It was true that most of the children in her time frame were a little more advanced. After the Great War, it had been hard for women to conceive, so each child was considered a gift to nurture into a contributing member of what was left of society. But Celeste had to admit that some things about her daughter seemed even more advanced than her post-apocalyptic peers. She had made a developmental leap in language, and Celeste wasn't sure about how to measure her abilities. And she had walked early. Separately, the two events meant very little, but combined, they cast doubt on her dismissal. Emma could truly be a genius.

Later, after Emma had fallen asleep with her new toy in her hands, Celeste stared down at her infant daughter. The gentle puffs of air leaving her body were a comfort to Celeste, and she tried to savor the moment. She tuned into Emma, blocking out other sounds until her daughter was almost magnified.

The toy slipped, and Celeste caught it before it landed on the floor, but not before it let out part of a melody. Celeste took her hand away from the button and turned it off.

Emma shifted in her sleep, but she appeared unaffected by the sound. Celeste laid the toy on the table and thought she heard a whisper.

She hurried back into the living room where it sounded as though Emma was repeating the gibberish she spoke when she told them secrets. She had turned around, ready to prepare herself for bed, when she heard something that turned her blood cold.

"Please don't take me back."

CHAPTER 37

Celeste sat in the witness box. She had placed her hand on the Bible, and she planned to tell the truth about everything except her name. She stated her host's name for the record and answered the prosecution's questions.

The reporters had to stay outside the courtroom, but there were throngs of people for them to interview while they waited for the court to adjourn. They seemed to know her as she was ushered past them, thankful for the deputy who guided her into the courtroom.

David and Lewis sat behind the prosecution, and no other seat remained on that side. She was placed in the seat behind the defense and closest to the door and stared at the back of David's head. He'd had a trim recently, and his tan suit washed out his features. Lewis was closer to her, and when her eyes fell on him, he scowled.

Time crept by slowly, but she was the first person to be called to the witness stand. She'd asked the bailiff, and she had informed Celeste that she didn't have to return to the courtroom after the day's proceedings as long as she was dismissed by the judge.

The hardest part was knowing that her attacker was in the room watching her. Willie James hadn't had access to as many drugs in jail, so his skin and hair were brighter, and his face had filled out. His boney stature had been replaced by bulky muscle.

She almost scoffed at his appearance when he was led into the courtroom in a sunset orange jumpsuit and shackles binding his wrists together on a chain that led to his ankles. Randy had wanted her to feel sorry for Willie's lack of food, but it seemed he had found a significant source of protein somewhere.

He searched out his ex-wife and blew her a kiss with his mouth. He looked back at her several times before the judge took the stand, offering her a wink. She stared at him with stone-cold hatred.

The Honorable Judge Brandon Marshal sat to her right as she gave her testimony. His white hair and stoic face made him appear seasoned, and Celeste hoped he was ready to give Willie the longest sentence possible.

No one was untouched by the proceedings, as the nurses had belonged to the community, and Celeste wondered why Willie's lawyer hadn't extradited the case to another county. Randy had mentioned visiting Willie and had tried to coax Celeste into going with him, but luckily, she was usually in class or at work during the scheduled visits. She thought Willie might have asked his lawyer to stay in the county so he'd have a better chance of seeing his ex-wife, but it may have been because Judge Marshal was from another county.

The defense lawyer had looked at the jury as he spoke about Hailey Hall's honorable discharge from the military and hinted that she wasn't the war hero the prosecution had described. What he said was enough to make Celeste hate him, but he kept bringing up Willie's children, and his lawyer's insistence that Willie was a great father made Celeste despise him. Caroline had talked to Celeste about Willie's children while they were in the hospital together, and she spoke about his occasional involvement with them. He had an eight-year-old son that he'd only seen a handful of times after he'd busted out the back windshield of his mother's car and rained glass down on his infant son as they tried to escape his abuse.

The defense attorney turned to her and ran a hand over his oily black hair. She had answered a few of his questions, and he seemed irritated by most of her answers. He was so close, and when he spoke, she could smell the onions he'd had with his breakfast.

"Would you say you left the defendant in a mentally unstable state?"

The prosecution called out an objection, but the slick defense attorney countered their claim until the judge allowed the question.

Celeste measured her answer. "Due to the drugs he takes, Willie James is mentally unstable, but he is responsible for the decisions he makes. It wouldn't have mattered when I left him. He would have been on drugs and unreasonable."

It wasn't the answer he'd hoped to get out of his witness, and he stared at her as if calculating the reason for her noncompliance. He smiled at the jury and put his hands together.

"Caroline, you seem angry today. My only guess as to your attitude is because you are upset about your husband's arrest."

"He's my ex-husband," Celeste corrected. "And I'm not upset. I'm livid that he took the lives of five people at the hospital."

The attorney nodded his head. "I think it's finally time to tell the whole truth."

"That is the truth," Celeste insisted, raising her eyebrows.

The attorney walked two paces before he spun around and pointed at Celeste. "Okay, if you're not willing to share your guilt in this, then it's up to me to make you. Caroline, will you please tell the jury why Willie James came to the hospital that day?"

Celeste thought it was easy enough to accept the blame of the woman who had left a psychopath, so she admitted it freely. "He came there to get me because I had left him."

The courtroom was silent as he leaned over the witness box and met her eyes. "And how did he know you were at the hospital?"

Celeste stared back at him with her mouth open. The answer hit her mind as if the attorney had rammed it there with a loaded truck. She thought back to Shelly's assertion that she had called Willie to pick her up at the safe house, and suddenly she knew. Caroline had called Willie to come to get her. Maybe she hadn't planned for him to come into the hospital with guns blazing, and she had been scared, but she had decided to go back to him.

"You called the defendant at 12:36 PM on May sixteenth. Would you like to elaborate on the conversation?" She didn't answer, so he spoke about Caroline's part in the disaster that befell the nurses and Hailey Hall until the prosecution landed on an objection that could be sustained by the judge.

At that moment, her eyes found Lewis's face and settled on David's grim expression. They both had every right to hate Caroline. She had always made the most self-serving decisions.

She wondered if she was any different. She'd lied to Zam about Emma's paternity, and she'd gone on a mission to tell David about his daughter and her love for him.

Judge Marshal dismissed her, and she left the stand on shaky legs. As she passed the scrutinizing faces of the people in her community, something else occurred to Celeste. Her last mission hadn't been a failure. The first mission had been to move Caroline away from Willie James, but she had gone back to him. The second time, she had called him to pick her up at the hospital, but Celeste had stopped him at the cost of her host.

She realized that Harvey Fletcher was financing her grandfather's time-hopping experiments, so Fletcher's wishes for the past led to certain missions to alter events, but she couldn't help feeling like her grandfather's plans were underneath several layers, and she had only peeled away the first one.

CHAPTER 38

"You have my heart," he told her as he traced a tear that had rolled down her cheek with his fingers. "I never knew love before you."

They exchanged rings, and the preacher pronounced them husband and wife. Mrs. Winsome had insisted on a wedding at their home church, and the hall was decorated in silver and navy blue. Ag wore the same colors as she stood by her side as her maid of honor.

He held their hands up in front of the congregation and cheers erupted. He ran her down the aisle and almost pushed her into the limousine where he fell onto her.

"My dress!" she shouted, mock scolding him. "We still have to go to the reception."

"Let's skip it," he whispered, growling and nibbling her ear.

She laughed at him, pushing him away, only to have him embrace her again. "It'll only be a couple of hours, and then you'll have me all to yourself in your room."

"*Our* room," he corrected her. "It's our room now."

Her eyes brimmed with tears. She wanted to share everything with him.

"What is it?" he asked, suddenly concerned. "What can I do to help?"

"You've already done it," she replied, wrapping him in her arms. "You've given me a home."

"To me, home is wherever you are."

Celeste woke with the taste of David on her lips, but it faded too soon. It had been a dream.

She'd often had them when she'd been jerked back into her time frame by her grandfather. Now, as she laid her head closer to Emma, she realized it was brief, and it could only remain in her memories.

David hated Caroline. She had destroyed his heart and hurt his family too many times.

Would he hate Celeste, too? She'd reasoned that their situation was unique, but it wasn't deplorable. However, now that she'd seen the way he looked at her over Caroline's decisions, she knew he'd never forgive her for her actions.

Celeste had lied to him since the moment she'd met him, and when she had told him the truth, she'd backpedaled when he mentioned putting her in a padded room. *How could he ever trust her?*

Celeste cried, finally condemning herself for her actions. She wanted to yell aloud that she was ready to go back to her own time frame. She doubted her grandfather would hear her, but she was willing to try it.

The only thing that held her back was Emma. She had to see through her decision to unite Emma with her biological father.

She hoped the DNA tests would be available soon. Even though she knew there would be a lot of questions, she was ready to deal with them.

Celeste had made selfish decisions, and they had put Emma in danger, but she was ready to put her in a place where she'd learn and grow to her fullest potential. Celeste cuddled her daughter, and Emma nuzzled her breast. Soon, she'd be with her father, and Celeste would have to return to her time frame. She had been selfish to think she could balance Emma between two worlds.

Celeste hugged Emma tightly and fell asleep. Too soon, she'd have to let Emma go, but for now, she'd hold her close.

CHAPTER 39

Celeste didn't receive a paper in the mail when Emma's paternity results arrived at the DHS office. She got a phone call from Rebecca Masters.

Her caseworker told her about the results and explained that the state would award her AFDC until after her court hearing with David. After that, it depended on the outcome of the custody arrangements as to how much, if any, money she'd receive.

Celeste tried to withdraw her request for AFDC. Rebecca attempted to talk her out of it, but Celeste insisted that she didn't want more money. "In fact, can you close my case altogether?"

"I can do everything except close your state insurance case," she told her. "Caroline, are you sure you want to do that?"

Celeste reiterated her request, and Rebecca told her about her conversation with David's lawyer. "He's been in contact with me regularly, so I called him when I received the results."

Celeste wondered why she wasn't contacted first, and Rebecca answered her question in her next statement. "I kind of felt him out to see their direction, and they plan to sue you for full custody."

Rebecca cleared her throat. "Do you have a lawyer?"

Celeste let her know that she couldn't afford one, and Rebecca suggested a pro bono attorney. Celeste made the appointment, and she already knew what she was going to tell her lawyer.

The knock was so light she almost didn't hear it.

It was well into the night, and Celeste wondered if it was a roaming animal who had sought warmth by lying against her door. Less than a minute later, the knock sounded again.

It echoed through the hall, lower than a usual knock, and she guessed that was the reason she had thought it was an animal. Celeste slid off the couch and placed her pillow on the floor in case Emma rolled over too far and fell off the couch.

She tip-toed down the hall and put her ear to the door. She only heard the wind whispering through the mountains.

"Who is it?" she whispered.

"Your ex-husband," a voice called from the other side. His amused laughter followed.

It felt like ice-cold water had been splashed on her, and it had run down her legs. She stood frozen on the spot.

"You're not gonna let me in," he slurred.

Was he drunk? Celeste tried to think if she had ever seen David drunk, and she drew a blank. Sure, he'd had a decent buzz a couple of times, but he'd never been truly over the limit.

She threw open the door and he almost fell on top of her. She pushed him onto the door frame.

"Why are you here?" she hissed. "Emma and I were asleep. I have to go to work tomorrow."

"Emma?" His brows lifted, but his eyes floated in their sockets. "Can I see my baby girl?"

"Absolutely not," she said. "You are in no state to see her." She cast a disapproving glance from his disheveled hair to his untied sneakers. "She deserves way better."

He put his hand to his eyes and swayed. "You're right." He put his hand down, and it slapped against his jeans. He must have liked the sound, as he did it again. "I need to tell you..." He trailed off, close to passing out, and Celeste shook him.

"I already know you're going to try to get full custody of my baby."

"*Our* baby," he corrected. "You took her away from me." He grabbed the doorframe and leaned in. Celeste could smell whisky rolling off him. "How'd you do that anyway?"

Celeste rolled her eyes. She didn't want to explain herself to a drunken man, but she spoke honestly.

"I didn't intentionally take her from you. She transferred with me when I time hopped."

David clumsily rubbed his eyes. "No, Caroline. I'm not going to listen to this time travel bull—"

"You'll listen to whatever I have to say!" Celeste whispered angrily. "You came to me. I didn't show up on your doorstep drunk."

He didn't say anything, so she took advantage of his intoxication to tell him everything. "I am from the future. My grandfather and I developed a way to travel in the past, but it only works if a host from that time period is used. Caroline's son funded my grandfather's project, so I was sent back to this time frame to keep Willie James from killing her."

She paused for his reaction, but David just kept rubbing his eyes.

"I wasn't supposed to fall in love with you as I created a relationship with you," she went on, hoping he was listening but doubting he processed her confession. "Your home was meant to be a haven for Caroline, but my grandfather couldn't find a way to ease the transition, so we kind of just popped back into our bodies. When that happened, Emma went with me. I carried her, and I gave birth to her. I came back as Hailey to tell you that I thought Emma was our daughter, but my grandfather wiped my memory."

David's head jerked up. "Don't talk about Hailey!" he barked.

She hadn't been prepared to see his grief in the form of anger. Celeste listened for Emma, but his voice hadn't awakened her.

"Fine. But I'm here now, and the only reason I came here was to tell you that Emma is your daughter."

David's jaw clenched. "There's only one thing you said that's true: Emma is my daughter."

He deliberately pushed off the doorframe and stumbled to the steps. "And I'm gonna take her from you. You're crazy, and you don't need to raise her to be a liar."

He tripped on the top step. Before she realized what she was doing, Celeste ran to help him. He shook away her hand, but he thanked her.

"Who brought you?" she asked, looking for a vehicle and hoping he hadn't driven there.

"No one," he replied. "I walked."

"From your house?"

He shook his head, and he grabbed the railing when the action threw him off balance. "I walked from the bar."

The closest bar was several miles away, and even if she woke up Emma and drove him to his vehicle, David didn't need to be driving it. She sighed heavily.

"You need to stay here."

"I'd rather sleep in a ditch than—"

"Shut up, David." Celeste didn't like to speak so roughly, but she needed to get his attention. "You're drunk. What was your plan?"

"I'll walk back and sleep in the SUV."

Celeste thought of another angle. "Why did you walk here? Mindy's house was closer."

Her question threw him off guard, but he recovered quickly. "I drank too much, and I didn't think about where I was going until I got here."

Celeste lived in a less populated area on the outskirts of town. The people who ended up on the road that led to her residence usually knew their purpose in coming there, and Mindy's house was in a different direction.

"You wanted to see me."

David wouldn't look at her. "I used to tell you all my problems, but when you left, I couldn't talk to anyone until—"

He tried to hide them, but tears rolled off his cheeks. He was still grieving for Hailey, but the woman he thought had been Hailey was standing right behind him.

"Emma and I were sleeping on the couch. Will you please sleep in the bedroom?"

He nodded, and Celeste led him inside. He lay back on the bed, and Celeste encouraged him to lie on his side.

Before she left the room, he told her, "I don't hate you, Caroline, but I won't let you ruin my daughter's life."

She spoke without turning around. "That's fine, David, as long as you remember I didn't have to tell you she existed. I brought her to you, but if you ever hurt her, I can take her away."

CHAPTER 40

She didn't think about sneaking David out until the next morning. She texted Kerry to let him know that she'd be late and waited until Randy left for work. Jonas and Jayden caught the bus soon after, so it helped her chances that they wouldn't be spotted as they left.

David said nothing about her concerns. She tried to keep Emma away from him, and David attempted to remain concealed, but Emma found him. It was almost like she could sense her father's presence.

"Daddy!" she cried when she peeked around the door to the bedroom.

David said something to her, and she squealed with delight. Celeste decided the damage was done, so she let them interact while she scanned Marlene's trailer for activity.

It didn't look like her neighbor was near her windows, so Celeste whispered to David that they needed to leave right away.

"We didn't do anything," David said to her. "Why does this feel like a walk of shame?"

"Maybe you need a little shame after the way you showed up here last night."

David tucked in his lip and looked away. Celeste was glad she'd made her point.

They drove in relative silence, except for Emma's occasional babblings. He climbed out of her car with a mumbled appreciation and walked to his SUV. Too late, Celeste realized she should have made him a pot of coffee, but she'd been too concerned with getting out of the trailer with him undetected. Besides, the coffee pot hadn't been used since she'd time hopped into Caroline, and Celeste doubted that she could have found coffee in the cabinets.

At the pawn shop, she apologized to Kerry again.

"Things happen," he said. "You don't need to take the day off, do you?"

Celeste's spirits lifted at his kind words. "No, it was just something unexpected that came up."

The rest of the day passed quickly, and Celeste's thoughts often returned to David. He had said some conflicting things. One moment he was threatening to take Emma away, and the next moment he was telling her that she had been his only confidant until Hailey, who, truth be told, was Celeste, too.

She understood his distress, but she was concerned about the route he had taken to express his confusion. Instead of drinking, he should have talked with his mother, sister, or Mindy about his feelings.

Celeste wondered what Mindy thought about the DNA test. David hadn't walked to her house the previous night, so had they fought when he had told her that he was Emma's biological father?

Kerry knew she was out of sorts, but he was polite enough not to pry. He told her to make the deposit at the bank, and when she returned, he told her to leave early.

"I'll need you to take over the shop for me again soon," he told her. "So you should take the afternoon off while you can."

It had been an unusually warm season, and snow had only fallen once. Celeste could feel the bitter air in her bones as she climbed out of her car, though, and she tightened her hold around Emma as she climbed her porch steps.

"Caroline," a voice called behind her.

Celeste's heart dropped when she saw Marlene hanging out of her door. The strained look on her face made it apparent that Celeste's trip to her car with David that morning hadn't gone unnoticed.

"Can you come over for a minute?"

Celeste sighed in resignation and hurried across their lawns. The smell of cigarettes hit her, and it was much stronger than when Marlene had smoked outside. Maybe she had chain-smoked today after she'd watched Celeste try to smuggle David out of the trailer.

Celeste stopped at the door, and Marlene opened it for her, stepping backward into her living room. Celeste unbuttoned Emma's coat, and the door shut behind her.

Behind her, a voice spoke. It was a sound that had haunted many of her worst nightmares since her first experience with its owner.

"Hey, Care. Are you ready to go?"

CHAPTER 41

Willie James approached her and put his arms around her waist. She saw the newest tattoos on his wrist and hands as they wrapped around her.

"Hey, Mar," he addressed her neighbor. "Could you take the baby so I can hug my wife?"

She wanted to shout at him that she wasn't his wife. Not only had Caroline divorced him, but the woman he thought he was holding was in another time and place.

She allowed Marlene to take Emma, and a new wave of terror seized her when she heard air brakes screech outside. Jonas and Jayden rushed inside, and Willie celebrated their return from school. The boys looked at their mother with uneasiness, but she smiled at them.

"Uncle Willie got out of jail early," she covered.

They returned his high fives anxiously, looking at their mother. She nodded her approval, but she seemed ill at ease.

Randy arrived home, and he regarded Willie with surprise. His shock melted into sheer joy, and he embraced him.

"I didn't know if Rowdy's plan would work, but I'm glad it did."

Marlene took the opportunity to get her children out of a potentially hazardous situation. "Boys, can you go over to Mrs. Floyd's house for about an hour? She looked at Willie, and seeing him still talking with her husband, she handed Emma to Jonas. "Take Emma with you."

Celeste couldn't move to touch or kiss her daughter before Emma was taken away. She was thankful for Marlene's suggestion, but it created a new set of worries for her. Celeste's most important concern was when she'd see her daughter again.

The boys hurried out the back door with Emma while Willie was occupied with their father. By the time his attention was back on the rest of the room, the boys had disappeared with the baby. Willie seemed unconcerned.

"Where's Rowdy?" Randy asked.

Willie moved to the living room window, dragging Celeste with him. He peeked out the blinds.

"He should be here any minute. He's picking up Summer."

Randy's eyebrows went up. "He's not taking Ruby?"

Willie smirked. "He's not like me." He pulled Celeste so close it felt like she was joined to him at his hip. "I'm a one-woman man."

"I just didn't think he was the type to abandon his wife and kids for a random chick," Randy said.

Normally, Marlene would have interjected a criticism against Rowdy for leaving his wife or at Randy for calling the other woman a "chick", but she didn't speak. Celeste was a little surprised that she was frightened by Willie, but he may have threatened her in the past. She'd certainly seen his handiwork on Caroline.

"It's not for me to judge him," Willie replied, shrugging his shoulders.

He brought Celeste around to hold her in front of him. Staring into her eyes, he kissed her, but he pulled back harshly when she didn't open her mouth.

"Aren't you happy to see your man?" he asked, squeezing her midsection painfully with his arms.

Celeste tried to smile. "Yes," she squeaked out.

"Good." He let her go, but he did it so forcefully that she dropped onto the carpet. "How much money do you got?"

Celeste looked up at him picking his teeth in the window. Maybe she could give him enough money to leave without her. She opened her mouth to speak, but he beat her to it.

"Just the cash on you. We ain't got time to stop at no bank."

"I might have some money in the car," she answered.

He regarded her with a slack jaw. "Where'd you get money and a car?"

Marlene helped Celeste off the floor without looking at her. "She's been workin', Willie."

He huffed. "Go get the money."

Celeste had hoped for this chance. Willie's greed outweighed his need to hold onto her, and it was the opportunity she needed to escape. She imagined running to the car and locking the doors before she started it and drove to Mrs. Floyd's house. Once there, she'd sit in the driveway and blow the horn loudly.

If her plan worked, Willie wouldn't approach her, as he feared discovery, and Jonas would run Emma out to her. Even if they stayed indoors as Celeste blew the horn, Willie would flee, as the police would be called due to her blaring horn. It was a good plan, and her hopes rose.

Willie pulled her to him again. "Where are your boxes?"

She had no idea how to answer his question. *Was she supposed to have gathered boxes for his getaway?* Willie was staring at her, and his arms moved with nervous energy. One wrong answer could set him off.

"She quit takin' Suboxone when she was pregnant," Marlene volunteered.

Celeste was both glad and horrified when she put context to Willie's request. *Did he want drugs?*

"It's been a couple of months since you threw my baby away," he said. "Haven't you been back to the clinic?"

She didn't address his statement. She only shook her head in answer to his question. He was upset over his son's mysterious disappearance, and Celeste was scared he was going to pounce on her like a wild animal, but he was interrupted.

A horn blew outside.

"That's our ride, baby." He grabbed Celeste's wrist and pulled her to the door.

"I'll miss you, brother," Randy said, and as they hugged, Celeste took in their similar noses and skin tones.

How could she have missed it? As if confirming her suspicion, she saw a bill clipped to the rack by the door. The name on the address label read: Randy James.

Her neighbors' over-involvement in her life made sense. They weren't just her neighbors. When Caroline had been married to Willie, they had been her family. She understood why they didn't want her with David and the reason Marlene and Randy chastised her for her lack of involvement with Willie.

Marlene hugged her, and Willie let her go. He seemed to approve of her relationship with Marlene.

"I'll take care of Emma," she promised. "That little girl will have a much better life in foster care than she'd have on the run."

"I don't want to go," Celeste begged, whispering desperately. "Please don't let him take me."

Marlene seemed sad, and she put her thin fingers on Celeste's arm. "It's what you wanted. You promised to be Willie's 'ride or die' woman, and now it's time for you to live up to your word."

Willie turned back to them. "Hurry up, Care. We gotta get outta here before the police come. You know they're gonna search our place first."

He dragged her down the steps and to the car. When she didn't walk quickly enough, he rewarded her by squeezing her wrist until she cried out.

"What about the money?" she asked, hoping she still had time for her plan. "It's in the car."

"Are you trying to get me caught?" he yelled at her. Spittle landed on her cheeks.

She shook her head.

"If I go down," he said, narrowing his dark eyes, "you won't live to see that little whelp you replaced our son with."

He jerked open the door to the backseat and pushed Celeste inside, almost falling on top of her. He bumped fists with the driver and nodded at the other occupant.

Celeste assumed the driver was Rowdy, and his thinning black hair was swept over the crown of his head. He was so tall that his head almost brushed the top of the vehicle's cab. He had wide eyes and a long nose that reminded Celeste of a bird. The woman who sat in the passenger seat had flaming red hair, curled into a wavy style. She wore pancake foundation which may have hidden her flaws, but it gave her an unrealistic appearance. Her bright red lipstick clung to her front teeth when she smiled.

The car was a rusty, late-model Honda. The midnight blue color had no distinctive markings, so it would escape the casual notice of police officers.

Celeste kept hoping she'd see police vehicles as they flew down the road, but none met them. *Why hadn't they started searching for Willie?*

"They haven't found them yet," Rowdy remarked, and Willie laughed.

Celeste hoped they didn't mean people had been killed in Willie's escape. It turned her stomach to think that there were bodies of dedicated law enforcement officers left behind in their wake.

Willie jabbed a finger at his temple, poking it several times. "They'd never think a cook was capable of it."

Rowdy smiled, obviously proud of whatever he'd done. "They didn't know we were cousins, though," he clarified, pointing back at Willie. "And they shouldn't have underestimated a food service worker."

Willie chuckled. "I thought I liked seein' Sheriff Murphy laid out on the floor, but I think pullin' Care's boyfriend into the jail was my favorite part."

Celeste's stomach dropped. Sheriff Murphy had been a father figure to her during the other times when she had time-hopped into that period. She couldn't think about how hard it would be on his family-especially his granddaughter-if something happened to him.

She imagined that anyone who showed interest in Caroline would be referenced as her "boyfriend", but Celeste was certain Willie meant Lewis Novack when he spoke of the officer he'd had to move inside the jail. After listening more, she heard that Lewis had been outside on the pavement where he could have collected attention, so they had dragged him into the jailhouse. Willie had stripped off Lewis's uniform, wearing it in Rowdy's car until they reached Marlene's trailer.

Celeste looked over at his black tee shirt and baggy pants and realized that he'd changed into Randy's clothes. The police would find Lewis's uniform in the trailer unless Randy and Marlene did something with it quickly.

"Gina's in the basement, so she shouldn't see anything until she clocks out," Rowdy said.

The men laughed at their well-executed plan, and Summer's profile revealed a half-smile of approval. Gina was the dispatcher, and if she didn't find the policemen until later, would they be dead, or was it already too late?

Celeste tried to discover the fate of the policemen, but every time she opened her mouth, Rowdy or Willie had something boisterous to add. Tears rolled out of her eyes, and she wiped them away as she stared out the window.

Celeste tried to look around in hopes of seeing Jonas run across the yard with Emma. Willie forcefully turned her head back around.

"You might as well face it, Care. That life is over."

The last time she'd visited David's time frame, Willie had killed her host. This time, he had her trapped with him, and the only way to survive was to pretend that she loved him.

Celeste thought she understood why her grandfather hadn't zapped her back to her time frame. He knew this was going to happen. He was angry with her, and Celeste had known he would retaliate, but she had expected him to simply pull her back before she could tell David about Emma. But he had found a better punishment, and she could almost hear him laughing as they zoomed away from Emma and any hope she had for a future.

CHAPTER 42

They stopped at a gas station in North Carolina.

Celeste had been keeping up with their direction, and she was almost certain that the Canadian and Mexican borders were in the other direction. She risked a question.

"Where are we going?"

Summer turned her head so Celeste could see her profile. "My uncle has a boat in Charleston, so we're gonna take it out far enough in the water to keep the police from following us."

Celeste was pretty certain that United States marshals and the coast guard could board the boat and arrest them, but she held her tongue. A flaw in their plan meant an escape for her.

Rowdy wore a black hat and sunglasses as he filled up the tank. Summer went inside and purchased cigarettes and a soda for each of them.

Celeste waved away the cigarettes when they were offered to her, but she accepted the soda. She didn't usually drink beverages with high amounts of sugar or caffeine, but she was dehydrated. The cool liquid stung her throat on the way down, but it satisfied her thirst.

"You're not gonna smoke?" Willie asked Celeste.

Summer turned around in her seat. "I'll take 'em back if she's not gonna smoke 'em."

Willie snatched them out of the seat. "We'll share them."

He took a red lighter from the console and lit a cigarette, blowing the smoke in Celeste's face. She coughed and waved away the smoke.

"What's your problem?" he said, his voice rising. "Why're you actin' different?"

"I just don't smoke anymore," she replied in a voice she thought was low enough to keep him from yelling at her. She was wrong.

"Do you want to know where we're goin'?" he thundered. "We're goin' to get my son!" He took an angry puff off his cigarette and threw up his other hand. "I mean, what woman gives up her son?"

Summer was quiet, but she seemed to agree with Willie. She nodded her head at his words.

Celeste kept her face blank, and Willie's temper fizzled. "We're not goin' to get little Henry, but if I ever find out where he is, I'll beat the door down to get him."

Celeste stopped herself from correcting Willie when he misspoke about Harvey's name. If he did not influence the baby's name selection, he had purposely said it incorrectly to rile Caroline, but Celeste wasn't going to take the bait.

Rowdy jumped into the car. "Keep it down, guys. There's do-gooders all over this place, and they won't hesitate to call the law."

"We got the answer for that in the trunk," Willie assured him, coughing out smoke as he laughed. Summer joined him, but Rowdy kept a straight face.

"I don't want to have a stand-off with the law," he said soberly. "We have a good plan. Let's stick to it."

"All I'm sayin' is that I won't go back to jail," Willie vowed, pulling Celeste close, and putting out his cigarette in his hand.

Rowdy turned on an Australian band, and the men sang along to the popular lyrics about a road destined for a place where Celeste wished she could send Willie. A bottle appeared from Summer's side of the car, and everyone drank from it. Celeste pretended to sip it, and Willie didn't study her actions when she put the bottle to her closed lips.

"Maybe it's better that you gave up the baby," he told her, kissing her with his nicotine-flavored mouth. "He can live on if somethin' happens to us." He pushed her against the door and put his body on top of her. The door handle was pressing into her back, as she tried to calm his lust with slower kisses.

"I have a feelin' we're gonna go down like Bonnie and Clyde," he breathed, as he trailed his hand up her shirt.

Celeste was repulsed by his touch, but she managed not to cringe. She tried to imagine David was gliding his hand across her body, but it didn't work. David's movements were different, and her body was used to them.

She thought about Zam. She hadn't been happy with him after she'd married David, but she felt pity for him. When she attempted to think the caresses were his, Willie jolted her back.

"You're different," he snarled, pushing himself off her. He lit another cigarette and hovered it just above her arm. She recognized the threat. "Who have you been with?"

"No one," she replied honestly. Other than her kiss with David at the hospital, she hadn't been romantically involved with anyone since she'd reassumed Caroline's body.

"You need to figure out if you want to be with me or not," Willie tested. "I don't want to spend the rest of my life with someone who doesn't want me."

Celeste's spirits lifted at the thought of another escape. She could tell Willie that she didn't love him, and they could let her out on the side of the road. It might take some time to walk to the nearest phone, but she could be back with Emma by tomorrow.

"We took vows, though," he went on, swiftly putting his hand up to her neck and then taking it away. "So, if you don't want to be with me, there's only one way out."

Celeste's hope diminished to almost nothing. She'd have to pretend she loved a monster to make it out alive. If she made it out at all.

Celeste was surprised when they stopped at a motel. Summer rented a room, as no one associated her with Rowdy or Willie, and they snuck in under the cover of darkness.

The room was as drab as the motel's exterior, with beige walls, carpets, and bedspreads. A small television sat on the dresser, and a phone was perched on a nightstand between two twin beds. A mirror reflected the beds, and a bathroom echoed whenever one of them entered it. A round wooden table and two chairs stood sentential by the door.

Celeste sat at the table, avoiding the beds. She was mortified by the prospect that Willie would press himself on her again and she'd be expected to have sex with him. Her stomach flipped at the thought, and she had to look away from the beds before she gagged.

How had Caroline fallen in love with Willie? Even if she had been attracted to his olive skin and dark features, his attitude was enough to push any self-respecting woman away.

"How much money does she have?" Rowdy asked Willie. He didn't address Celeste directly, as she was seen as Willie's possession.

Willie sat down on one of the twin beds and stared at her. "What did you bring with you?"

Celeste had left with her clothes and the coat on her back. "You didn't let me go to the car before we left."

"Don't you have a couple of bills, a bank card, or nothin'?" Summer asked. She applied lipstick and popped her mouth at the mirror.

Willie jumped up and stuffed his hands into Celeste's coat. He withdrew a bank card and the receipt for the bank deposit she'd made for Kerry. She had forgotten to give him the receipt before she'd left for the day.

Poor Kerry. He'd think Celeste had left her position there without notice, and they didn't know each other well enough to justify him tracking her down.

Celeste was certain that people would say she'd abandoned Emma to go on the run with Willie. She wondered if Kerry would believe the rumors when they circulated.

Who was she kidding? Everyone would believe the rumors. It was part of Caroline's pattern of behavior. She had always dropped everything for Willie.

"Won't they be able to find us if she uses it?" Rowdy asked.

Willie nodded his head, but he gave the card to Summer. Celeste felt irritation bubble up inside her. Why did Willie think he had a right to any funds on her bank card? She'd worked for the amount in her checking account, and even though it wasn't a sizable chunk, it was hers.

"I'm starving," Rowdy said. "We're gonna have to get some food soon."

Willie glanced at him before turning his attention to the large window. He had pulled the curtains closed, but he left an area where he could peak through without moving them.

"Does she have any connections here?" he asked Rowdy, pointing his finger to Summer.

Summer nodded at Rowdy, and she made a phone call. Celeste didn't pay attention to it, choosing instead to investigate the bathroom. It had concrete walls, a porcelain sink, a toilet, and a tub with a paisley shower curtain. Her heart fell when she realized there were no windows.

Summer and Rowdy left, promising to bring back food and drugs when they returned. She was alone with Willie. He grabbed her by the wrist he had already bruised and pushed her onto the bed.

He stared down at her like a predator ready to consume its prey. "Alone at last."

CHAPTER 43

The complimentary shampoo and soaps the hotel provided would never erase the stench of Willie's kisses on her skin. She showered slowly prolonging the time before she had to be with him.

She had delayed his advances by claiming that she needed a shower. She'd had to use an extra sultry voice that she'd hated, but it had worked. He'd released her so she could clean up for him.

Celeste hoped Rowdy and Summer would be back before she was forced back onto the bed, but for now, she was under the faux protection of the water. She worried that Willie would try to join her, easily overcoming the almost useless lock on the bathroom door, but he left her alone.

When she could delay the process no longer, she steeled herself and joined him. She found Willie in front of the window, peeking through a tiny space in the curtains.

"I think they're here," he whispered.

Relief washed over Celeste. She wouldn't have to lie down with Willie yet.

"That was fast," she responded.

He narrowed his eyes at her before he went back to looking through the window at different angles. "No, stupid. Not Rowdy. The police are here."

She was flooded with relief. They could save her.

Her hopes were dashed when Willie pulled a gun from underneath the bed. In Celeste's time, guns were given to upscale military officials by the government as a sign of trust. She had learned to shoot a gun when her father took her into the woods for banned community events, but she couldn't classify the types of guns Willie revealed when he lifted the bedspread. She wondered when the others had brought in the guns from the trunk and realized it could have been while she was zoned out.

"I love you, Care," Willie said.

Celeste echoed the words to keep his attention off her. He saw another threat, so in his eyes, it strengthened their bond.

The door swung open, and Willie turned the gun, unclicking the safety. Rowdy held his hands up, dropping fast food bags onto the carpet.

"Did you see them?" Willie asked him, flicking the safety back on but still carrying the gun.

Rowdy looked truly scared for the first time since Celeste had met him. His bird-like eyes were huge. "N-No, man."

Willie seemed to brush off his suspicion. He picked up a bag and scarfed down a cheeseburger before handing half of one to Celeste.

She shook her head. "I'm not hungry." It was true. The smell of meat sickened her.

He ate it in two bites, wadded the wrapper, and threw it at her. It hit her just below the eye.

"You're different," he said.

Celeste was tired of hearing that she was different. She was tired of getting subjected to his abuse, and she was tired of being scared. She walked to the open door and stepped into the night air. No sooner had she felt the bitter breeze on her skin than she was jerked back into the room.

"Not another lover's spat!" Rowdy tutted. "You guys will end up killing each other on the boat."

Willie jerked her onto the closest bed and stood over her. "Where did you think you were going?"

Celeste didn't respond. He reared back his fist, and she prepared herself for the blow.

"Hey!" Summer shouted from the door. "I didn't just stand out there and miss eating warm food to see you beatin' a woman when I got back. My ex used to beat me bloody, and I won't stand for it."

Up to that point, Celeste had thought Summer had agreed with Willie's treatment of her. Apparently, she drew the line at physical abuse.

Willie abandoned his assault on Celeste. "What'd you get?"

Summer visibly relaxed after he stepped away from Celeste. "I could only get ice."

Willie took the baggie she offered him. "I usually do crystal."

His drug preference didn't seem too critical because he disappeared in the bathroom for an hour.

Chapter 44

Celeste woke up with Willie's butt pressed into her back. She loathed him, but it was easier to allow the touch than to hear him yell in a slurred speech at her.

As she lay in the stillness of the morning, she wondered if Emma was okay. *Did she sleep well without her? Had Marlene already turned her over to child services?*

She knew the baby wouldn't enter foster care. David had filed a custody suit, so Emma could be given to him. Celeste wondered if he was stable. He may have broken up with Mindy, but she hoped her daughter would be able to benefit from the woman's kindnesses.

She heard a sound like a stick snapping, and she wondered if the maids were already there to clean. Judging from the low light entering the room, it was just after sunrise.

Pounding knocks fell on the door.

Willie jumped from the bed, throwing the blankets over her as he stood. He found a spot low to the ground and inched up to the window. Rowdy and Summer sat up straight, pulling the comforter over their nakedness.

"It's the law," Willie whispered.

"Open up," a booming voice commanded. "We have you surrounded, Willie. Come out with your hands up, and no one has to be hurt."

Rowdy hopped out of bed and crouched on the floor. He picked up his jeans and slid them on. Summer asked for her clothes, and he threw a handful of them at her.

Willie had told Celeste that he wasn't going to go back to jail, and he had a collection of firearms under the bed. She moved to the floor and crawled into the bathroom. She could hear their voices echoing off the concrete walls.

"Last chance, Willie!" the voice shouted. "You don't want Caroline to get hurt, do you?"

"You won't take me alive," Willie yelled back at them. "I AM THE NIGHT!"

Celeste heard the metallic clicking of guns as they were passed out. She wriggled herself into a space between the toilet and the bathtub and held her hands over her head.

"Where's Caroline?" Willie asked.

"Hidin' in the bathroom," Summer answered with indifference.

"Care!" he shouted. "Get out here and grab a gun!"

Celeste didn't move. She had no intention of helping them fight off the police, even if it meant that Willie beat her unmercifully before they managed to break down the door.

The movement in the room had stopped like Rowdy and Summer were waiting on Willie's orders. "We'll fight our way out, and I'll get Caroline before we go to the car," Rowdy volunteered.

That must have been enough for Willie because he didn't seek her out.

The gunfight didn't begin right away. The police tried to negotiate with Willie and size up the situation, using a mega horn to broadcast negotiations to the group. They found Summer's car and reasoned that she was in the room with them, but they didn't mention Rowdy.

Again, Celeste found herself wondering what Rowdy had done to help him escape. *Were cameras set up in the jail?*

A loud banging sounded from the room. There was a pattern to it as if the person causing it was deliberately waiting before striking again.

"What are you doing?" Summer hissed. "Do you want them to hear you?"

"I don't know about you two, but I'm gonna live to fight another day." Another bang followed Rowdy's assertion.

"Do you think the room next door is empty?" Summer asked him. "They've put rangers in it."

Celeste doubted that the police were rangers, but she silently agreed with Summer's rationale. She hoped Rowdy would continue to chip away at the sheetrock between their room and the room next door. Once he breached the barrier, the police could roll in and take them to jail.

Celeste wouldn't mind being lumped into a group of outlaws if it meant she could get away from Willie. She hoped it would be sorted out when they were taken in for questioning, but she knew better. Caroline had attached herself to Willie, and she'd abandoned the attempts to rescue her from his abuse on numerous occasions. Most times, at the physical, mental, or emotional cost of others.

Rowdy stopped banging on the wall. "We shoulda kept goin'. Why'd we even stop?"

"You were hungry, and Willie wanted drugs," Summer said simply.

At the mention of drugs, Willie straightened up. "Do you have any more?"

The question was directed at Summer, and she answered, "What! You've already gone through what I gave you? That was supposed to last you a while!"

"Do you have any more?" Willie repeated.

Summer sighed, and Celeste heard plastic crinkling. "I guess you can fix me some, too."

"I thought you were off it," Rowdy asked her, notes of anger in his voice.

"I was, but this morning I woke up to an ambush, so I think I'll have a little before I die."

"You think we're gonna die?" Rowdy asked fearfully.

"Let's see." Sarcasm dripped from her tongue. "We have a good selection of guns and bullets, but we're surrounded by law enforcement officers with bullet-proof vests and rifles. My guess is that they have people on the outside and in the room to the left and right of this one. Are you with me so far?"

Celeste could imagine Rowdy's face paling. He joined in on Willie's boasts, but he didn't have the countenance of someone whose bravery or loyalty had been tested. It seemed whatever he had done for Willie had been undercover, but now that he truly risked death or prison, he blanched.

"And if that's not enough," Summer finished, "they have at least one sharpshooter. Once a shot comes from this room, they have no reason to pull any of us out alive."

She was casually cool as she spoke, and Celeste wondered why it was so easy for her. Just like everyone else, Summer had a story, and her experiences had led her to this moment.

The megaphone boomed in the background as the police spoke to them from outside. They'd tried to call the phone in the room, but it hadn't helped them. Willie had answered it "Joe's Pizza", and ripped it out of the wall after yelling expletives at the caller.

"I love you, Care," Willie called from the next room. His voice was softer, and she imagined the drugs were starting to make their way through his body.

Maybe they'd depress his system so much that he'd pass out, and she could talk Summer and Rowdy into surrendering with her. She doubted Summer would give herself up, though. She was too calm about the possibility of their death.

She had shared part of her story with Celeste. When the guys went out to find ice, Summer had told her about her pregnancy at a young age and the family member who had claimed paternity. She had been a young minor, and he had claimed she'd tricked him into sleeping with her, so he'd taken full custody of their son. Summer had watched her son grow from afar, and when she had become an adult, she had expected to have visitation rights. The court system had refused her claim, stating that the child had a balanced home.

At the time, Summer hadn't dabbled in drugs or alcohol, but she had flung herself into the lifestyle to forget about her hard life, moving from boyfriend to boyfriend to help her support her habit. She'd had abusive boyfriends, and the one before Rowdy had almost killed her. After she'd suffered broken ribs and a few missing teeth, Summer had decided to take her life back. She had tried to kill her abusive partner, setting his house on fire. The man had lived, but he'd suffered second-degree burns.

The police had exercised all their tricks to get Willie to surrender. They had tried to negotiate a particular prison so his children could visit him and mentioned Caroline's safety several times. It had all fallen on deaf ears.

"What I want to know is how they found us," Willie said.

"It was probably the drugs," Summer pointed out.

"You told your connection about me?"

Summer laughed like they were at a party instead of a potential shootout. "No, silly. You gave me Caroline's card so I could buy you the drugs."

Rowdy sucked in a breath. "You both knew we could get caught if you used the card. What were you thinking?"

"I thought we'd be on the boat before they traced it," Summer answered, but she didn't sound convincing.

The police boomed a communication that included a plea to Summer, but Celeste hadn't heard most of it. They mentioned a child, but Celeste hadn't been able to pick apart more. Sometimes, the words were muffled, and other times they were amplified like the person was standing in the next room.

Finally, the police were finished. "I'll count down a minute," the voice cautioned. "Then we're going to come in there and get you."

Willie yelled and cussed them for almost sixty seconds. Celeste didn't hear the sound of the metal clips over the rod, though, so she knew he hadn't revealed himself.

Celeste used the time to pray that she'd make it out of the situation unhurt. She wanted to see Emma again.

The counting stopped, and there was a silence that stretched out for an eternity. The door slammed open, and the first shot echoed against the wall.

CHAPTER 45

Celeste pulled her hands more tightly against her ears and squeezed her arms over her ribs. The sounds were deafening.

Celeste had heard gunfire. It had been part of her reality until the tensions of the Great War had settled in her time. The firefights she had witnessed in her youth did nothing to protect her mind from the fear of the bullets whizzing through the hotel room.

She thought it would last much longer, but it ended in just over a minute. As the uninjured crunched through the debris in the hotel room, Celeste carefully loosened her grip on her ears.

"There she is," a partially muffled male voice cried out.

Celeste was guided to her feet and held firmly by each arm. She found she couldn't use her legs. It didn't matter, because the officers who flanked her carried her so that her feet dragged across the ground.

She didn't want to look at the results of Willie's poor decision, but she almost stumbled over a pale arm on her way out. Summer lay on her back with her eyes frozen into a stare. Her olive-green tee shirt was riddled with bullet holes and soaked with blood. Bile threatened to rise into her mouth, but Celeste pushed it back down.

When she was pulled outside, cold air blasted her face. She was drenched in sweat from fear, and the bitter wind cooled her way below her normal temperature. She knew better than to ask for her coat. The police still thought she was part of the resistance.

Screams echoed off the buildings around them, and she glanced at the source of the noise. Willie had survived the shootout and was receiving medical care. The EMT was professional and methodical as Willie shouted obscenities at her. He'd been shot in his midsection, but Celeste was too upset that he was still alive to investigate the exact location of his injury.

"Your boyfriend's been shot," the policeman on her right said.

"He might die," the other one told her.

Celeste could only hope he was right.

Celeste had found a cockroach when she was a young child. She'd enjoyed the way it tickled her fingers as it ran across her hand. After she brought it to her father for examination, he flicked it off her palm and stomped his foot on it. Celeste had cried until it had popped back up and scurried into the grass.

"They'll rise out of the ashes after humankind has destroyed itself," her father had remarked.

Celeste thought Willie was a lot like the cockroach her father had tried to kill. No matter how many times people tried to stop him, he lived on to pop back up again and destroy more lives.

Thankfully, no police officers were injured during the standoff.

Celeste sat in a well-lit room with gray walls and a darkened window directly in front of her. She kept her head bowed so whoever was on the other side of it wouldn't see her face.

Her grandfather had similar windows all over his facility, along with minuscule security cameras he'd asked her to install after he'd reached the first milestone in the creation of his time travel machine. Celeste had put them in the most innocuous places, like in the faces of artificial flowers and on the sides of rolling tables.

She slumped into a metal foldout chair. A large rectangular table had a plastic cup of coffee with steam lazily drifting into the air.

She waited so long that she started to drift to sleep. She jerked just before she slid out of the chair and landed on the laminated floor. She dozed in and out for what seemed like hours before an officer in plain clothes entered the room.

He was taller than most of the people in his time frame, and his six-and-a-half feet lengthened his legs and torso, causing his body to be much thinner than it might have been at a smaller length. He wore a pewter shirt and light blue jeans, and he carried a camera with him.

"I'd like to record our conversation," he stated. "Is that okay?"

Celeste nodded her consent.

He folded himself into the chair in front of her and leaned down so he could meet her eyes. "I'm Detective Johns, and I want to ask you some questions."

Under different circumstances, Celeste thought she'd like the dark-eyed man with dishwater blond hair and an array of freckles. However, the blinking red light reminded her that he was there to gain her confession about the role she had played in the events between Willie Jones's escape and capture.

After they'd established her identifying information, Detective Johns began the interrogation.

"Were you aware that Willie James planned to escape?"

Celeste decided she was going to answer honestly. She didn't care how anyone else was affected.

"My neighbors, Randy and Marlene James, told me that Rowdy planned to get Willie out of jail."

"By Rowdy, do you mean Timothy Stills?"

Celeste shrugged. "I never knew his real name."

The door opened and an officer brought in a box and laid it between them. Detective Johns pushed the box to her. The smell hit her, and her mouth watered. She didn't want to dive into the pizza, but her stomach growled its need for sustenance.

"Go ahead," Detective Johns encouraged her.

She opened the box and was only a little disheartened to see pepperoni on the pizza. She picked off the meat quickly and bit into the gooey cheese and crispy crust.

Detective Johns pointed to her pile of discarded meat. "Most people like pepperoni on their pizza."

"I'm a vegetarian," she explained.

He resumed his questioning as she ate and waited patiently for her answers between bites. "Did you play a role in Willie James's escape?"

Celeste shook her head.

"Did you expect him to retrieve you yesterday?"

"No," Celeste snorted. "I expected him to stay in jail."

"You sound angry about his escape," Detective Johns observed. "If you weren't happy about it, why did you leave with him?"

"He forced me to go."

Detective Johns eased back into his seat. "I want to believe you, Caroline. I really do. But the facts suggest otherwise."

Celeste put the piece of pizza she'd been holding back into the box and brushed the crumbs off her hands. "I didn't try to shoot you guys when you came into the hotel room. I was happy you were there."

"I wasn't there," Detective Johns said. "But the lack of gunpowder residue on your hands and arms confirms that part of your story." He leaned forward and steepled his fingers on the table. "You weren't the only one who chickened out when the officers kicked in the door."

"Willie?" His name was out of her mouth before she could stop it. She supposed he could have been shot in the crossfire as Summer sprayed bullets from her gun.

"No," he grimaced, raising his golden eyebrows. "When the responding officers conducted their search, they found Timothy Stills hiding under the bed."

Celeste spent hours answering questions as Detective Johns attempted to dissect her statements. She was placed in a cell at night, and the questioning resumed each day.

After the first day, Detective Johns didn't bring her special treats. She was given water and the same meals as every other prisoner in the jail. She ate her way around the meat and choked down the water.

After three days, Detective Johns sighed with the weight of his responsibility. "Do you have someone who will pick you up?"

Celeste was shocked by the question. She was convinced she'd remain in jail until she was tried for whatever charges she'd received from her association with Willie.

"I don't know," she responded, fumbling for a name. "I guess I could call Marlene."

By that time, Detective Johns was well aware of the names of everyone Celeste knew. He shook his head.

"If you mean Marlene James, she's been detained by the Unicoi County Sheriff's Department." He explained that the James' had been taken in for questioning after Rowdy had admitted to picking up Willie at their trailer and Celeste had told Detective Johns that they had known about his escape.

"Just because they heard rumors about it, doesn't mean they were in on it," Celeste argued. Tears swelled in her eyes when she thought about Jonas and Jayden in foster care. Maybe they had been placed in the same home as Emma.

Detective Johns nodded along. "They'll be released if they're innocent."

Celeste racked her brain for any other person who'd pick her up. She could call Kerry, but she didn't know his feelings about her. Finally, her mind landed on the only person who might not fully hate her.

CHAPTER 46

Ag picked her up in the family's SUV. When Celeste climbed inside, she was aware of her smell and the state of her appearance.

She hadn't asked if she could shower, fearing Detective Johns would change his mind and keep her locked in the cell. She had waited for Ag to arrive on a wooden bench while the sheriff's department buzzed around her.

She had glass in her hair, and she wore the same clothes she'd had on when Willie had kidnapped her. Her last shower had been in the hotel room, and she smelled unsavory scents each time she moved.

Ag didn't say anything as the miles passed by, except to ask her if the temperature was comfortable. Celeste nodded in response and tried to think of something to break the silence.

Detective Johns had told Celeste that Rowdy had played a role in her release. He was a convincing victim, giving the officers a detailed account of Willie blackmailing him into poisoning the lunch at the jail with sleeping pills. He had described a hostage situation, where Willie had held him at gunpoint, first making him drop him off at Marlene's home and then demanding that he go to Summer's house.

He denied his involvement with his mistress, claiming that Willie had threatened his family if Rowdy didn't follow his orders. According to Rowdy, Summer was one of Willie's girlfriends.

Celeste was ready to destroy Rowdy's false statement, but Detective Johns told her that his description of the events supported Celeste's kidnapping claims. Celeste held her lips together tightly as Detective Johns said that Rowdy upheld her abduction, citing that Willie had dragged her around by her wrists and threatened her child. Detective Johns had inspected Celeste's arms and seemed to be satisfied with the angry marks on her wrists.

Celeste wanted to contradict Rowdy's claims of innocence, but her release hinged on his credibility, so she was stymied. She wanted Rowdy to receive jail time for his actions, but she also wanted to go home. In the end, she had dropped a hint that Rowdy was Willie's cousin, and the look on Detective Johns's face confirmed that he'd follow up on her intentional slip.

Celeste was relieved that the officers were unhurt, even though they had been knocked out by the sleeping pills for several hours. Their extended nap was the worst thing that had happened to any of them, aside from Lewis waking up in a jail cell without his clothes.

She was thankful to be riding in the Winsomes' SUV with Ag. Although it was awkward, she was glad to be with her closest friend.

Ag opened her mouth several times, but then she'd close it, and shake her head. There were many questions Celeste imagined she wanted to ask, but she knew David's sister would get to it in her own time.

"Did you leave with him?"

Ag had finally asked her question, and Celeste was glad to hear it. She wanted to plead her case to Ag, but she didn't wish to launch into it before Ag had asked. It would have sounded too desperate and forced.

"He took me."

Ag sighed heavily. "That's hard for me to believe when you've run to him every time there was an opportunity."

Celeste looked at Ag. Her eyes were swollen, and lines ran down her mouth that were usually lifted into her cheeks. Ag was dressed in a smart tan suit, and she'd applied a little eyeshadow and lip gloss, but she looked haggard, as if she'd driven longer than three hours.

"I understand why you'd feel that way, but I blocked his letters from the jail, and—"

"You still lived in his home, Caroline."

"Yes, but I was planning to move," she defended. "I didn't have the money—"

Ag waved away her explanation. "You could have transferred your housing assistance to another place."

"I've stopped receiving benefits from the state."

Ag cocked her head to the side without taking her eyes off the road. "They finally realized you were perfectly capable of working and supporting yourself."

"I told them to cancel my benefits," Celeste told her. "I've been working with Kerry Shelton, and—"

"I'm well aware of everything you've been doing," Ag interrupted. "Not only is it all over the news, but I had to sit at the police station with everyone who had any connection with you or Willie." She shook her head. "Thank God they questioned Mama at home."

"I'm so sorry," Celeste said, looking at her lap. "I wish no one would have had to go through interrogations."

Ag shook her head, blowing a scoff swiftly out her nose. "They hardly questioned me."

Celeste glanced up at her, but Ag's profile gave little away. She only seemed sad and tired.

"They asked Mama and me about your relationship with Emma, but Mama couldn't tell them a lot. She got agitated halfway through their questioning and yelled at them to 'bring him back'."

"Who? Willie?"

Ag shook her head once. "Detective Roll asked if that's what she meant, but she denied saying anything."

Celeste remembered her time with dementia patients. "She seems to be going downhill fast."

Ag's tone softened. "No, Caroline. I lied about how long it's been going on. She's been having trouble for years, but she asked me to hide it from everyone, so I did."

"That's why you told me she changed after the wreck."

Celeste colored when she realized her slip. Ag had told Hailey about the wreck that had claimed her father's life and injured Mrs. Winsome.

If Ag was confused by Celeste's reminder, she didn't show it. "It was a convenient way for people to dismiss her oddness."

"I'm sorry, Ag." Celeste thought about touching her hand, but she doubted the attention would be well-received.

Ag's voice cracked. "I'm not ready to lose her."

Celeste put her hand on Ag's shoulder. "Your mother could be around for a while."

Tears rolled down Ag's cheeks. "But in what condition?" she cried. "Will she remember what she had for breakfast or the characters in her favorite shows?" Her voice was just above a whisper. "Will she remember me?"

Ag pulled over and allowed Celeste to comfort her while she wept. The afternoon sun stared at them through the windshield by the time Ag pulled back onto the road.

"I'm such a mess," Ag said by way of an apology. "I don't know how we were allowed to keep Emma."

"Emma?" Celeste exclaimed, rising in her seat. "You have Emma?"

A flush crept up from Ag's neck. Celeste wasn't supposed to know the location of her daughter.

"Actually," she replied carefully, "David received emergency custody of the baby."

Celeste could hardly contain her relief. She'd imagined hundreds of foster care scenarios, and none of them had ended well. She was glad David's DNA test results had helped him gain custody of her.

"Is she at your house? You have to take me to her!"

Ag's eyebrows climbed with her words. "No, Caroline. You—"

"I was kidnapped!" Celeste yelled. She hadn't expected her sudden anger, but Ag's refusal had sent her past frustration.

"If you'll let me finish," Ag spoke in a stronger tone. "I was going to say, that you need to shower first."

Celeste relaxed and fell back in her seat. As if to prove Ag's point, a shiny sliver of porcelain fell from her hair.

"I guess you're right."

"And even then, I'm not certain David will let you see her."

"Why?" Celeste could think of no reason she'd be kept from her daughter.

"He doesn't know if you abandoned her for Willie."

"That's ridiculous! I would never have left her for that man!"

To Celeste, it seemed rational, but to Ag, her words may have seemed debatable.

"You have to see it from his perspective," Ag tried.

"But I love Emma, and I wouldn't abandon her."

"You loved David." Ag's voice was hoarse and hollow. "And you abandoned him."

The consequences of Caroline's actions washed over her again. *Would she never escape her host's terrible decisions?*

"It's different with a child," Celeste argued.

"Is it?" Ag countered. "Where's Willie's baby?"

She had backed Celeste into a corner. If she told David's sister the truth, Celeste would sound crazy, and Ag wouldn't take her anywhere near Emma. She had to let her believe the lie. She hung her head, completely defeated.

By the time Celeste had showered and they were back in the car, the sun was low on the horizon. Ag had waited for Celeste to dress while she sat in her living room, reading a book from an app on her phone.

Celeste had dropped the keys to the trailer and her car inside Emma's diaper bag. It was still by the door when they'd arrived, protected from the elements by the awning over the porch. No one had known Celeste's keys were in the bag, or she did not doubt that they would have pilfered through the trailer and her car.

The women pulled into the Winsomes' driveway, and Celeste's heart flipped into her stomach. *What would she do if David refused to let her see Emma?*

She pushed open the passenger side door, extremely unsure of herself. She hadn't eaten much in the last four days, and combined with her anxiety, her lack of nutrition was catching up to her. She gripped the handrail on the stairs a little too tightly, and a splinter pricked her skin. She cried out, and Ag stopped unlocking the door.

"It's just a splinter," Celeste explained.

"You look a little pale. Are you sure you're okay?"

Celeste nodded and waited for her to open the door. Ag put a hand on her arm.

"You should probably stay out here until I can let David know the circumstances."

Ag disappeared into the house, and minutes later, feet pounded down the steps. Celeste braced herself for his rage, and she worried that she couldn't withstand his anger. A sudden loss of breath and a light sweat signaled that she was physically weaker than she'd thought.

The door burst open, and David ran through it. Celeste almost closed her eyes in fear of what he might say to her.

David ran so hard at her that he almost knocked into her. And then he took her into his arms.

CHAPTER 47

"I'm glad you're okay," he whispered, kissing her head. "I was so worried about you."

Celeste wondered if she had slipped into an alternate time zone or traveled to another world. She was certain David hated her. If it wasn't because of her slights against him after Caroline had abandoned him, then it derived from his belief that she had hidden Emma from him.

David had loved her, and there had been certain moments when she'd thought they could rekindle their romance, but she'd thought the DNA test had ruined her chances with him. She was confused by his arms around her even though she welcomed their warmth and strength.

"Are you okay?" he asked leaning back and surveying her.

"I'm fine," Celeste told him carefully.

Ag appeared behind him, and when David noticed her, he pulled his sister into their embrace. It was uncomfortable to have Ag's face pressed up to hers, and she was glad when David loosened his grip.

Ag stood at the door with her arms crossed loosely. David continued to hold Celeste and stare at her.

"Are you sure you're unhurt?" he repeated.

Celeste nodded, afraid that anything she said would end their moment together. She was still feeling weak, but she willed herself to remain standing so she wouldn't miss a moment of David's attention.

"I thought the next time I saw you—" He let the rest of his thought remain unfinished, taking his hand and burying his face in it.

"We didn't know what was going to happen to you," Ag elaborated. "We saw the news and heard what the police were saying." She glanced at her brother who still seemed to be overcome with emotion. "At first, we were mad because we thought you'd left Emma behind." She stared hard at Celeste. "And we were still skeptical when Sheriff Murphy said you may have been involved against your will."

David picked up where Ag left off. "If your neighbors hadn't confessed to giving Timothy Stills their sleeping pills, and he hadn't said you were with Willie, then you would have been transported from that jail in South Carolina to the one here."

"Or the sheriff could have tried to leave her in the jail there," Ag interjected. "He told me that he doesn't want Willie back here."

"He's going to live," Celeste said, sighing with resignation. "I'll never be safe."

David squeezed her midsection. "You will be as long as you're with me."

There was only one thing that could break her desire to be held by the man she loved. "Where's Emma?"

Ag went inside and David led Celeste indoors with his arm still around her. Celeste stepped carefully into the living room.

"Mommy!" Emma shouted.

Within seconds, her blonde-haired child ran into her outstretched arms. Celeste squatted and felt Emma's little arms encircle her neck. She breathed in her hair, expecting a strawberry scent, but not surprised when it echoed the smell of David's eucalyptus bath products. Either Ag had bathed her in David's soap or David had held his daughter close to him.

"Mommy here," Emma said, stroking her mother's hair. Celeste wondered if Emma's touch was more of a consolation for Emma or herself.

Celeste sat on the floor, holding her daughter until she fell asleep in her arms. David offered to take the baby, and Celeste stood.

Then the world went blank.

Soft sounds whirled around her, like machines buzzing by the beds in the hospital. Panicked, she shot up and found herself in darkness. *Had her grandfather popped her back through time?*

A hand reached out and touched her arm. She flinched, backing her way out of the blankets over her legs.

"It's me," David's voice whispered. "You're with me."

Celeste relaxed before her thoughts landed on Emma. "Where's the baby?"

"Ag's sleeping with her tonight," he told her. "We ordered a bed for Emma, but it won't be here for a few days. Then she'll sleep in the room next to us."

Celeste thought about what he'd said and what it meant for her. Her elation bubbled over until she remembered Mindy.

"What about your fiancé?"

David breathed out into the darkness. "I broke up with her. She was upset over Emma's DNA results, so I ended it."

Celeste was surprised. She'd never imagined Mindy would be upset over the results. She'd thought Mindy would be overjoyed, taking Emma into her home and raising her as her own.

David's announcement caused Celeste concern. Before she'd been kidnapped, he had almost hated her, but now he was lying beside her in his bed.

David had always been quick to trust people and to get angry, so it wasn't shocking that he had decided that Celeste should move in with him. She was certain, though, that she needed time to straighten out her feelings before she moved back into the Winsome house.

She shared her doubts with David, and he listened to her without interrupting or forcing his thoughts on the issue. After they spoke about her need to live alone for some time, he took her into his arms and kissed her.

The kiss was soft and sweet, and it left Celeste breathless. He pressed himself to her, eager to kiss her again.

"I should sleep on the couch," Celeste said, surprising them both.

She had dreamed of nothing more than she, Emma, and David together as a family, but now that the opportunity was a possibility, something didn't feel right. She moved up in the bed.

David sat up with her. "You don't have to live here right away, but I thought you'd want to be close to Emma."

Celeste had forgotten that David had been granted sole custody of their daughter. She paused in her consideration. She wanted to be close to her daughter, but she needed to establish some boundaries.

"I'll stay, but I'm going to sleep on the couch." David was silent until she added, "At least for a while."

"Okay." He touched her shoulder and traced his fingers down her arm.

The sensation gave her chill bumps, even though her skin was covered by her sleeves. She wanted David to continue his soft caresses, and he seemed to read her mind.

He kissed her again, long and slowly, running his hands lightly over her body. With more insistence, he tugged at her shirt, and it came off before Celeste knew it had happened.

He stopped his physical advances, waiting for her consent. "Let me show you that I love you," he breathed.

Celeste's resolve melted with his words, and she pulled him to her. "Okay."

CHAPTER 48

Celeste stood at the sink with a glass of milk and a peanut butter sandwich. After David had fallen asleep, she had crept downstairs in search of food.

Usually, David would have insisted on feeding her after she passed out, treating her more like a patient than a lover, but he had been so overcome with emotion that he'd just been happy to see her alive.

She took another bite of her sandwich and chewed through the thickness of the peanut butter. She'd made it into a thick layer in hopes of gaining some energy.

She thought about checking on Emma, but she dismissed the idea. She trusted Ag to care for her.

She delayed going back upstairs to David's room. She ate slowly, intentionally chewing several times before she swallowed. *Why wasn't she in a rush to be back in her lover's arms?*

If she was honest with herself, it was because it felt weird. She was convinced David was her soul mate, and she longed for his touch, but something wasn't right. The passion was there, and he had worshipped every part of her that needed attention, but there was a missing element.

It occurred to her that the first time she had used Caroline as a host, she and David had fallen together naturally. Celeste was so caught up in the emotional connection, that the physical aspect of their relationship was a bonus. Now that she'd desired David from the standpoint of another host, she had a deeper focus on the physical relationship. This time she'd had more than a few days to become accustomed to the biology of Caroline's body, so she was more aware of her body's reactions.

David hadn't seemed to notice a difference, and she was glad for it. If he would have asked her about her experience afterward, Celeste couldn't have been honest about her reaction without diving back into her futuristic origins. It would have taken away from the moment.

Celeste heard shuffling from Mrs. Winsome's room, and the lady appeared in the kitchen. Celeste tried to blend in with the shadows, but Mrs. Winsome's eagle eyes spotted her.

"So, you're back," she commented.

Mrs. Winsome had spoken at her usual volume, and it echoed through the quiet house. Celeste hurried to close Ag's bedroom door, fearing the conversation would wake Emma.

"I fainted, so David took care of me," Celeste responded.

"I'm sure he did," Mrs. Winsome conceded. "He seems to be an expert at fornication."

Celeste was glad she was in the dark so her face couldn't be seen. She was certain it was a shade that resembled a firetruck. She struggled to find any conversation starter that led Mrs. Winsome away from sexual references.

"I-I ate a sandwich," she stuttered.

Mrs. Winsome huffed. "It's not the first time you've taken from me, and it won't be the last. You blonde women are all the same."

Celeste didn't know what to say. Caroline had hurt David deeply, and Mrs. Winsome didn't know that Celeste was a different person. In her state, it might be too much for her to understand. At times, the idea of time hopping was almost overwhelming for Celeste, and she knew the mechanics of it.

The lady shook her head. Ag had rolled curlers in her mother's hair, and one of the spool-shaped tubes fell to the floor. Her eyes had adjusted to the low light in the room, and Celeste could see it on the kitchen floor.

Ag's door opened and she tied a violet robe around her as she rushed to her mother's side.

"Mama, what are you doing out of bed?"

Mrs. Winsome pulled her arms tightly to her sides. "I don't need permission to visit the little girls' room."

Ag held her hands out around her mother, but she didn't touch her. "No, Mama, but it's a little early-even for you."

"My bladder doesn't have a clock," came her smart reply.

An uncomfortable silence followed as Celeste and Ag waited for the strong-willed woman to speak or move in the direction of the bathroom. Mrs. Winsome's head stayed fixed in the stillness until she decided she'd made her point. Her cane stabbed the floor with gentle thuds.

She mumbled as she went. "I can't go to the bathroom in my own home, but the kids can have sexual congress and rattle the roof over my head."

Celeste wished she could go outside and crawl into the first hole she spotted. Her legs tingled from the embarrassment, and she could almost see Ag's mouth and eyes widening with her mother's revelation.

"I'm sorry," Ag told Celeste when her mother was out of earshot.

"It's fine," Celeste replied. "How's Emma?"

"She's tossed and turned tonight, but she's settled now. David was sleeping with her until last night, and then he let me take over."

Celeste was glad that Emma had been able to spend some time with the Winsomes. It looked like they both would be seeing more of the family.

"Has he asked you to marry him yet?" Ag laughed.

"Don't be silly," Celeste said, but her heart leaped at the idea.

Ag got her laughter under control and spoke in a lower tone so as not to wake the baby. "I mean, after what Mama just said, you can probably expect a proposal by the end of the week."

"He did ask me to move back in."

Ag sucked in a breath. "Did he really?"

Celeste backpedaled. "It was mostly over Emma. He wants her to have two available parents."

"You see," Ag chortled. "A ring won't be far away."

They were interrupted by a banging in the bathroom. Ag ran to assist her mother and Celeste stood by in case Ag needed her help.

"Tell him to bring back my boy," Mrs. Winsome cried.

She thrashed around, knocking the soaps and a candle off the porcelain sink. Ag held Mrs. Winsome to prevent the elderly lady from hitting her head, but she was struggling. Celeste moved quickly, grabbing her legs.

Mrs. Winsome's fuzzy house shoe hit Celeste's cheek as she tried to kick away from her grasp. Celeste locked her arms around her legs and helped Ag balance her mother onto the kitchen floor.

Emma heard the commotion, and she wailed. Ag nodded at her, and Celeste ran to Ag's room.

Emma stood on the bed, crying in the direction of the door. When she saw Celeste's form in the shadows, she held her arms out. Celeste lifted and held her. She was conflicted about whether she should walk back into the kitchen with the baby. Now that her toddler was awake, she didn't want to leave Emma unattended, but it wasn't safe for her to take her around Mrs. Winsome during one of her fits.

The sound of a slap bounced off the wall and Ag cried out.

Celeste put Emma on Ag's carpeted floor. "Can you stay right here for Mommy? Auntie Ag needs my help."

She thought she saw Emma nod, but it could have been a trick of the light or a product of her tired mind. She shut the door to Ag's room and ran back to assist her.

The sun had peaked over the mountain, and Mrs. Winsome had quieted. She lay on the floor with her head in Ag's lap. Ag's cheeks were dripping blood from three slashes just under her eye.

Celeste stood over them, waiting for a cue from either lady.

Mrs. Winsome groaned, trying to lift herself into a sitting position before finally giving up.

"You have to get him back," she pleaded. Her voice was small and helpless. "Please bring him back to me."

"Daddy's gone, Mama." Ag consoled her mother, but Mrs. Winsome twisted away from her.

Ag thought Mrs. Winsome was talking about Mr. Winsome, but Celeste had another idea. The realization was swift and heart-crushing. Mrs. Winsome wasn't talking about her dead husband.

She was talking about David.

Chapter 49

Celeste watched the sun light his face. It dusted his cheeks with golden rays and showed the stubble on his neck and jawline.

He wore a small smile that Celeste had helped place on his mouth, and he clutched the pillow she'd laid on when she woke in his bed. It wasn't his bed, though.

She placed a gentle hand on his shoulder. He opened his eyes at her touch.

"I missed you," he said holding up her pillow. "I had a poor substitute."

She pretended to be amused. He stretched and she tried to work out what to say to him.

"So, everything is okay between us?" she asked hesitantly.

He sat up and wrapped her in his arms. She forced herself to relax in his embrace. He smelled like David's musky cologne, and he had the same freckles on the top of his hands and a strong chest, but the pressure of his arms was wrong. It was restrictive and controlling, not comforting and loving.

Celeste had believed it was her acclimation into Caroline's body that had made her sexual experience with David different, but she'd been wrong. It had been different because she hadn't been with David.

"Of course," he responded. "I saw you on the news, and I knew you didn't choose to go with that—"

"Willie is a deplorable human being."

His chin moved against her head. "I wish I could have gone after him myself and taken you out of there."

"What if I had chosen to go with him?"

He bent his head to look at her profile. "But you didn't. He took you."

"Maybe I didn't know he was going to take me so far. Maybe I wanted to see him again," Celeste went on, picking up on a thread of conversation that seemed to agitate him. "He *is* my ex-husband."

Celeste was waiting for him to clench his jaw. She prayed that she would look at his face and his mouth would be set in a grim line. It's what David would have done in response to her faux admission. When she looked back at him, though, David's mouth moved into a playful smile.

"You never would have done that."

"How do you know what I'd do?" She purposely goaded him. "Maybe I'm tired of living a boring life. Maybe I wanted to have an adventure. And maybe," —she narrowed her eyes at him— "I was waiting for an excuse to get away from you!"

"Stop it, Celeste." He'd kept his voice low, treating her like an unruly child, but it didn't matter. She had him. Without knowing it, he had revealed more than she'd expected, but Celeste had known him for a long time, and she knew exactly how to unravel him.

"Who's Celeste?" she asked innocently.

He slid out from behind her and stood. The early morning light showed an outline that usually made her heart do a double beat, but she wasn't excited by his form.

"You knew before I said your name." It wasn't a question.

"I know my lover."

He scoffed, grabbing a pair of boxers that had been tossed to the floor in the heat of the moment. "Do you mean me or him?"

"You don't want me to answer that, Zam."

Celeste shouldn't have been upset with him. He had been her long-term boyfriend when she'd left, and he deserved better than her haughty attitude. But he had invaded David's body, tricked her into believing David wanted her, and slept with her. It was one of the worst deceptions she had encountered, and she'd invaded the bodies of several different people.

After he pushed his legs through the boxers, he sat on the end of the bed. He leaned over and put his head in his hands.

"I just had to know," he said miserably.

Celeste didn't ask him for clarification. He'd wanted to know if she had cheated on him.

"When you came back after your first trip here, you were so different." He sat up straighter, but he wouldn't look at her. "You still shared my bed, but you were distant." His shoulders dropped. "It was like you never left here."

Zam waved his hand in the direction of the door. "I thought if I could be a good father to Emma then you'd stay, but you told me you were going back on another mission. I knew you and I were finished when you left the last time."

Celeste considered the years she'd spent with Zam and the pain he must have felt. She tried to keep her role in his decisions in mind when she spoke.

"I loved you, Zam, and we had a lot of good times together."

"But," he said.

"*But* I was never passionately in love with you." She paused. "I never took vows with you."

"Funny you should say that—"

They were interrupted by a knock at the door.

"I don't mean to interrupt anything," Ag said nervously from the other side of the door, "but Emma's awake."

"Could you give her a little cereal, and I'll be down to eat with her in a few minutes?" Celeste called.

Ag's footsteps receded. Celeste didn't have to worry if she heard anything. Ag would have spoken up if she'd thought someone had invaded her brother's body.

"Why are you here?" she asked Zam. "My grandfather wouldn't have let you come here unless it benefitted him."

He had looked at her when she'd asked her question, but he turned his gaze on the blue and white rug at his feet.

"I was supposed to do something, but I couldn't do it."

Celeste sighed. "I don't have time for vague responses. What were you supposed to do?"

Zam jumped up. "What does it matter? I couldn't do it!" He paced the room and waved his arms. "I'm not made for blackmail and secret time-jumping missions!"

Celeste liked to think she was observant, and as she watched Zam, she could see the difference between the way he and David moved. Ag had mentioned the change, but Celeste had been concerned with gaining access to Emma and the effects of her lack of nutrition had distracted her.

"Blackmail?"

He stopped pacing and stared at her with his eyes burning. At that moment, Celeste noticed David's flecks of gold were missing.

"Do you think it's beneath him?"

Celeste didn't put anything past her grandfather, but she wondered what he had used to gain Zam's cooperation. She echoed her thoughts to him.

The rage fell off his face. "Are you kidding me?"

"He threatened to erase you, didn't he?"

"He called it 'murder without a smoking gun'." He used air quotes around one of the old phrases her grandfather liked to say.

"That's what he did to Harvey Fletcher," Celeste commented.

Zam laughed dryly. "He just shifted him into a different timeline."

"I don't understand how he made that move and he still received financing for his time machine."

"Really?" Zam lifted David's dark eyebrows. "He just schmoozed another billionaire."

Celeste stood up, opening her arms to Zam. She hugged him, pulling away when his hands roamed below her waist.

"I need to go downstairs and eat with Emma, but I want to clear up a few things with you."

He put his hands on his hips, an action completely unfamiliar on David's body. "I guess this is where you tell me you want to end things with me and spend the rest of your life with David."

"Not exactly," Celeste hedged. "It's unethical for me to live in Caroline's body. You're right about one thing, though. I want to be with David."

He rushed to her. His hands grabbing her elbows were the only thing that kept her from falling backward.

"Then be with David." His eyes were darting left and right, and his breaths were desperate. "I'll stay here with you, and we can raise Emma as Caroline and David."

Celeste pushed him away, rubbing her elbows as she put more distance between them. "Zam, you took the same ethics classes as me. You know it's wrong." She pulled on the blue and white comforter, hoping the action of making the bed would force Zam into helping her and keep him at a distance. "Besides, I love David. I'm not just after his body."

Zam flicked the comforter up, but he didn't help her as she'd hoped. "It didn't seem to bother you last night. You liked his body then, and I was in it, so what do you think that means?" He gave her a self-satisfied smile.

Celeste's anger boiled over before she could contain it. She forgot Zam was her past lover and friend, who was being blackmailed by her grandfather. In their discussion, he had revealed his true intentions. He had planned to stay with Celeste and keep David and Caroline imprisoned in their forms in the future. Celeste's sympathy for Zam flicked off like a light switch.

"It means that you tricked me! It means you used me for your narcissistic pleasures, and it means we're done! I never want to see you again."

He gave a derisive snort. "You don't have to *see* me again. You can look at David while I stay in him. I think if I kill the person Dr. Maze wants me to then I can 'write my own ticket'. If you know what I mean." He put air quotes around another one of her grandfather's phrases.

Celeste never thought she was capable of physical violence, but at that moment, she formed a plan. Zam was blinded by his obsession with her, and her grandfather had played him like a wild card, trumping her efforts to unite David with Emma. He would be perfectly happy to let Zam remain in David's body, briefly retrieving him for debriefings and giving him orders.

She dropped the blanket. She had to be convincing. Zam knew her, and the smallest slip would give away her true feelings. She had to make sure she spoke as little as possible while she used his infatuation with her against him.

"You're right. David will never love me for who I really am." Even though her body screamed in defiance with every step, she made her way over to Zam's side of the bed.

She kissed him, and he tried to lean her back onto the bed, but she turned him until they fell onto the mattress with her on top of him. She hated his hands roaming over her body and despised his tongue as it searched her mouth. She waited until he was taken over with lust before she suggested tying his wrists to the bedposts.

He slipped out of David's boxers. She'd had to take off her shirt before he'd complied, but once he was securely fastened to the wooden posts of David's bed, she made her move.

"How long were you going to wait to tell me it was you?"

He gave her a sheepish grin. "How long were you going to wait to tell David you weren't Caroline the first time you used her as a host?"

His smug reply strengthened her resolve. "It's over, Zam. I'm never going to be with you again, and Emma's not your child."

She'd expected shock and a pained expression. Zam rolled his eyes.

"I would have been a fool to think you delivered a fully developed baby at seven and a half months pregnant." He pulled at his bonds, but they held him. "I guess you thought I took care of her while you were gone, too." He laughed. "Your grandfather kept her at the facility, studying her like the lab rat she is."

Celeste grabbed the pillow-the same one Zam had held in his sleep-and put it over his face. He jerked at his bonds, and one of them almost released him until she grabbed his wrist and held it back. She put all her force on the pillow over his face and the hand that held his wrist. He bucked beneath her, banging her spine with his knees.

His efforts were in vain. He wasn't fully accustomed to David's body, and Celeste had been inside Caroline's form for months, measuring her strengths and weaknesses.

She imagined the Predictor her grandfather carried. It was thin-almost like a tablet in her current time frame-but it had a stand he used so he could keep his eyes on the changes his alterations made in the past. She thought about it alerting him to a significant change.

Perhaps he was working at his office desk, preparing another arrangement for the people who he used like marionettes in a play. He'd hear the notification, and his eyes would widen in surprise as he saw David's death skew the timeline outside his favor. Celeste didn't want to end the life of the man she loved, but she had to commit to his murder to send the message to her grandfather.

David's body began to relax beneath her. *Would her grandfather take Zam before David died? Would she know when they switched?*

Just as she released the pressure around David's wrist, Dr. Maze made a decision that stopped David's murder. But it wasn't Zam that he switched back.

Chapter 50

"Celeste."

Timberly's desperate voice pulled her into the present. "Celeste. Please get up. I need to tell you something."

Celeste opened her eyes, expecting blurry vision and tingling limbs, but her vision was clear, and her arms and legs felt fine. She sat up immediately and stared at her friend. "Why do I already feel acclimated?"

"You've—"

Timberly stopped speaking when the door opened, and Dr. Maze flew into the room. He tried to control his temper, but he could hardly contain his rage against his deliberate movements.

"I hope you're proud of yourself," her grandfather ranted.

"You're dismissed." He shooed Timberly away with a flick of his bony hand. She backed her way to the door, shooting worried glances at Celeste.

"He's alive," her grandfather continued, fixing her with his blazing emerald eyes. "You knew if you killed Zam that David would have remained in his body here."

"I'm aware," she responded defiantly.

"Did you think I'd let him live?"

Celeste had been so upset she hadn't thought further than getting her grandfather to switch Zam back into his own body. "You can't kill him."

It was an uncertain bluff, and her grandfather's smile was the only confirmation she needed to know she was wrong. She felt her heart drop as she realized the man she loved had less protection than she'd assumed.

Her grandfather glanced at the device he kept close to him. "The timeline has remained on track," he confirmed. "David's death wouldn't have upset the larger balance, but it would have thrown off a potential player in the grander scheme."

It was more than he'd shared with her since he'd recruited her for the missions. Years ago, he had won her over with promises of a less decimated planet and a brighter future. He'd even promised her that he'd send her to a time when she could meet her mother.

He noticed her eager attention. "Once again, Celeste, you've missed the forest for the trees. You're so oblivious and trusting that you make yourself easily controlled."

She narrowed her eyes. "You didn't control me when I chose to take Emma into the past."

His eyebrows shot up. "I didn't?"

A smile inched up his thin face. "If you'll remember, Caroline was pregnant when you entered her body the last time. Where is the baby now?"

Celeste looked down at her body. Not only was she the same shape she was when she left, but there weren't machines attached to her, feeding her as her body slept.

"Were you trying to kill me?"

Dr. Maze feigned surprise. "You think I was neglecting your nutrition?" He picked up a cord, twisting it in his hand. "Even after you left without secure attachments or IVs, I arranged for the care of your body. Caroline was given the best care until she delivered her son." He let go of the cord. "But I guess you knew about his delivery since you were the one who went trough the labor and delivery."

The confirmation concerned her. What if Emma had needed her while she had been in her body delivering Caroline's baby?

"Why didn't you let Caroline deliver her baby?"

"She was scared of the pain," he answered simply. "And people are so much easier to control when you take a Hedonistic approach."

"Maximize pleasure, reduce pain," Celeste said before another realization dawned on her. "Caroline was awake?"

Her grandfather straightened and pointed at her. "You got it. How could my plans have worked without her cooperation?"

Celeste suddenly felt sick. "She's been living in my body?"

He tutted. "Don't be so disgusted. *You* were living in *her* body."

He had a point. Celeste had been using Caroline's body for several months and she was her host for almost a year the first time. Her grandfather's explanation raised more questions, though.

"I thought you didn't want anyone from the past to be aware of this timeline?"

He flipped her question away like it was an annoying bug. "She's easily controlled. She won't be a problem anyway."

"Why?" Celeste asked, fearing the answer.

"Because she's you."

Chapter 51

"You want me to stay in Caroline's body?"

He shrugged his shoulders. "I haven't decided yet. You have become a rouge player in my plans."

"You're going to kill me?" She jumped off the bed, realizing her dexterity was due to Caroline's inhabitance in her body up until she popped into the current time frame. "But I'm your granddaughter."

"It means very little to me. What means more is that you're a soldier."

Celeste decided to work that angle on her grandfather. She was too nervous about her potential demise to be upset by his indifference to her.

"It would be hard to train another person with all the information I've gathered."

Her grandfather chuckled. It sounded dry and forced. "You think you can manipulate me to your will. I'd love to see you try." He held up the Predictor. "You helped me develop this. It tells me the course of history based on certain decisions." He stared at it with a snarl on his lips. "Humans think they have free will, but the truth is, they follow the same pattern. It's repeated in one way or another from one generation to the next." He flashed the screen at her, but all she could focus on were dark red and black lines and a flashing green light.

She was starting to get tired. She wondered if it was her or the body Caroline had inhabited. "Send me back now." She gave up and leaned back on the bed. "Just let David go and send me back."

Dr. Maze opened the door to the room. "I don't think I will."

Celeste jumped off the hospital bed and ran after her grandfather. The hall was empty of any other person, so she felt confident enough to call after him. He didn't turn around.

"I have to go back!" she yelled at him. "Emma's still there."

"You should have thought of that before you time-hopped out of here with her."

"But she needs me," Celeste pleaded. Tears sprang to her eyes when she thought about Emma waiting for her to come downstairs and eat breakfast with her. "I will not leave her there!"

"It's not your decision to make."

"She's my daughter!" Celeste reasoned.

His strides stopped, and his lip licked up in a smirk. "Not in the traditional sense."

"I carried her, I gave birth to her, and I'm raising her," Celeste countered. "She may not share my blood, but Emma is my daughter!"

A dry puff of wind escaped him, and he continued to speak with his own brand of haughty condescension. "Emma does share your blood. Well, your blood type," he clarified. "She also pulled one-fourth of her DNA from you."

His proclamation didn't surprise her. Celeste had guessed Emma had inherited her chin, but she also had Caroline's nose. She echoed her thoughts to her grandfather.

He turned around, facing her. She had finally asked a question that had gotten his full attention.

"Many things about the time jump are still a mystery, but the DNA results from David Winsome's time frame paired with the tests

I administered to Zam and Caroline confirmed Emma's parentage. David is her father and you and Caroline are her mothers."

Celeste had felt a connection to Emma that she knew was stronger than an outside bond. Part of her insisted she was Emma's mother, and her body cried out to the child she'd left in the past.

"How is it possible?" It was hard for Celeste to wrap her head around the specifics when human reproduction had been straightforward.

Her grandfather's shoulders peaked. "It may come down to simple science. When you're transferred, your consciousness goes with you, but your brain stays here. Zam reported that your tattoo showed up when you were Hailey Hall and that Caroline has a mole that appeared on your back when she assumed your body. It's possible that Caroline's eggs spliced and received some of your genetic material. I'm studying it, but I have many pressing engagements that require my attention right now."

"How did Zam know about Caroline's mole?"

Her grandfather smiled and dipped his head, glancing at his Predictor. "I'd tell you to ask him, but you may have burned that bridge when you tried to kill him." He turned on his heel and continued down the hall.

Celeste wanted to jump on his back and claw out his eyes. She wanted to bash his head against the wall and make him send her back. She wanted him to know the pain she felt.

But the best way to get Dr. Maze to do what she wanted was to make him think it was his idea. She swallowed every ounce of her pride and squared her shoulders.

"What will you have me do?" she asked. "If all I am to you is a soldier, what are my orders?"

He stopped walking, and his face softened. Now that he was getting his way, the lines on his face relaxed into a more agreeable expression. He was still unmovable in his declarations, but Celeste's circumstances would be more negotiable.

"Don't be melodramatic," he scolded. "You're still my granddaughter, and I prefer you in your body as opposed to that vile creature who has been running around in it these past months."

As she did with everyone else, Celeste stayed silent to see if she could garner more information. It did very little to satiate her curiosity.

"She spouts out so many crude colloquialisms." He glanced at Celeste who tried to make her face impassive. "Her language made some of the nurses blush. I was fortunate they knew she wasn't you."

Celeste risked a question. "How many people know about your time travel machine?"

"Machines," he corrected. "After all, if you were using one, how could Zam have visited you?"

Celeste hated the cruel smile that played on his lips. She pushed down the urge to use the battle training from her youth to pummel him into the brick walls that lined their way.

He went on, answering her question in his extended way. "The circle of believers is still small. I have only extended the range to include more support for myself, and each new member of the team has signed a contract."

"Did you make them sign with their own blood?" She couldn't resist a jab after he'd made it seem as though working with him was like joining a cult.

Her grandfather clucked at her retort. "Let's just say they know how important it is for them to cooperate."

Celeste scoffed. "Yeah, Zam mentioned blackmail."

"Zamuel needed extra encouragement."

Celeste rolled her eyes, but she didn't let him see her do it. "How long are you going to keep Zam in David's body?"

He glanced at his device. "Zamuel will stay until his mission is complete."

Celeste could hear the finality in his voice. Her grandfather's patience with her was waning again, and their conversation was nearing its end.

They walked in silence until they reached his office. In order to play the role of a compliant soldier, Celeste forced herself to remain at his door without speaking as he unlocked it. Before he stepped inside, he turned to her and placed a thin hand on her shoulder. It was his most endearing act.

"I will call for you when you are needed," he told her. "I think it's best for you to remain locked in a room at the facility, but after your mature response in the hall, I am willing to let you go home." He held up a finger next to her face. "Provided that you don't cause any more mischief."

"Yes, sir," Celeste responded, attempting to keep her face free of emotion.

Her heart leaped. All she had to do was wait until she knew her grandfather was at his home or attending a public event, and she could sneak in and rescue David. Her hopes were dashed when her grandfather spoke again.

"After Caroline moved into your body, I revoked your pass, so you'll have to call and make an appointment if you wish to see me. If you have trouble acclimating, schedule a session with Sioban or Reece."

He took his hand away, and it was her cue to walk away. However, she couldn't stop until she tried one more thing. "Did Harvey travel back with Caroline?"

"He did not."

Dr. Maze was a busy man, and he valued forthright conversations. With that in mind, Celeste made her proposal.

"I was still breastfeeding Emma. Could I take the infant with me and feed and care for him?"

Her grandfather stared at her as if he were trying to dissect her intentions. "It is a good idea. The child is unremarkable, except for his leap in the womb between time frames, so it may be best for him to remain with you. It will be less of a drain on the facility's resources."

Celeste's move had been a good one. She didn't chance the smallest smile, though.

"I will make the necessary calls," he said.

With that, he jerked open the heavy wooden door and stepped inside. The smell from the room met Celeste's nose and it reminded her of her youth. Lemon astringent and pine almost jogged a memory, but it was gone before her mind fully recognized it.

Her grandfather would monitor her moves until she left his building, so she didn't throw open doors or backtrack to the room in which she'd awakened. Her plan to get David would take more time, but it was worth it.

In the nursery, Harvey was handed to her without fanfare. She assumed it was commonplace for the nurses there, as they weren't privy to the body-swapping that happened in their workplace.

Harvey was one of two babies in the nursery. Even though there were a dozen bassinettes, the facility had never seen full capacity. Handling more than five infants over the space of a year was rare, so the same three nurses rotated shifts, with two during the day and one at night. When they weren't caring for babies, they were placed in other areas of the hospital, particularly in the portions that dealt with Slover's Disease and extended wound care.

Zara, the youngest of the nurses, handed Harvey to her. Her dark eyes sparkled from the joy of caring for him.

Celeste almost felt guilty for robbing her of the opportunity. Zara might never have a child. After the chemicals from the Great War spread around the world, the population had taken a significant hit, and their community was no different.

"Take good care of little Zam," Zara chirped.

Thankfully, she glided away, because it would have been nearly impossible for Celeste to mask her surprise. *Why had Zara called Harvey by her ex-boyfriend's name?*

Celeste looked down at the infant in her arms. It was clear that he'd have Caroline's button nose, but aside from inheriting Willie's olive skin tone, the baby's deep cupid's bow and dimpled chin appeared to be his own.

He was wrapped in a blanket with the facility's signature color: yellow. It represented the sun and the start of a new day.

Celeste opened the doors to the facility and was unsurprised to find that it was almost evening on a humid day. Seasons and time of day didn't match up when she time-hopped, so she'd grown accustomed to the switch from a cold winter to spring flowers. Her best guess was that she had popped back in time just before Independence Day.

After the Great War, Independence Day held a new meaning. No family had been spared the loss of a loved one during the last war. Even her grandfather responded to the celebrations with reverence, closing his facility to attend the parades and fundraisers for the few remaining veterans.

Celeste had been alive when the generations-long struggle had ended with a shaky treaty, but she could remember very little of it. All she understood at that time had been that she was lucky her father's leg had been maimed in a hunting accident, or he would have been sent to fight.

He'd died when she was young, but he had left behind his notebooks for her. Dr. Maze had taken them, placing them in his library, but Celeste would have them one day. He never revealed his age, but her grandfather couldn't live forever.

She took the baby down the main street of Erwin. The travel agency had just closed, and they'd turned on the sign that flashed vacations with animated attractions and classic characters and tours of honored battle sites.

The building across the street caught her eye. She glanced down at her wrist and the ink on her arm swirled in a pattern of flowers around Emma's name. She had gotten it from Magic Man's Tattoo Parlor, and the artist had been the owner, Movey Shelton.

She'd been curious about the transfer of the tattoo between two time frames. Caroline's tattoo had remained when Celeste had entered her body, so Celeste rationalized that it was something Movey had used when he inked the tattoo onto her skin.

She didn't give it a lot of thought before she stepped into the door of Movey's shop. Harvey —as she refused to call him Zam— let out a cry, and she thought better of entering the parlor. It was a decent environment, as Movey didn't allow fighting or vulgarity. There was some foul language, though, as patrons experienced the first pricks of a tattoo needle or cried out from repeated piercings. She decided she'd visit the business at another time.

Just as she'd abandoned her hope of asking her tattoo artist about her relocating tattoo, she bumped into him. Movey was returning from his dinner break, a Zigi's pizza box in his hand.

He was only a year older than Celeste, and the town considered him a young business owner. He wore jeans and a tee shirt that mirrored the band who sang the song for which he'd named his tattoo parlor.

He was a brilliant artist, and his swollen fingers and the rainbow of stains on his hands reflected his passion. He had a dark smudge under his chiseled nose, and she resisted the maternal urge to wipe it away. His long dark hair fell freely down his back, and it was clear he kept it meticulously brushed and parted down the middle. His attention to detail didn't stop with his hair, as his snowy eyeshadow matched his shirt, and his dark eyebrows were lined into easy arches over his violet eyes.

Movey's eyes were blue, but he had insisted on changing their color when he was in school with Celeste. They had been dating at the time, and she might have stayed with him if her grandfather hadn't pushed her into a relationship with Zam.

Celeste and Movey had shared a passionate relationship. He was an artist, and everything they had done had a unique rhythm. In his arms, she had felt like a muse, and he had painted all her colors. They had shared all their secrets, and when they hadn't been together, they had carried vials of their blood attached to necklaces.

Even after almost a decade had passed, residual feelings remained on both sides, so the pair stood awkwardly on the sidewalk. Movey was the first to speak.

"Were you going to get another tattoo?" He touched the top of the baby's head. "Maybe you'll want one with this little guy's name."

Celeste shook her head. "I actually want to talk to you about this tattoo." She held up the wrist with Emma's name.

"Don't tell me you want a refund," he joked.

Celeste smiled politely and asked, "Do you have a place where we can talk? Maybe like a back room?"

Movey smiled good-naturedly, revealing a set of gleaming white teeth. "After all these years?" He waggled his eyebrows. "I thought you were married?"

Celeste was used to his jokes, so she laughed lightly and followed him into the parlor. No one glanced up until she followed Movey to a door at the back of the room. Two of the tattoo artists looked up at each other as if they were silently communicating between themselves.

The back room was clean and monochromatic. Movey noticed her surprise.

"I add the color in my work." He pointed to an easel in front of the window. An accordion of paints sat next to it.

"You know I love your work," she started.

Movey offered her a padded chair and sat on the edge of his desk. His perfume held citrus notes, and it seemed to linger on everything in the room.

"But there's something strange about the tattoo."

His already-arched eyebrow flew up.

Celeste had shared some of the details of her mission with him when she'd commissioned him to design the tattoo with Emma's name. He'd been surprised, but he'd listened to her with an open mind. At the end of their session, he'd hugged her, earning him a scowl from Zam who had been waiting on the other side of the spacious tattoo parlor.

"When I traveled to the past, the tattoo traveled with me."

His eyes widened, and he popped off the desk. "You're kidding me!" He picked her up off the ground, but remembering the baby in her arms, sat her down gently. "That's incredible!"

He paced to his easel and shook it in his excitement. "Do you know what this means?"

Celeste softened her voice to deliver the blow. "It's truly fantastic, but we're the only ones who can know about it. I didn't even tell my grandfather."

He deflated immediately, his posture dipping until he slumped onto the round swivel seat in front of his easel. "That's my luck." He looked up at her, resigning himself to a smile. "I guess fame and fortune will have to wait."

"Why do you think it happened?"

He shrugged, standing up and settling in the same position in front of her. "I don't know. I'm not the scientist."

Celeste rolled her eyes. "I studied engineering, not biology or physics."

"Sure," he agreed. "And now you live the glamorous life you always wanted."

"Hey," she whispered, standing up and cupping his cheek with her palm. "I wanted to do something I loved, just like you."

He turned from her and sniffed. "I would have given up art for you."

She smiled at his toddler-like profession of love. "No, you wouldn't have." She searched for his eyes. "And I wouldn't have made you."

Movey locked his hands around her waist and looked into her eyes. If the baby hadn't been between them, Celeste may have rekindled the spark of her old flame.

The moment passed, and he dropped his hands. "Promise not to get mad."

Celeste inwardly groaned. "I'll make no promises."

"Then I can't tell you." His playful humor had returned.

"Fine," Celeste consented. "What is it?"

"Do you remember those vials of our blood we had when we were kids?"

Celeste rocked Harvey, who was beginning to wake from a nap. It would be time to feed him soon, and she wanted to be home when she did it in case he had a hard time adjusting to her.

"Please hurry and tell me," Celeste said. "I think the baby will need to eat soon."

He put his index fingers to his mouth. "I may have used our blood in the ink."

"What?" Celeste cried, succeeding in fully waking Harvey. "That blood must have been seven or eight years old. Why did you keep it?"

He shrugged one shoulder. "I held out some hope that..." He paused, letting Celeste fill in the rest.

"Oh, Movey," she said. She didn't touch him again, but she wanted to hug him. "Hasn't there been anyone special in your life?"

He tossed his head. "I can find anyone I want for the night, but the one I want for the rest of my life was taken from me."

How poetic. She'd expect nothing less from her locally famous artist friend.

He looked down at his feet, kicking the tile with the tip of his sneakers. "I shouldn't be talking to you like this. You've made your choice."

She debated on telling him that she had broken up with Zam, but it wouldn't matter. She'd only have to follow it up with the admission that she'd fallen in love with a man from another time.

"Thank you for telling me about the blood."

"I have some more if you want another tattoo," he responded with a sly grin. He must have seen the alarm in her eyes, as he followed it by saying, "I'm just kidding."

She didn't believe him.

CHAPTER 52

She was living in a world with few resources, and it was hard to divide them among the two billion people on the planet. The people in her community received credits to buy items that weren't a necessity, and she was uncertain how many of those allowances had been used by Caroline while she was in Celeste's body.

Caroline seemed to be an impulsive person, so Celeste doubted she'd have credits until the current cycle ended. She passed several places, including Zigi's, where she wished she could pick up some ready-made food, but she walked past them. She could only hope Zam had stocked some of her favorite foods at home.

She stood in front of the two-story duplex for a moment before she walked to the door. The mint green vinyl stood out from the other brick homes on the block, but she valued the originality. She wished her father would have been waiting for her inside, but he had been dead for over a decade.

Her fingerprint was accepted, and the apartment door opened. "WELCOME, CELESTE AND LITTLE ZAM. YOU NEED JUICE," an automated voice boomed. She always needed juice.

She gasped when she saw the disarray. Zam was a good housekeeper, so she didn't understand how he'd allowed the apartment to get so messy. It was possible that he'd moved out, though, electing not to share his living space with a stranger.

She discarded that idea when she picked up a pair of his briefs from beside the couch. It was hard for her to stand the smell in the apartment, and she vowed to clean it after she fed Harvey.

The baby took to her nipple immediately. Physically, nothing had changed, and the way she held him must not have been much different than the way his mother did.

After Harvey fell asleep, Celeste started cleaning. As she shifted through the mess of wrappers, dirty clothes, and soiled diapers, she could almost recognize her apartment. She found her sapphire dress on the bathroom floor next to a full bathtub of gray water. She wished Caroline hadn't worn her best clothes or she had taken better care of them.

She worked on disinfecting the bathroom well into the night. Harvey woke several times, but after a diaper change and some milk, he was ready to fall asleep. She had to make a space for him on the floor while she tidied Emma's room. It didn't seem like it had been dusted or mopped since her departure, but the worst part was that Caroline and Zam had left dirty clothes on the floor, and used diapers had been tucked into the sides of the crib.

By the time Celeste was ready to faint from exhaustion, the apartment looked better, and the bathroom and Harvey's room were completely clean. She fell onto the couch and slept soundly until Harvey woke for a feeding.

She remembered how often Emma had awakened when she was a newborn. Despite her exhaustion and the tears stinging her eyes, she stayed awake for over an hour thinking about Emma. *Had she sensed a change when Caroline took back her body?*

Suddenly, a panicky feeling hit her, and she had to wait a moment before she realized its source. *If Caroline and Zam had been indifferent to Harvey's care, as the state of the apartment suggested, how will they treat Emma?*

Her anxious mind ran through several scenarios where Emma was left alone to play outside, or sharp objects hung off countertops. However, there was a difference between Harvey's and Emma's situations. In the current time frame, Harvey wasn't valued as much by Dr. Maze. As long as he was given reasonable care, Caroline could get by with attending to her baby when she wished. In the past, though, Emma had Mrs. Winsome and Ag. Mrs. Winsome's mental health was fading, but she wouldn't allow her son and his girlfriend to neglect their child. Ag would be just as vigilant, and Celeste hoped Emma's bed would be placed in her room. There were a few hazards on the floor, but Ag seemed to be more attentive than Caroline.

She drifted back to sleep as she thought of Emma's smiling face when she hugged her and the way her blonde curls bobbed when she ran to encircle her arms around her mother's neck. Biologically, Caroline and Celeste were Emma's mothers, and Celeste could only hope that Caroline would treat her sweet girl with the love she deserved.

A loud banging at her door woke the baby and her. Celeste stumbled to answer it, with Harvey's hungry mouth searching her shirt for food. A tall man with paper-thin skin regarded her before he spoke. "I see you have the same sleep habits as the other woman."

Celeste was shocked at his knowledge of the situation until she realized that he was her grandfather's trusted butler, Fanto. Over the years, he'd opted for a few body modifications, and the change in his eyes had thrown her off. She tried to stand straighter, but he only looked at her with disdain.

"Little Zam is late for his monitoring session at your grandfather's facility."

Celeste's eyebrows rose. "I wasn't told about a monitoring session."

He shook his head and smiled down at her as if he were speaking to a small child. She had known him since she could remember, and she despised his condescension.

"You should remember from your first child that the doctor likes to see his children on a regular basis."

Celeste resisted the urge to scream. Her grandfather had only sired one child, but he insisted on calling the offspring he doctored his "children". The parents who brought their children to Dr. Maze stared at him with an expression akin to hero worship, so she doubted they felt the same bubble of bile rise in their throats when they heard their progeny referenced in that manner.

"In addition," Fanto went on, "you are to dine with your grandfather this evening." He had stared at a space above her head as he recited the invitation, but he looked down and met her eyes when he added, "And do not bring the infant."

Celeste wasn't surprised by the order. Her grandfather would wish to maintain appearances by having her visit him at his home. He had been fascinated by Emma, so Celeste and Zam had been encouraged to bring her with them when they received the regular dinner and holiday invitations, but Dr. Maze had considered Harvey unremarkable, and he wasn't related to him, so he was left out.

Celeste closed the door on Fanto. It was an act that brought her more happiness than she'd admit.

After feeding Harvey, she bathed and clothed him. He was asleep before she snapped the last button on his romper, his legs falling limply. She placed him in Emma's crib and hurried to her room.

After her intense cleaning session, Celeste was ready to soak in a hot bath, but she settled for a shower since she had to crunch time. She towel-dried her hair, wishing not to wake Harvey with the noise, and tip-toed into the bedroom to find clothes.

Many of her tailored outfits had been lying on the floor, so she was limited on choices that were comfortable and suitable to wear to her grandfather's facility. She opened her underwear drawer, and she was shocked to see her lace thongs and pretty bras were missing. She didn't understand how Caroline could have worn them while she was nursing, but she assumed it was because the woman hadn't had a lot of experience with lingerie. She selected cotton undergarments and opened her closet. A few teal suits and two dresses hung on her side, while Zam's portion of the closet was stocked with his formal and informal clothes.

The members of her community wore clothes that signified their station. They were cut in the form of the "scrubs" hospital workers had worn in the past. Even though Celeste was an engineer, she was considered an employee of her grandfather's medical facility, so she wore teal suits.

Artistic community members, children, and university students could wear the clothes of their choice, but it was considered a status symbol to wear a suit of a particular color. Teal and purple were regarded as the most respectable colors.

Celeste threw on a suit and cast a weary look over her bedroom. She didn't know if it was going to be a long day, so she decided to strip the bed and put on clean sheets. She'd want to fall into it right away if the day was taxing, and she wouldn't want to take the time to remove Caroline's impression on the pillows or sheets.

As soon as she pulled off the comforter, piles of lingerie spilled out. She tried to remind herself that the clothes had been next to her skin, but it was hard to shake the nasty feeling that erupted when she confirmed that Caroline had worn her most intimate pieces.

When she pulled back the sheet, her stomach dropped. Two pairs of Zam's briefs lay on top of the fitted sheet.

When she'd found some of his clothes next to the couch, she'd assumed that he had slept there, giving Caroline the bed. It seemed they had shared the bed in more than one way.

Celeste needed to sit down, but she didn't want to touch the bed. It was tainted in a way she couldn't explain. She and Zam had shared their love in the same bed many times, but...

She could hardly process it. Her mind whirled around the deceit as she tried to put it in order. Zam knew Caroline was in Celeste's body, and he wooed her into bed with him. Then, after he took possession of David's body, he tricked Celeste into having sex with him.

She determined that she would pack up his belongings and send them to his mother. Through tears she didn't feel like she deserved to cry, she started grabbing his personal items and throwing them into a duffle bag she found on his side of the closet.

She skipped the dirty underwear. She planned to burn it along with the lingerie Caroline had worn and the bedsheets. She might throw the mattress on a bonfire, too.

As she tossed the books on his bedside table into the bag, her eyes landed on a framed picture. She picked it up with tingling fingers and held it without really seeing it.

The picture showed Zam and her in a field of spring flowers. He was pointing at the sky like he was describing a bird that had flown past. She was looking at him with love and adoration, a bouquet of tiger lilies in her hand. Her grandfather and some people she didn't recognize flanked them, holding champagne glasses.

The picture had been taken of the two of them, but Celeste hadn't worn the indulgent smile or the white A-line dress that stretched to the ground. She had cared for Zam, but she had never held his hand with such affection.

Celeste dropped the picture, and it landed on the mattress without a sound. She shook her head and backed away until she bumped against a wall and slid to the floor.

Zam and Caroline had taken vows. That meant Zam and Celeste were married.

CHAPTER 53

Celeste's vision cleared when Harvey cried. She retrieved him from the crib and held him as he fed.

She'd ended her relationship with Zam, but not before he had taken vows with another woman. Well, maybe he had united himself with Celeste, but she hadn't spoken the words that had sealed their union.

Drawing on what she knew about Zam and the experience she'd had with him when she'd figured out he'd inhabited David's body, Zam hadn't been in love with Caroline. Celeste was sure he had manipulated the situation to tie Celeste to him upon her return to her body.

Zam was smart, but he wasn't quite diabolical enough to have figured out that plan on his own. She knew exactly who had led him down the path that he had taken, and she was going to confront him about it as soon as she saw him.

Dr. Maze had used her for years, but it was finally time for her to fight back with everything she had.

Dr. Maze had loved someone so much that he still carried around a picture of her in a locket around his neck. Some may have glimpsed the simple silver chain, but only Celeste's father had known about the contents. He told her the story of her grandmother with somber tones and soft words.

Dr. Alexander Maze had studied medicine and physics, graduating with the highest marks in his class. Before he started practicing, a government official had pulled him away to work on a war project. There, he met a spirited undergraduate student who had won his heart.

Even in his youth, Dr. Maze was stiff and stoic, and the woman he admired ignored him. Then, however, after a spirited debate on the project, he surprised her by kissing her.

Her father had always ended the story by saying, "And the rest is history."

When she was young, Celeste admired the youthful picture of her grandmother that hung in the grand hall of her grandfather's massive house. To her, it had been a mansion, but the contemporary brick home was just over three-thousand square feet of livable space.

Fanto opened the door, and she stepped into the airy foyer. She had worn her royal blue silk dress that stopped just above her knees. Choosing to walk to the facility to drop off Harvey and then to her grandfather's house, she had selected flat sandals that fastened around her ankles. Fanto asked her to remove them before he guided her down the hall.

Her grandmother's picture no longer hung in the hallway. It had been taken down after her father's illness had claimed his life. Celeste assumed her grandfather didn't want such a large reminder of death staring at him every day as he left for work. Instead, an old picture of him hung in its place. Even though the portrait had been painted years beforehand, her grandfather still looked the same as he did in the picture. After the war ended, modern aesthetic surgeries improved every day.

"Your grandfather is already seated," Fanto relayed.

Celeste was ten minutes early, but she hadn't expected her grandfather to wait on her. He ran on one time: his own.

He rose when she walked into the room, an old-fashioned courtesy many men of his generation extended to women. Celeste appreciated the gesture and took her place to his right. Fanto offered to take her clutch, but she waved him away, placing it in the seat beside her.

He sat down at the head of the long, polished dining table. When he had dinner parties, as many as twenty guests sat around it comfortably.

Dr. Maze lifted a silver spoon to his lips and sipped a green soup. Pea soup was his favorite, and Celeste sipped hers gratefully when Fanto delivered it.

"Did you leave the baby at the facility?" her grandfather asked.

"Yes," she replied.

"You can leave him there overnight." He dropped his spoon into the bowl and sat back in his seat, indicating he was ready for the next course. "Caroline often did."

His statement wasn't much of a revelation to Celeste. Caroline hadn't seemed maternal.

"If it's just the same, I will take him home with me."

Dr. Maze's silver eyebrows shot up as the next course was served. "It's acceptable. It helps keep down costs at the facility, and it allows the boy to be raised by a member of my inner circle who realizes his purpose."

Celeste chanced a snarky remark. "Yes, I know I'm raising a lamb for you to slaughter."

He put both of his hands on the table palms down. "You knew what you were getting into when you agreed to be part of my project."

"No, I didn't!" Celeste shouted, jumping out of her seat.

Fanto came into the room, but her grandfather waved him away. The butler stood just inside the door, ready to throw Celeste out if her temper became unmanageable.

"You act like I signed some sort of contract, but I never agreed to do your bidding across time until it ruined every life I touched. I didn't like deceiving David into believing I was Caroline, and it wasn't fun to get him reconnected with his daughter."

He smiled at her, picking up his napkin and tossing it onto his uneaten salad. "You knew we were going to alter history, and you didn't seem to have a conscience when you told Zam that Emma was his child." He rose to his feet, and at his height, he looked down at

Celeste as they argued. "Your temper is unjustified. You wanted David to meet his daughter, and you accomplished it."

Celeste shook her head. "But now he's a prisoner inside Zam's body."

"He makes good leverage," Dr. Maze said, smiling deviously. "You won't leave this time frame without him."

Her grandfather was right. She wouldn't slip back into the past until she knew David was safe.

"What's your plan?" Celeste spat at him. "Do you want Caroline and Zam to have more children for your army?"

As soon as the words were out of her mouth, her stomach flipped. She hadn't really thought about it, but she might have a point. It was hard for women to get pregnant in her time, so maybe her grandfather had tried it.

Dr. Maze stroked his smooth chin. "I had considered it." He paused for a dramatic effect while Celeste mentally checked her body for signs of pregnancy. "But Zam's on birth control."

Celeste breathed an audible sigh of relief.

"I guess you know about their happy union," he said.

It wasn't a question. He had deliberately sent her to their love nest.

She crossed her arms. "What does this mean for me?"

Her grandfather smiled. He sensed that she was becoming more submissive when the opposite was true.

"It means that you have choices before you."

Celeste waited for him to speak again. He took his seat and indicated that she should do the same. She plopped into her chair with her arms crossed.

"I can bring Zam back, and you can live with him, raising Caroline's baby alongside any other progeny."

"That's out of the question," Celeste asserted. "He crossed a line."

Actually, Celeste had crossed a line when she'd tried to smother him to death. She thought Zam would forgive her, though, and the idea made her dislike him even more.

"You can go back into the past and live with Zam inside David Winsome's body, raising Emma and awaiting the Great War."

That option was more appealing, but only because she missed Emma so terribly. Her grandfather would still buzz her back at his will, so she'd never be free of him. Worst of all, David would be inside Zam's body, living only through medicated slumber.

"An option without David is not an option," she decided.

"I can release David and Caroline, and bring Zam back to the present."

"What are you trying to do?" she yelled at him. Fanto cracked his knuckles, but Celeste continued in the same tone. "Do you seriously think I'm going to abandon David or Emma?"

"You can't have them both," he said simply.

"Let me travel back in time and get Emma," Celeste pleaded. "I'll take Harvey with me and reunite him with his mother, and I'll bring Emma back."

"That might work," her grandfather admitted, "but we both know you won't stay away from David Winsome. Just like the last time you left, you'll convince yourself that Emma needs to know her father, and you'll find a way to jump through time."

It was true. There was a pull that had dragged her back through the years to be with David and she was powerless against it.

She didn't want to cry, but tears made a course down her cheeks, forming dark patterns as they landed on her silk dress. She put her arms on the table and buried her face in them, sobbing.

Fanto and her grandfather held back from comforting her. After a few minutes, Celeste sought to regain some dignity, and she excused herself to rinse her face in the bathroom.

She stayed within the silent walls for some time, smelling the floral scents and rubbing her bare feet against the fluffy pink rug. She fished out some makeup from her clutch and relined her eyes with ebony eyeliner. Finally, she decided to rejoin her grandfather, still uncertain about the choice he wanted her to make.

She paused outside the door to her grandfather's study. He didn't lock the doors in his home as he did at his facility, so she pushed it open and walked inside.

Ornate bookcases lined the walls with stacks of books she'd read and many she couldn't understand. His Brobdingnagian cherry desk sat in the center of the room, offering little space on either side to get around it.

Celeste slipped to the side, placing herself between a bookcase and the desk. She stood on her toes and made herself as small as possible, but her butt brushed the bookshelf, and a copy of The Universe and Expansion pounded the floor.

She stood still for almost a minute, imagining footsteps running down the hall. When she realized she hadn't been caught, she stepped over the book and moved behind her grandfather's desk.

Like everything he owned, it was painfully neat. Pens and pencils were lined up in order of length, and a planner lay across the top. However meticulous he was with his items, Dr. Maze's handwriting was atrocious, and Celeste couldn't make out the words scribbled on the lines.

She tried a drawer, and it opened easily. It contained office supplies, like notepads and staples. She moved them around, but nothing was buried.

What was she looking for anyway?

Her grandfather had mentioned that David was leverage against her, so Celeste wanted to find anything to make him release David. Part of her doubted he'd hide anything noteworthy in his home; he'd keep it at the facility, where he spent most of his time.

She yanked another drawer a little too hard, and it pulled open to the end, exposing all the contents at once. If she had only tugged on it, the drawer would have appeared to have extra pens and pencils, still wrapped in their packaging. At the back of the drawer, however, lay a handgun.

Celeste didn't know a lot about the different types of guns, but she knew how to shoot them. She picked it up and weighed it in her hand. She could determine the distance she'd need to hit a target just by that simple act. She replaced the gun and closed the drawer.

It wasn't a surprise that her grandfather had a gun. Many people had hoarded collections of them before the government seized firearms. Celeste's father had collected an array of guns. He had taught her to shoot them, but Celeste hadn't concentrated on the names of the pieces she had fired.

She leaned back in her grandfather's chair, and it issued a small squeak. She swiveled in the direction she'd entered, intending to pick up the fallen book and abandon her efforts, but her eyes fell upon a picture on the shelf.

The five-by-seven photograph was framed in what Celeste assumed was a pure gold frame. The glass over it was thick, and it reflected the light in the room. Celeste plucked it off the shelf and brought it to her eyes, studying it.

It didn't take her long to realize she had already seen it. The photograph was old, and it hadn't been taken in her current century. It was a black-and-white picture of a group of people around a table with their heads bent over books.

She looked at it from different angles, wondering if it was a replica of an iconic moment, but it wasn't a famous photograph. It was a meaningful one.

And it was the same picture that sat on Mrs. Winsome's bedside table.

CHAPTER 54

The air held some humidity, but a cool breeze brushed over her intermittently as she walked down Main Street. She passed Movey's shop and pondered walking inside. A lonely patron sat waiting on his appointment with his hands clasped together and feet bouncing. She didn't want to visit her old boyfriend two days in a row, as he seemed to carry stronger feelings for her than she'd realized. He might misread her confidences as an attempt to get closer to him, and she couldn't afford to confuse her situation more.

Her grandfather had told her that she could leave the baby at the facility overnight, but she'd asked to take him home with her. Her grandfather had made the necessary calls, and the door of the building was opened for her by a night watchman when she arrived.

The night nurse handed over a tightly swaddled Harvey, and he sucked merrily on a pacifier.

"He had some stored breastmilk about an hour ago," she told Celeste. "He may sleep another hour or two."

Celeste wandered down the halls. Her access was restricted, but she couldn't help stopping in front of the manilla door that led to where the man she loved slept. She stared at it, willing it to open, and she was shocked when it did.

The door let out a low buzz as Timberly rushed out. She had two files in her hand, and she almost bumped into Celeste before she realized she was there. When she noticed her friend, Timberly's almond eyes grew so large that Celeste wondered if they'd pop.

"You can't be here," she whispered.

Celeste nodded to the baby in her arms. "I was picking up Harvey, and I thought I would—"

Timberly was shaking her dark hair. Her curls bobbed against her chocolate skin.

"You were thinking about pulling Zam out of David's body."

Timberly had known her for years, and she understood her motives. Celeste hadn't confided her love for David to her friend, but it had been clear when she had awakened from a time jump with his name on her lips.

"I just want to see him." At its core, her statement was true. She just wasn't certain what she would do afterward.

"You can send him back, you know," Timberly said, flipping the files under her arm. "Dr. Maze told us about your choices, and I think you're being selfish."

"What?" Celeste was surprised. Timberly was usually agreeable and supportive.

Celeste assumed her aggressiveness was a product of the late hour. Timberly had a young daughter, and she was probably attempting to return to her before bedtime.

Timberly dipped her head into her hand, rubbing one of her temples with her thumb. Timberly had frequent headaches, and Celeste didn't want to be the cause of one.

"Look," Timberly started. "You can go back to your baby, or you can stay here with Zam and raise that one." She pointed to Harvey.

"It's simple, really," she shrugged. "Just make the decision that's best for everyone."

Celeste thought about it. Any of the choices her grandfather had proposed landed her in an undesirable situation. She'd be stuck with

Zam in David's body, or she'd be married to him in her current time frame, raising a baby who didn't belong to her. Allowing Zam and Caroline to raise Emma wasn't an option, and David would hate her for imprisoning him in the future.

"I have to let go of both of them," Celeste concluded. "I have to let David go back and raise Emma."

Timberly closed her eyes. When she opened them, she put her hand on Celeste's arm. Her sympathetic friend had returned, motivated by Celeste's reasonable decision.

They hugged with the baby between them, and Celeste cried. She thought about Emma's arms reaching for her when she'd come back from class, and the way her daughter would call for her whenever she woke, finding Celeste wasn't on the couch with her. She considered her relationship with David and recalled their pillow talks and whispered promises.

"At least you have this little guy," Timberly declared, caressing the downy peach fuzz on the baby's head.

Celeste nodded, unwilling to admit that he was a poor substitute for the child she'd lost. There was a little girl who would forever be waiting for her mother to come down and eat breakfast with her.

Timberly urged her down the hall, and Celeste turned her back on the door that led to the man she loved. Just before they moved into the next hallway, Celeste grabbed Timberly's arm, causing the folders to slip onto the floor.

"Please let me see him!" she begged.

Timberly looked down both ends of the hall, scared that they had been heard. She turned fearful brown eyes on Celeste.

"I can't," she hissed. "You don't know what you're asking me to do."

"I'll be in and out," Celeste promised. "I just want to tell him I love him and pass along a message for Emma."

Celeste thought she had lost her. Refusal was stamped across her features.

"Wouldn't you want your daughter to know you existed?" Celeste tried. "Once Dr. Maze switches him back, David won't know I ever truly existed, and Caroline will be..." She trailed off, uncertain about the way to describe the woman she had lived inside for months.

Timberly held up her hand. "I've met the girl. She's... not like you."

"Emma knows that I'm not there anymore," Celeste said miserably. "I'm sure she can see the difference between Caroline and me, but how long will it be before she forgets?"

Timberly took a deep breath. "There's no guarantee that David will tell her what you say or even remember it. You know how disoriented you are when you wake up."

"I have to try," Celeste said, hoping her pleas were enough to shift Timberly.

"I'll give you five minutes," Timberly told her. "And you have to adjust the security camera, so the night watchman won't see us."

The women hurried down an adjacent hallway. Celeste adjusted the equipment to replay the same five minutes of footage for twenty minutes and rushed back down the hall to the wing her grandfather reserved for his time travel project.

Timberly led her straight to David's room, and when she opened the door, Celeste was surprised to see four beds with time-hopping equipment beside them. She resisted the urge to ask about it and focused her attention on the man in front of her.

Zam's body was tied to a hospital bed with his eyes closed and his jaw slack. She waited for Timberly to attend to the machine that held David in a medicated sleep.

"Five minutes," Timberly reminded her. She turned off the sedative and added the drug that "popped" time travelers into consciousness.

It was hard for Celeste to look at Zam's body and imagine David inside it. Zam's short limbs were the only similarity between Zam and the man Celeste loved. They both had dark hair, but David's had a healthy sheen, and Zam's was mousy. Zam's face was unmarked by blemishes or hair, but David had a rash of acne scars across his jawline and he grew stubble an hour after shaving. David had stubby fingers, while Zam's fingers were long and thin.

Celeste put her fingers around Zam's hand. David moaned as he started to wake, and his eyes popped open.

He tried to sit up, but his restraints kept him in place. He said some nonsensical sounds before he yelled, "I can't see."

"I'm here, David," Celeste told him, pressing and releasing his hand. The pressure could distract him enough for the eyedrops to work.

"Caroline?" he asked, searching for her with sightless eyes.

Celeste and Timberly exchanged a look and Timberly shrugged. Timberly placed the solution in his eyes, and his vision cleared.

"What's going on?" he asked, looking from Celeste to Timberly.

He was a trained health professional, so he understood he was in a medical facility. Celeste could have spent days helping him acclimate to his surroundings, but she was going to chance his mental health to let him see the truth.

She balanced Harvey in her lap. His sleep was undisturbed as he sucked his pacifier.

"David, I need to tell you some things very quickly," she began. "Will you look at me?"

He stared at her and blinked. Golden flecks reflected in Zam's blue-green eyes. "Who are you?"

"I'm Celeste." She found herself smiling after she spoke her name and almost in tears over finally showing David her true form.

She continued. "I'm from a time in the future after the Great War. I traveled back in time to change the future of Caroline Fletcher, but I fell in love with you. I got pregnant with Emma in your time, but when I was pulled into this time frame, I carried her with me. When I realized that she was yours, I hopped back into time and tried to unite you with our daughter. In between those jumps, I was Hailey Hall. We went ice skating and attended art classes together, and you were jealous when you thought I'd slept with Lewis Novack."

David moved his hand until she was forced to let go. "What is this place? Get away from me!"

Celeste glanced at Timberly. There was a small hand mirror by each machine. It was placed there because looking at herself in the mirror after her first time hop had allowed Celeste to better acclimate. Timberly shook her head as she handed the mirror to Celeste.

Celeste held the mirror in front of David so he could see his reflection. David narrowed his eyes as if trying to get a clearer view and then glared at the women.

"You aren't going to fool me with a trick mirror."

Celeste was running out of time. "Look at your hands!" she told him, directing his attention to them. She rubbed his face with her hand. "You haven't been shaved for hours, but your skin is smooth."

He jerked his head away from her hand, but he looked at his hands. He stretched the fingers and bent them.

"This can't be happening," he whispered.

"He freaking out," Timberly warned.

Celeste jumped into his field of vision. She held the baby close to her so his head wouldn't loll.

"David, I love you," she told him. "Remember my face and tell our daughter about me. Let her know that she has my chin." She pointed to the dimple and pressed.

His eyes were starting to lose focus. He was chanting the same sentence repeatedly. "This is not happening."

"He's getting loud," Timberly cautioned.

Celeste's head was spinning. She didn't have the time she needed to properly convey the situation to David, and she was going to lose Emma and him forever. At that moment, she found a new choice, one her grandfather had never wanted to provide as an option.

She reached into her clutch and pulled out the gun she had taken from her grandfather's study. It wasn't loaded, as she couldn't think of a reason to kill another person.

Timberly's hands went up automatically. "What's wrong with you, Celeste?"

She glanced at David. "Give him the sedative."

Timberly shrugged and pushed a button. Within seconds, David's eyes fluttered, and he relaxed against the bed.

"You didn't have to threaten me for that," she murmured.

"Yeah, but I'm not finished." Celeste leveled the gun at her friend and severed the tie to one of her last allies in her time frame.

Timberly showed Celeste the date and time on the machine. Celeste held Harvey in her arms as Timberly affixed the equipment to her.

"The baby won't transfer," she predicted.

"Emma did," Celeste commented. "And I think you know that."

"I hope you're right," Timberly said. "You know what will happen to that little baby if your grandfather can't use him."

"Put him back in the nursery, and don't tell anyone about it," Celeste suggested. "The baby is blameless."

Timberly didn't make any promises.

Celeste watched her switch Zam, bringing him back to their time frame. As soon as he woke, he looked over at her in surprise. David's brief period of wakefulness had physically awakened Zam's body, so he wasn't as disoriented and blind.

She didn't want to hate him, but she could no longer look at her ex-boyfriend without feeling a sense of loathing. He had taken advantage of her vulnerability even though he had taken vows with Caroline. She didn't want to think of him enjoying her body when Caroline reentered it, but switching bodies with Caroline was the only solution she could see that would give her access to both David and Emma.

He looked at her, and his eyes grew wide. His eyes, Celeste noted, did not have golden flecks. He tried to get off the table to prevent her from going on another one of her own missions, but he was still strapped to the bed.

Celeste smiled at him haughtily, and Timberly pushed the button that sent her back into Caroline Fletcher's body.

Chapter 55

Dr. Maze stared at his granddaughter's sleeping form. "Did she try to take the baby with her?"

Timberly answered quickly. "Yes, but I pulled him from her arms before the switch was complete." A quick review of the tape confirmed Timberly's assertion.

"Emma was a significant loss," he related to Timberly and Zam. "I'm going to uncover another way to get her back."

"I was holding her," Zam told him. "Caroline and I kept her with us the whole time."

"There's no reason she shouldn't have transferred with you," Dr. Maze seethed. It was clear from his subdued tone that he was angry. "Are you sure you didn't give her to your great-grandmother so you could enjoy your new wife?"

Caroline had started to wake, and she'd heard the question. "Ag was busy with her mother," she relayed. "That old lady has some real problems." She fingered one of the leads before Timberly detached it and glared at Zam. "Besides, I have no plans to be with that man for a while after I caught him with his pants off when you switched me back."

Zam's head jerked in her direction. "I told you she tricked me."

"You were naked, and she was on top of you," Caroline shot back.

"She was smothering me!"

Caroline crossed her arms and purposely addressed Dr. Maze. "If you want to send me back, I'll sleep with David, and you can have another kid for your army."

"Nice, Caroline," Zam muttered. "Really mature."

"Leave," Dr. Maze said to Caroline. He was tired of the bickering, and she was the main cause of it. He'd let Zamuel suffer for his mistakes, but only after he'd spoken with him.

As she stood, Caroline opened her palm, revealing a gift Celeste had left for her grandfather. It appeared that she had taken more from his study than the handgun.

Caroline dutifully handed over the picture to the doctor. He glanced at the writing on the back: *I know.*

He maintained his stoic posture, placing his keepsake in his pocket. Caroline knew him well enough to silently leave the room without inquiring about the photograph. She left the baby with Timberly without a backward glance.

"I think it's time to move to the next phase of our plan," he announced.

"I'm done," Zam said, ripping off and throwing down the transdermal patch used to regulate his insulin disorder. "I said I'd pretend to be David, and I did it."

"Yes, and you will do it again." He sighed. "And you let Emma slip through your fingers."

Zam jumped up, swayed, and sat back on the bed with a thud. He pointed at Dr. Maze. "I told you that I was holding Emma when I was switched. It's not my fault!"

Dr. Maze regarded his employee. "Maybe you're right. Perhaps the child can only travel with one of her mothers." He glanced at the Predictor. "Were there any new developments?"

"The baby's bigger," Zam remarked.

"That generally happens over a period of months," he mocked.

Zam rolled his eyes but not where the doctor could see him. "I mean, Emma's bigger than she should be."

Timberly adjusted the monitors behind them, attempting to appear insignificant.

"That must be the cost of a time jump for her," Dr. Maze observed. "How much was she affected?"

"Maybe a couple of months," Zam answered. "Is that what happens to me when I jump?" Suddenly anxious, he grabbed a mirror from beside the monitor. "Do I lose months of my life?"

The doctor thought Zam might need a gentle reminder about his role in the bigger plan, so he renewed his threat, "You will do as I say, or I will eliminate Laura from the timeline. She will be dropped on her head as an infant, dying instantly. Thus, your father and you will never be born."

Zam hung his head as a tear rolled off his cheek. "When will it stop? When will it ever be enough for you?"

"Is it really so bad, Zamuel?" the doctor asked him, enjoying Zam's suffering. "You were able to marry the woman you adore, and everyone thinks that the two of you are so deeply in love that you were able to have two children." He chuckled. "That's almost a record in this day and time!"

"Caroline is not the woman I love," came Zam's bitter reply.

Dr. Maze smiled. "Neither is Celeste." Before Zam could object, Dr. Maze continued, and his was the only voice that carried meaning in that room. "Obsession is not love." Unknowingly, he squeezed the picture in his hand. "Sometimes, you think you're in love, but the other person doesn't feel the same. You need to wake up and count your losses before you end up completely alone."

Zam's tears had stopped, as he understood Dr. Maze's intimate reflection. The doctor's words revealed a pain from his past that was so great that it seemed to motivate him on his time-altering mission.

"She thought I'd brought David back here to punish her," he sneered as he stared at the picture. "Ha! She is hardly a blot on the page of my bigger plan."

He threw the picture into the trash and smacked one hand against the other as if ridding them of imaginary dirt. "She thinks she has the last laugh. Well, we'll see what she thinks when she finds out what I planted in David Winsome's mind."

Zam was tasked with delivering the baby back to the nursery. He could take his namesake home with him, but he didn't feel a connection to the baby. He needed to have it out with Caroline anyway, and even though the baby might be too small to understand the subject of the discussion, he shouldn't be around a potential argument.

Rows of empty bassinets greeted him. He pushed a buzzer, and the night nurse appeared with her only charge. He was greedily sucking a bottle and wriggling around fiercely. It was clear that the nurse had her hands full, but Zam decided to leave the baby without another thought.

The nurse pointed to a crib in the far corner and the infant cried out. That caused the other baby to wail, and Zam took it as his cue to leave.

He smiled apologetically at the night nurse as he left, reaching out to shake the chubby hand of the other baby. "Try not to give her a hard time," he told the infant.

The baby stared back at him, and Zam was amused by his startling features. The infant had ivory skin, a tone that was uncommon since before the Great War, but his most defining features were his contrasting blue and green eyes.

Chapter 56

She woke in bed next to David. Her arms were empty, and she immediately felt Harvey's loss.

She had failed the baby. She wished she could have transported him to his original time, far away from the influence of Dr. Maze. Worse still, she didn't know if she could have carried him with her, as Timberly had pried him out of her arms as her body began the transfer. She could only hope that he'd be okay, and she could risk rescuing him from her grandfather if she was ever pulled back into the future.

The possibility that she'd be whisked back at the most inopportune times was likely. Her grandfather would be livid over her jump, and he'd watch his Predictor for signs of an altered future.

She could almost see him scanning his device and scouring genealogy records for a possible pregnancy. He had mentioned that he was building an army, and Celeste believed he wanted her to provide him with children who could time jump without using hosts. The idea made her want to take every birth control available, but she quieted her anxiety by reminding herself that David was beside her, and Emma waited for her downstairs. As long as she inhabited Caroline's body, she had the power to make her own decisions.

She could hear Ag and Mrs. Winsome discussing dinner plans over breakfast. She smiled, despite her awkward situation.

She'd been with Zam while he was using David as a host, so David had no recollection of their intimacy. Furthermore, she had no idea when Zam had taken possession of David. Her best guess placed it sometime between after she dropped him off at his SUV and when Ag said he started acting differently to her.

Zam's behavior around Ag had been strange. She didn't have time to dissect it, though, as David began to stir.

David sat straight up in bed. He looked back at her, his eyes wide.

"What are you do— Did we—? "

Celeste lifted her eyebrows. She was dressed from her trip downstairs, but all that covered him was a thin sheet.

"No wonder I had bad dreams," he said, resting his head in his hand. "I dreamed I was in your futuristic—"

"Shut up, David," Celeste barked. She was surprised by her brazenness, but it had gotten his attention.

She sat up, straightening her hair from lying on the pillow she had used to smother Zam. "You love me." When he opened his mouth to object, she spoke over him. "You can feel it. You know you love me when you look at me. You think about the times we shared in this bed and the plans we made. You remember our trips to the creek and the long walks I took with you. We held hands down the same road where you and your dad shared long talks. I know you feel that way and think about those things because I feel that way, too." She pointed her hand at her chest, hovering it over her heart.

"That doesn't change what you've done," he argued. "I don't know how drunk I got last night, but this" —he motioned between the two of them— "isn't going to work."

Celeste swallowed hard. "I'm willing to accept that, but I have two favors to ask first."

"If it's about money—"

Celeste put her finger to his lips. "It's not about money."

He was quiet so she could proceed.

"First, let's raise Emma together. I want us to get along and show her that we can be there for her without killing each other. I'll get an apartment nearby, and we can co-parent our daughter."

He nodded his head. "As long as you don't make decisions that keep me from Emma or endanger her."

Celeste shook her head. "We covered all that last night," she hedged. "Willie kept me from telling you about Emma because he was jealous, and he abducted me when he escaped from the jail."

Celeste felt guilty for the lie she told him. He had seen her—truly seen her—in her time, but his mind couldn't process it. It was best to let him believe it had only been a dream.

He looked down at himself. "I guess we would have cleared that up before we—" He raised his eyebrows at her, and she laughed.

She was glad to watch the smile that stretched across his face. It had been so long since she'd seen it, and it danced across her heart, instantly wiping away the fear she felt over her grandfather and his ulterior motives.

"What's the second thing?" he asked.

Celeste leaned in and locked eyes with David. She slid her hand into his and felt the heat radiate off him when she inched closer. "Kiss me."

The moments that followed their kiss were filled with the passion and love David and Celeste felt for one another. Afterward, there was no denying their need for each other, but they agreed to take it slow, even though Celeste knew David never traveled at that speed.

Celeste was in time for breakfast with Emma, and her little girl's eyes lit up when they clinked spoons over their cereal bowls. David joined them, sitting on the other side of Emma and rubbing his neck.

"I feel like I strained something," he commented.

"It's all that amorous activity," Mrs. Winsome called out from her chair. "It's too late to have Irish twins, but the two of you seem to be workin' on stair steps."

"Mama!" Ag admonished, jumping up from the breakfast table.

She touched Celeste's arm as she took her bowl to the sink. "I, for one, am happy for the two of you."

Celeste smiled up at Ag and busied herself by pouring more cereal into Emma's bowl. She hoped David's neck discomfort hadn't resulted when she had tried to smother Zam. She should have gone back to a time before she'd fought with Zam in David's bed, but she wasn't certain all events could be erased once they were lived, and she had a feeling Zam remembered the attempt on his life very well.

Midway through the meal, as Emma was jabbering to them and waving her spoon around, David scooted his chair next to Celeste and encircled her in his arms. He rested his chin on her shoulder and gave her a brief peck on her neck.

Emma squealed with delight as her father showered affection on her mother, and Ag leaned against the counter, smiling at her niece. David enjoyed the peals of laughter Emma issued when he kissed Celeste, and soon he was covering her with kisses as the baby encouraged him with her giggles.

It was the family moment Celeste never thought she'd experience. She could almost imagine their lives together, and she'd never been happier than when she was laughing with Ag, Emma, and David as Mrs. Winsome chided them for interrupting her morning programs. It felt like family.

A knock at the door startled them. They grew quiet as each person wondered who could be at the door so early.

"If it's a vacuum cleaner salesman, tell him to suck money outta someone else," shouted Mrs. Winsome.

David chuckled as he ran to answer the door. "There haven't been vacuum salesmen for decades, Mama."

His good-natured face fell when she responded, "I just got rid of one last week. Your father gave him a ride to the gas station. That man's heart is too good."

David pulled open the door while still looking at his mother, so Celeste was the first person to see Mindy standing on the porch. Tears streamed down her face, and she clutched her hands in front of her chest.

When he turned to her, she sobbed, "I th-think we need to talk."

Celeste waited while David and Mindy spoke in his room. It was almost an hour before they walked down the steps. Mindy hugged David at the door, and Celeste thought the woman smiled smugly at her as she looked over David's shoulder.

Perhaps Mindy's view of her had changed. After all, she had caused their breakup and taken David away from her.

David walked Mindy to her car, and Celeste paced in the kitchen while Emma played on the floor. Occasionally, Emma would say something, but Celeste was too distracted to try to decipher it.

What had they talked about for so long? Had Mindy found a way to win David back?

"You're gonna wear a hole into the linoleum if you keep pacin',," Mrs. Winsome called from the living room.

Celeste joined her, sitting on the couch opposite Mrs. Winsome's chair. Mrs. Winsome seemed clearer than she had that morning. Much more time had passed for Celeste than it had for the elderly woman, but she seemed to feel much better than when she was screaming on the kitchen floor.

"You're back," she commented.

Celeste lost her breath until she remembered that Mrs. Winsome hadn't properly spoken to her since she had been kidnapped. She smiled wanly.

"Yes, ma'am. I'm so glad to be home."

Mrs. Winsome raised her penciled-in eyebrows. "Home?"

Celeste backpedaled, feeling the heat rise in her face as she spoke. "I meant I'm glad to be back in Unicoi County. It was a terrible experience."

"I don't doubt it." She stared back at her television, and Celeste thought she was finished speaking.

"It was my fault, you know," Mrs. Winsome said, still watching the characters on the screen. She had slipped back in time, but only in her mind. "He told me it was dangerous, but I thought my calculations were flawless."

Celeste had never heard Mrs. Winsome speak that way. Most of the dialect of the region was absent, and her voice was much younger, as if it were projected from her youth.

"He can't come back," she went on, turning to Celeste. "But I can see the way he meddles with my life. He sends his blonde women to haunt me and mess up my family."

Celeste thought back to Mrs. Winsome's mentions of blonde women. She had said it when she thought she was speaking to Caroline and Hailey, whom she knew as Emma at the time. Celeste was willing to bet Mindy had heard the same comment from Mrs. Winsome, although, she doubted it was as applicable to the conversation they were having. There was a connection Celeste wasn't making, and she was worried that it meant more than she could fathom.

After minutes that seemed like hours to Celeste, David slumped back into the house and dropped onto the sofa with his head in his hands. The couch sagged and brought Celeste involuntarily closer to David. Ag had heard the door open, and she wandered into the living room, standing where she could hear David speak, but she could also watch Emma playing in the kitchen.

David peeked over his fingers before burying his head again. He straightened his spine and stared ahead, not meeting any of their eyes.

"I might as well tell everyone at the same time," he accepted, closing his eyes. "Mindy's pregnant."

Celeste felt like she slipped off the edge of the world. Everything that had been in focus an hour ago flew from her grasp.

She tried to control her breathing as David explained that he and Mindy thought it was best to get back together so he could be with Mindy during her pregnancy. He wouldn't look at Celeste as he spoke, and she wished she could move away from him without making her intentions obvious.

"There aren't secrets in this house," he observed, "so I'll tell all of you my idea."

"I'm sure it's a doozy," Mrs. Winsome muttered.

"I think I should move in with Mindy and Caroline and Emma can have my room."

Mrs. Winsome chuckled. "That's awfully chivalrous of you, considerin' you were fornicatin' in the room all night with her."

David looked in the direction of the door as if Mindy could hear their conversation over the miles between them. Celeste stared at her lap until Ag lifted her chin.

"You have no reason to be ashamed," she told Celeste. "I saw the way my brother acted around you last night, and I thought he was in love with you again."

David's head swiveled around, and the crease between his eyebrows deepened. "How drunk was I?"

"You're a jerk!" Ag yelled at him. "You slept with Caroline, and now you're running off to be with Mindy!"

David stood. "She's pregnant!" he shouted back. "What am I supposed to do? I can't abandon the baby!"

"But you don't have to live with her," Celeste squeaked out. All heads turned to her before she realized she was crying. "You could stay with me and see the baby after it's born. It's what you're proposing to do with Emma. How is she any different than Mindy's baby?"

David tried to hold her, but she pushed him away. Ag wrapped her arms around Celeste and stroked her hair

"Sleep on it," Mrs. Winsome suggested.

"It's not even noon, Mama," David told her, rolling his eyes.

"I know that, son," she spoke harshly. "I'm not an idiot. I meant you should spend the day with Emma as a family. Give that poor child at least one day before her life is divided."

Celeste had raised her head out of Ag's arms. She had no hope of spending the day with David, but she was surprised when it seemed he was considering it.

"Will you spend the day with me, Caroline?" he asked.

Before Mindy had knocked on the door, he wouldn't have had to ask her permission. Now, they sat on opposite ends of the couch, with him relaxing against the armrest and her bunched up in Ag's arms, but they might as well have been light years apart.

She could only choke out one word: "Okay."

CHAPTER 57

Celeste was silent until Emma fell asleep in the new car seat David had gotten for her. It was convertible, and Celeste believed he had purchased it because he planned to be active in Emma's life as she grew.

She thought her words would be hesitant, but they flowed freely, revealing the hurt she felt. "We love each other, David. Why are you going to be with Mindy?"

He cringed, not expecting her to be so bold. "I've already talked about my reasons."

"And I made very good points against them."

He clenched his jaw. "Look, if I'm not with Mindy, she'll have the baby on her own. How is that fair to her?"

"So, you're going to run your life on playground rules," Celeste mocked. "It's not fair for poor Mindy—"

"Stop it," he interrupted. "You didn't have to be alone when you were pregnant with Emma. You had me, and then you ran off to be with your ex-husband."

Celeste felt like she had been doused with cold water. "Are you trying to get back at me?"

David shook his head, but Celeste wasn't convinced. Her grandfather's observation about people and their patterns came back to her.

"Why did you break up with Mindy in the first place?"

David's grip on the wheel tightened. "It's really none of your—" He stopped, staring intently at the empty interstate. "I broke up with her because she told me to take Emma away from you."

For the second time that day, she felt like the breath had been knocked out of her. Mindy had been so kind to her. Why would she suggest that David seek full custody? She voiced her thoughts to David.

"She wanted another baby," David told her, glancing over to measure her reaction. "I guess she got her wish."

Celeste stared at the floorboard where a lonely can of coffee rolled with the curves of the road. "It's hard for me to believe that you broke up with her over that."

David sighed. "It was a little more than that. It's like Mama says, 'It was the straw that broke the camel's back.'"

Celeste was familiar with the saying. Her grandfather had spoken it when she had done something small that had pushed him over the edge.

"How do you expect to stay with her if things were already going downhill?"

David's grip on the steering wheel tightened. "I'll find a way to work it out, and honestly, it's none of your business."

Celeste's mouth dropped open, and before she closed it, she told him how she felt. "You're a coward, David Winsome."

He wasn't baited by her accusal. "At least I don't abandon the people I claim to love."

Celeste crossed her arms as she watched the passing maple and oak trees. "But that's exactly what you're doing."

David changed the radio station, and a familiar song by the Dave Matthews Band played. It carried special meaning to both of them, but he didn't know he had shared that song with her when she was using Hailey Hall as a host, so Celeste remained indifferent as he changed it to a more upbeat selection.

"I'm not abandoning you and Emma. You're going to be staying at the house with Mama and Ag."

"And I'm sure you'll visit when you feel like it," Celeste spat.

"Mindy and I think it's best if we gradually intermingle Emma with the boys."

"And who's idea was that?" Celeste was upset, and she wasn't surprised by her cattiness. She couldn't stand to hear David speak about Mindy as if they were a respectable couple, making decisions that were best for their family when he had been with Celeste just before Mindy drove to the Winsome's house.

She shook her head. "Anyway, I'm not going to live there. I'm going to get my own—"

"But it's a free place to stay with free childcare for whenever you get a job or go on a date." He said the last part with a forced smile.

"Yeah, right," Celeste scoffed. "I don't move as fast as you."

He glanced at her with his eyebrows drawn down before refocusing his attention on the road. "What's that supposed to mean?"

David was aware of the way people talked about him. He fully understood that he jumped into a relationship and ran at full speed.

Celeste didn't mince words. "It means that you were with me in your bed this morning, and as soon as you see Mindy again, you'll be in her bed."

David's jaw clenched and unclenched several times. He saw the road, but he wasn't concentrating intently on it. "I'll admit, it's a strange situation, but it's nothing I can't manage."

Celeste clapped her hands. "Well, good for you. And while you're managing your *situation*, I'll be picking up the pieces you left behind."

"Then we're even," he said with finality.

The day passed too quickly. Even though she was hurt and upset with him, Celeste savored every moment with the man she loved.

They took Emma to an indoor amusement park in a nearby city. Celeste encouraged David to go into the batting cage and drive the go-carts, but he was more interested in spending time with Emma.

David bought a basket of fries, and they shared them at one of the metal tables. Emma liked fries as much as her mother, and she used them as swords, battling her father with each of them.

Celeste loved to see David and Emma together, and she felt like she had accomplished her mission. David and Emma knew they were father and daughter, and they had years of loving interactions ahead of them.

They played bowling and arcade games with her, but Emma preferred the inflatables. They watched her bounce on them until the older children got out of school and began to fill the building and release their pent-up laughter and energy. One child landed on Emma's ankle when she fell, and she didn't even apologize when the baby let out a wail.

Emma didn't stop crying when they got her to the car, and David peeled off her socks.

"It might be broken," he announced, and Celeste's stomach dropped.

Even though they were fifteen miles away and the nearest hospital was within three miles, David insisted that they take Emma to the hospital where he worked. Celeste agreed that Emma would receive better care there, and David phoned ahead to let them know he was on his way.

Celeste had elected to ride in the backseat with her daughter. Emma let out shrieks that broke her heart and looked up at her like Celeste could do something to take the pain away. All she could do was elevate her foot and hope Emma would find relief soon.

"I should probably tell you that Mindy's there," David said, meeting her eyes in the rearview mirror. "I don't want you to be blindsided when we go into the ER."

After a full day of play and the pain from her injury, Emma fell asleep just before they reached the hospital. Celeste tried to tell herself that her daughter was experiencing a pain-free slumber, when in reality she had probably passed out from her suffering.

David picked Emma up and carried her into the emergency room with Celeste on his heels. As soon as Debbie, the receptionist, saw him, she spoke into the call button on her shirt, and Mindy met them at the door that led to the exam rooms.

Mindy didn't cast spiteful glances at Celeste as they hurried past rows of empty rooms. In fact, she seemed worried and sympathetic.

Dr. Sing was waiting for them at the door to the exam room. She assessed the injury and ordered an x-ray. Celeste thought they'd wait on the technician for a while, but he wheeled in the x-ray device while Mindy was taking Emma's vitals.

Emma lay across her father's lap and Celeste held her hand as the technician set up the equipment. She didn't wake up, but occasionally, she'd grimace or cry out in her sleep.

"Any chance you could be pregnant?" he asked Celeste.

She saw Mindy look at her out of the corner of her eye.

"I'll walk out of the room," Celeste volunteered.

Mindy followed her. Celeste thought they would stand in uncomfortable silence, but Mindy opened her arms and embraced Celeste.

Celeste kept her posture closed, and the hug was brief. When she pulled away, Mindy's tear-filled eyes stared up at her.

"I don't want to have animosity between us," she said. "On one of the shows I watch, two sisters fought over the same man, and it didn't end well."

Celeste didn't bother to tell Mindy that they weren't sisters. They weren't even friends.

"I think this will all work out," Mindy told her as she covered her with conciliatory touches that Celeste didn't want.

Mindy would believe that. After all, she was the one who had won David's heart.

The door opened, and the technician ushered them back inside. He left, and Celeste kept waiting for Mindy to follow him. She was horrified when she concluded Mindy was going to stay, already assuming her role as Emma's stepmother.

Mindy cleared her throat. "I spoke to Caroline in the hall," she informed David. "We've decided to be friends."

David raised his eyebrows as if he didn't believe it. Celeste was glad he wasn't fooled by his girlfriend's optimism.

Silence rang through the room. Celeste tried to ignore it, but she felt the pressure to fill it with conversation.

"You're working on a daytime shift," she commented in Mindy's direction.

David squinted as if he were trying to piece together how his ex-wife was privy to his girlfriend's work schedule, but Mindy didn't miss a beat.

"I started working the day shift when I found out I was pregnant." She lowered her eyes. "I just made the change yesterday. I thought it'd be easier if David and I were on the same shift."

The silence resumed, but Mindy found another topic. "Hey, I heard something through some of the other nurses today."

David and Celeste looked at her without excitement.

"There's a night shift janitorial position open," she began. "Caroline, didn't you take some CNA classes and drop out?"

Leave it to a scorned woman to bring her rival down in front of the man they loved. Celeste bit her tongue to keep from speaking, only nodding once to answer Mindy's question.

Noticing Celeste's disinterest, Mindy spoke mostly to David. "Well, Sandra's getting ready to retire, but the man on the janitorial staff is only on family leave, so I thought Caroline could take over for him until he got back. She could retake the CNA classes by day, and she'd be ready to fill Sandra's position when she retired.

"If they hired her," David said.

Mindy rolled her eyes. "You can put in a good word for the mother of your child." She nudged David. "I will if you will."

David nodded his approval of the plan. Celeste had to admit it was a better option than waiting for another opportunity to fall into her lap.

"We'll all be on the day shift together," Mindy almost cheered.

David glanced away, unwilling to encourage or stifle Mindy's positivity. Celeste gave her a small smile. Mindy was a good person, and it took a lot to be unfailingly kind to a potential adversary.

Dr. Sing returned and relayed that Emma had a broken leg. Celeste was shocked that such a small accident had led to a terribly significant injury.

Dr. Sing told her that they saw the injuries all the time. Emma's leg was set in a neon pink cast that resembled a boot, and when she woke up, Mindy gave her medicine to control her pain.

Mindy kissed David when she handed him Emma's discharge papers. "Will I see you tonight?"

Color blotched David's cheeks. "Mama wants me to stay home tonight. I'll be over tomorrow."

Mindy caressed the back of his neck with her fingers. "I hope you plan to stay a while." She pecked his lips softly. "Like forever."

Emma looked between Mindy and David quizzically. "Mommy?" She pointed to Celeste.

"I need to get them home," he told Mindy briskly, kissing her forehead and carrying Emma out.

Celeste followed him to the car, and he buckled Emma into her car seat. After they had been on the road for a minute, Emma's head lolled, and she fell asleep.

"You're really great with her," Celeste admitted.

David nodded. "I wish I could have gotten to know her sooner."

"Me too," Celeste replied.

David snorted. "I'll never forgive you for taking her away from me."

They'd shared a beautiful day, but neither of them could work past their resentment. Celeste was angry that David had chosen Mindy over her after he learned Mindy was pregnant, and David couldn't let go of his idea that his ex-wife had hidden their daughter away from him.

Celeste felt depressed and emotionally exhausted. If there was a way for her to win back David's favor, she didn't feel like thinking about it yet. It seemed like too much work for her tired mind.

While they were in the hospital, cornflower blue skies had been replaced by pressing gray clouds and harsh winds. Celeste looked out the window as angry clouds released the emotion she felt.

"Then maybe it's better that you're with Mindy."

Chapter 58

Celeste opted to sleep on the couch. David offered to let Emma and her sleep in his bed, but she couldn't stand to stay in the bed she'd shared with him that morning. The pain was too fresh.

Mrs. Winsome shuffled to her room at her usual time with Ag behind her like a doting parent. From her angle on the couch, Celeste could see the upper part of Mrs. Winsome's bed. She insisted on sleeping on the side nearest to the edge, leaving a space for her deceased husband.

Ag sighed, unwilling to argue with her mother. She pulled the gray comforter up to her shoulder and kissed her mother's cheek.

"Send your daddy to bed when he gets home," Mrs. Winsome voiced before Ag left the room. "He's comforting a parishioner tonight. The man's a saint."

Ag sat down on the couch at Emma's feet and let out a long puff of air. "This is going to be the death of me."

Celeste had heard that the health of caretakers of people with Alzheimer's Disease often depreciated faster than their charges. The anxiety and constant care proved too taxing for their bodies. Celeste wondered if she should rethink David's suggestion about living there. She could fix up the room next to David's bedroom, and she'd be available to relieve some of the pressure off Ag.

As unhealthy as the situation was for her mentally and emotionally, Celeste felt the drive to help David's family. No matter her host, they'd been good to her, and she felt like she owed them. They were Emma's family, too, and Mrs. Winsome and Ag had loved and cared for her before they knew she was David's child. However, Celeste believed they had suspected the truth from the day Celeste showed up on their doorstep with Emma in her arms.

Emma inched up to Ag and laid her head in her lap. Her cast prevented a range of motion, so Emma had to crawl wherever she went unless she was carried, and David had done that a lot since they'd returned from the hospital.

The doll Mrs. Winsome had sent her at Christmas was in Emma's hand. She climbed onto the couch and moved down it to nuzzle Celeste. She kissed her mother and caressed her face before she settled into her chest. Celeste took the cue and gave Emma her nipple. It wasn't good for Emma's teeth when Celeste nursed her to sleep, but it was hard to resist her daughter when she was sleepy and sweet. Emma was asleep in moments, and David came downstairs, planting a kiss on his daughter's cheek before he went into the kitchen.

"She babbled all day today," Ag said about Mrs. Winsome after her brother left the room.

Celeste took in the difference in Ag. Over the past several weeks, the spaces beneath her eyes were darker and she hardly ever shared her usual banter with her brother. Her short hair had grown long enough to be pulled into a ponytail, and her nails were never painted. She'd abandoned her bright dresses for comfortably neutral clothes, and she wandered through the house like a ghost most days, tending to her mother without saying a word.

Ag cataloged a difficult day that had started with Mrs. Winsome's morning outburst and ended with the exchange Celeste had witnessed.

"She said you and David had been different people, but you were back now," Ag related. "She kept going on about David being possessed by some man in the future, and that you were from the future, but—" She stopped talking and forced a dry chuckle. "I think I may need to go to bed."

Celeste's face had drained of color as Ag had relayed her mother's ramblings. First of all, with her declining health, how did Mrs. Winsome recognize the differences in her son and his ex-wife? Zam had been so careful when he had assumed David as a host that he'd fooled Celeste. And next, when Celeste traveled back to the moments before she strangled Zam in David's bed, it should have erased the timeline where Caroline and Zam went through the day in that time frame. Had she missed something, or did Mrs. Winsome's illness afford her the ability to see both timelines? That would certainly be a weight on an already tired mind.

David passed his sister on her way to her room and squatted in front of Celeste. He stroked his hand tenderly through Emma's hair.

"I'll keep my phone on tonight." He held it up. "If Emma needs anything, call me and I'll come right down."

Celeste was certain she could handle anything their daughter needed, but she smiled at David's attentiveness. He was exactly the type of father she had predicted.

Celeste hadn't noticed him staring at her, and she was surprised when he kissed her. Her mouth opened and he reached his tongue inside to connect with her. The kiss was long, without pretense or suggestion, and Celeste had no idea how much time had passed when they broke away.

David scratched the back of his head. "I need to go to bed. Do you want to come with me?"

Celeste laughed. "Good try, but no. I'm not interested in having my heart broken even more when you leave for Mindy's house tomorrow."

David's sheepish grin turned into a thin line. "It's not fair to you, is it?" He put both hands on the couch, preparing to lift himself. "I love you, but I don't know the right decision to make in this situation. I'm just doing the best I can. I can't see the future, you know?"

Celeste almost laughed at the irony. She wished she could show him the outcome of his actions on her grandfather's Predictor, but he had thought his trip to the future was a nightmare, so she doubted he would understand the implications of the technology. Celeste wasn't certain she could read the Predictor anyway.

David climbed the steps to his room alone that night, and Celeste was thankful for her willpower. She loved him deeply, but she was unwilling to allow him to use her, even if he claimed to love her.

She heard a sound from Mrs. Winsome's room, and she eased off the couch to check on her. It was dark, but the lady's breathing was sharper than it had been when she was asleep.

"I remember you," she spoke.

"Are you okay?" Celeste asked her.

"You came to me on the night we sent him away," Mrs. Winsome said, ignoring Celeste's question.

Celeste tried again to ask about her well-being, and when she received no answer, Celeste resolved to get Ag. As she turned to go, Mrs. Winsome froze her in place by saying, "I destroyed it, you know. I took the time machine apart piece by piece, and I never went back. I was the only one who knew the code. They all tried to get it out of me, but I wouldn't say a word."

It was several moments before Celeste could move. When she did, she went straight to the couch and settled down beside her daughter. She was unprepared for what Mrs. Winsome had said.

She slept fitfully, waking through the night, convinced she heard voices. At first, she thought David was talking to Ag, and then she surmised that Ag and Mrs. Winsome were conversing in the elderly lady's room. She dismissed it all until she heard an ear-piercing scream.

Celeste ran to the source of the outcry. Mrs. Winsome's room had been dark when she'd last been inside it, but the moon had moved in its nighttime pattern to bring silvery light through the cracks in the closed blinds.

A figure stood over Mrs. Winsome's bed, bent over her with a knife in his hand. A dark, sticky substance dripped from the blade.

Celeste's first instinct was to attack him. She wanted to drive the knife through his heart and end his life, but then she recognized Eleanor Winsome's attacker.

Her legs gave away, and she fell to the floor. "No!" she cried out.

Suddenly, the reason her grandfather hadn't whizzed her back into the present time frame was clear. Not only had he seen Mindy's pregnancy on his device, but he had planted directions in David's mind in much the same way as he had erased Celeste's memories when she had assumed Hailey Hall's body.

David dropped the knife, shaking in the moonlight. "What did I do?" he asked her. "Celeste, help me."

Did You Like This Book?

If you enjoyed this story, would you please write a review on Amazon, Goodreads, and/or BookBub? Something as simple as "I liked it!" helps the author so much! Your feedback can make the book more visible to other readers, and it gives the author a reason to dance a jig when she sees your review!

You can sign up for Courtnee's newsletter, and you will receive exclusive bonus content, like cover reveals, sales, and news about upcoming releases.

Thank you for reading Solomon's Tears!

Acknowledgments

Tosha, thank you for pushing me to write this book. You have given me valuable input, and I'm thankful for your unwavering support.

Stereling, I hope you read this book one day. It may not have anything to do with you, but it's one of my better novels.

Kinidy and Stereling and Tosha and Matthew, the four of you form two couples that model the most loving and supportive relationships. Matthew, you and Kinidy answered my prayers for Tosha and Stereling. I appreciate and love both of you.

Mama, thank you for your love and encouragement. I always look forward to hearing your thoughts on my stories.

Legacee and the rest of my wonderful children are the reason I keep writing. My work and the love I leave with my children are my legacies.

Stephanie Edwards, I appreciate your enthusiasm and positive spirit. You're a great author, but you're also a cheerleader for authors everywhere. Thank you for suggesting the Bless Your Books Blog and inviting me to join you on it.

To Stephen King, this may not be a horror novel, but you influenced it. Thank you for writing the books that inspired me to become a writer.

Readers like Linda, Lisa, Elaine, and Judy bring my heart joy with their thoughtful reviews. In addition, TATTERED PAGES and Read More Books Facebook Pages have helped me significantly.

To you, dear reader, thank you for reading my story. You make it possible for me to share my thoughts with the world when I must stay in one place.

About the Author

Courtnee Turner Hoyle is a travel agent, mom, multi-genre writer, and an award-winning author of the books in the Pale Woods Mystery Series, It's About Time Series, and Rasputin's Dynasty Trilogy, in addition to several stand-alone novels and a few short stories that have been anthologized. The first book in her Pale Woods Mystery Series, My Brother's Keeper, has won five awards. The culture and views of her Tennessee home have forced her to find her own perspective. While she may embrace the traditions of her area, she has set non-negotiable boundaries, especially against sweet tea, chocolate, and unannounced visitors. Courtnee graduated from East Tennessee State University with multiple undergraduate degrees and a master's degree and developed unique ways of dividing the personalities of the people in her life to create quirky, relatable characters. She belongs to the Lost State Writer's Guild, and she volunteers with several local organizations. She encourages you to write splendid reviews of her books on any platform, especially on Goodreads, BookBub, and Amazon. Good reviews from her readers make her jump up and down in her kitchen and spin her children around happily. Courtnee lives with her husband and numerous children, braving the adventures of homeschooling and tree climbing, and believes there is a story in every experience.

Learn more about Courtnee, her hometown adventures, and her books by visiting www.courtneeturnerhoyle.com, plucking the leaves of her Link Tree (linktr.ee/Courtnee_), and on Instagram @pale_woods_mysteries to discover her Facebook, BookBub, Goodreads, TikTok, YouTube, and other accounts.

Celeste's Mashed Potatoes

Celeste was raised during a time when the use of animal products could cause Slover's Disease, so her mashed potatoes may seem a little different than the ones our grandmothers made for us. However, I use this recipe when I make mashed potatoes, and my husband doesn't notice a difference. I hope you enjoy them!

Ingredients:
*Potatoes (Quantity is dependant upon dining party, but this recipe assumes five pounds of potatoes.)
*Two sticks of vegan butter
*1/16 cup of plain soy milk

Procedure:
1. Boil potatoes until tender

2. Add soy milk and butter

3. Mash with a mixer for five minutes or until clumps were gone

4. Serve warm and season to taste

5. Enjoy!

Also By Courtnee

Hollis's Hobby
A Killing Quills Book

Do you trust your lover?
After an abusive childhood and soul-splitting heartbreak, Hollis hovers around her hometown, secretly killing the men who are unfortunate enough to fall for her charms, until her lonely friend, Josie, asks Hollis to move in with her. Hollis attempts to drop "Holli", the alter ego who dispatches her unsuspecting lovers, but she finds it difficult to function as a teacher when she sees the evidence of abuse on a student. To veer away from her murderous path, Hollis forms a relationship with the father of one of her students, Quillen, but he's running from a secret Hollis may not understand.
Hollis's sad and twisted past has never been unearthed, but will Quillen's influence cause her to dig up details that could risk her capture? When all Hollis's secrets threaten to come to the surface, will she continue to live under the guise she's created, or will Hollis's hobby be revealed?

Also By Courtnee

Solomon's Tears
A Pale Wood Suspense Novel

Are the ghosts in her house or her mind?
Ketron Gouge is puzzled when she feels like one of her children
is missing. A quick check calms her panicked mind, but the
uncomfortable thought continues to concern her.
Ketron and her husband, Marvin, bought a home they hoped would
be perfect for their growing family. Soon, however, Marvin develops
a drinking problem and Ketron becomes more anxious about the
mysterious shadows and disembodied crying in the house. Most of
her five children seem to be conscious of the uncanny events, giving
credence to Ketron's worries, but her best friend and therapist think
it may be a product of her overstressed mind.
Ghosts from her past and memories of her childhood tumble to the
surface, reminding her of her mentally unstable mother, and she
begins to wonder if there's truth to the nagging idea that someone is
missing. And when she begins seeing things in her house, she thinks
it may be time to accept an inescapable truth.

Also By Courtnee

Rasputin's Scorn
Rasputin's Dynasty Trilogy

What if there was a drug that could cure your terminally ill mother, but it could also take away her humanity? Fourteen-year-old Razz enjoys the freedom of his single-parent household until his mother becomes ill. Without involved relatives, he worries about what will happen to his sister, Lexi, and him when their mother dies. Feeling powerless, he seeks out Scorn, a drug that can give the user unlimited strength, but its effects are short-lived and the consequences of taking it are high. The user may seem unaffected by it for some time, but eventually, almost all those who take the drug become exceedingly aggressive, using their new strength to tear apart anyone in their paths, especially those closest to them. The government collects the users who have pushed past the limits of their strength and taken a life or lives and places them in a facility from where only one person has returned. Simply feeling the vial in his hand makes Razz feel more dominant, and he decides to keep the amber powder close to him. He starts having dreams about blood, and strange physical changes make him wonder if he's going through the natural stages of adolescence, or if touching the Scorn in the vile has caused an irreversible reaction. Will Razz use Scorn to help him cope with his mother's failing health, and keep Lexi and him together after his mother's death? Or is there something more to Scorn, and is his family somehow responsible for it?

9 789898 764683